GASH

Firefly Gadroon

This story begins where I did something illegal, had two rows with women, one pub fight, and got a police warning, all before mid-afternoon. After that it got worse, but that's the antiques game for you. Trouble.

It can only be Lovejoy speaking – Lovejoy the antique dealer, 'one of the happiest creations of recent crime fiction' (*Oxford Mail*), 'who likes females almost as much as flintlocks' (*The Times Literary Supplement*), and 'has a diviner's instinct for telling the genuine from the fake' (*Irish Times*).

The trouble began when what was described as a 'small portable Japanese box. Maybe bamboo' was sold at auction under Lovejoy's nose. He wanted that box, which was a genuine antique firefly cage, but someone else wanted it even more, because an original might provide a clue to the secret of a model, and that secret was worth murdering for. Unfortunately the victim battered to death on the Essex marshes was a friend of Lovejoy's, and though he is not above faking an antique or two (and telling the reader how to do likewise), Lovejoy always ends up on the side of right when the chips are down. So he embarks on a campaign of personal vengeance, culminating in one of the most exciting episodes of his career.

Whether Germoline the donkey is also on the side of right is one of the many things the reader will discover – about antiques and about human (and animal) behaviour – in Lovejoy's latest narrative.

by the same author

THE VATICAN RIP
SPEND GAME
THE GRAIL TREE
GOLD FROM GEMINI
THE JUDAS PAIR

JONATHAN GASH

Firefly Gadroon

A Lovejoy narrative

COLLINS, ST JAMES'S PLACE, LONDON

William Collins Sons & Co. Ltd
London · Glasgow · Sydney · Auckland
Toronto · Johannesburg

First published 1982
© Jonathan Gash, 1982

British Library Cataloguing in Publication Data

Gash, Jonathan
Firefly gadroon. — (Crime Club).
I. Title
823′.914 [F]   PR6057.A728

ISBN 0-00-231296-4

Photoset in Compugraphic Baskerville
Printed in Great Britain by
T. J. Press (Padstow) Ltd

For

A story for Susan and Germoline, Erica and Betty, with thanks to Paul for the rock bit.

CHAPTER 1

This story begins where I did something illegal, had two rows with women, one pub fight, and got a police warning, all before mid-afternoon. After that it got worse, but that's the antiques game for you. Trouble.

I was up on the auctioneer's rostrum. But all I could think was, if that luscious woman crosses her beautiful legs once more I'll climb down through the crowd and give her a good hiding. She was driving me out of my skull.

As soon as I clapped eyes on her I knew she'd be trouble. We'd turned up for the auction that morning to find Harry the deputy auctioneer was ill. That caused a flap. Gimbert's auction rooms had three hundred assorted antiques—some even genuine—to auction off before the pubs opened. Old Cuthbertson caught me as I arrived and quaveringly asked me to stand in for his sick assistant. It's not exactly legal to do this but, we antique dealers often ask ourselves, what is?

'Why me, Cuthie?' I asked sourly. It was one of those mornings. I felt unshaven, though I'd tried.

'You're honest, Lovejoy,' he'd said earnestly, the cunning old devil. It's a hell of an accusation. That's my name, incidentally. Lovejoy. Crummy, but noticeable.

The trouble is I'm too soft. Anyhow Cuthbertson's too senile to lift a gavel these days, and he offered me a few quid knowing I'd be broke as usual. So, amid the jeers and catcalls of my fellow dealers, I took the rostrum and got the proceedings under way.

Gimbert's is a typical auction, such as you'll find in any sleepy old English market town. That means corrupt,

savage and even murderous. Beneath the kindly exterior
of contentment and plaster-and-pantile Tudor homeli-
ness there beats the scarlet emotion of pure greed. Oh,
I'm not saying our churches hereabouts aren't pretty and
the coastline invigorating and all that jazz. But I've
always found that when antiques come in at the door
morality goes out of the window. You can't blame people
for it. It's just the way we're made.

It was a blustery September market day with plenty of
people in town, refugees from the stunning boredom of
our unending countryside. Gimbert's was crowded.
Naturally the lads were all at it, shouting false bids and
indulging in a general hilarity as soon as I'd got going. I
soon stopped that by taking a bid or two 'off the wall'
(dealers' slang: imagining an extra bid or two to force the
prices higher and faster). I got a few million glares of hate
from my comrades but at least it brought orderliness, if
not exactly harmony. Old Cuthbertson was at the back
silently perforating his many ulcers.

'Here, Lovejoy,' Devlin called out angrily. 'You on
their side?'

'Shut your teeth, Devvo,' I gave back politely, and
cruised on through the lots. The girl crossed her legs
again. Devlin's one of those florid, vehement blokes, all
front teeth and stubble. You know instantly from his
dazzling waistcoat and military fawns that he's a white
slaver, but even his eleven motor-cars can't prove he's not
thick as a brick. He's supposed to be Midland porcelains
and early silver, which is a laugh. Like most antique
dealers, he couldn't tell a mediæval chalice from a chip
pan. I once sold him a Woolworth's plate as a vintage
Spode (you just choose carefully and sandblast the marks
off). Pathetic. Devlin's been desperate to get even with me
for two years. Thick, but unforgiving.

By Lot Twenty-Nine we'd settled down to a grumbling
concern with the business of the day. Between bids I had

time to suss out who had turned up and let my eyes rove casually over the crowded warehouse while the next lot was displayed by the miffs (dealers' slang, to mean the boozy layabouts who indicate to bidders which heap of rubbish comes next). There was the usual leavening of genuine customers among the hard core of dealers, but most were housewives. The lovely bird with the legs didn't seem a dealer, yet . . . She crossed her legs. Everybody noticed.

'Next lot,' I intoned. 'Regency corner shelves, veneered in walnut.'

'Showing here, sir!' The miff's traditional cry turned a few heads.

'Who'll bid, who'll bid?'

They were quite a good forgery. Most of us there knew that Sammy Treadwell makes about one set a month in his shed down on the waterfront. A grocer from East Hill started the bidding, thank God, or we'd be there yet. He got them for a few quid, cheap even for a fake. A minute later there was the usual bit of drama. An American chap in a fine grey overcoat was bidding for a manuscript letter which some rogue had catalogued as being from Nelson's father, the Reverend Edmund, the year before Trafalgar. Even from my perch I could see it had all the hallmarks of a forgery. From politeness I took a bid or two but the Yank seemed such a pleasantly anxious bloke I decided on a whim to protect him and knocked it down to a loud antique dealer in from the Smoke. I didn't know it then, but I'd just given myself a lifeline. The Yank looked peeved because I stared absently past his waving arm, but I'd done him a favour. By Lot Fifty the bird was worrying me sick.

I kept wondering what the hell she was up to. She was neither bored housewife nor dealer, which leaves very little else for a good-looking bird in a sleazy auction to be. She'd obviously sat down merely to flash her legs more effectively, which is only natural. She'd dressed to kill, with that kind of aloof defiance women show when it's a specially risky occasion. Throw of the dice and all that. And her gaze kept flicking back to the same place in her catalogue, something on the seventh page. Items in the high hundreds at Gimbert's are usually portabilia, small decorative household objects or personal pieces, snuff-boxes, scissors, needle-cases, scent bottles and visiting-card cases, suchlike. There's always a display case full.

I started looking about at Lot One Sixty to give Tinker Dill my signal. He's my barker and 'runs' for me. A barker's a dishevelled alcoholic of no fixed abode whose job is to sniff out antiques wherever they may lurk. Tinker has a real snout for antiques. I pay him for every 'tickle', as we dealers say, though most other barkers only get paid when a purchase is completed. As Tinker can't afford to get sloshed twice a day without money, you realize how strong the stimulus actually is.

I needn't have worried. At Lot One Sixty-Two in he shambled, filthy and bleary-eyed as ever. He has this sixth sense, helped no doubt by a few pints in the Ship tavern next door. I suppressed a grin as dealers near the door edged away from him. Tinker pongs a bit. Outside it was coming on to rain, which made his woollen balaclava and his old greatcoat steam gently. Still, if you're the best barker in the business you've talents Valentino never dreamed of. He gave a gappy grin, seeing me on the rostrum. I signalled in the way we'd arranged for him to bid on Lot One Eighty. To my relief I saw him nod slightly. He was still fairly sober. It would go all right.

We plodded on up the lot numbers. Helen was in, being amused at the way I was struggling to keep my eyes off the flashy bird's legs. Helen's too exquisite and stylish to worry about competition. She gave me one of her famous looks, a brilliant smile carefully hidden in a blank stare. Helen's good on porcelain and ethnological art.

We'd be together yet but for a blazing row over a William IV davenport desk about which she was decidedly wrong. I was in the right, but women are always unreasonable, not like us. Anyway, we split after a terrible fight over it.

Big Frank from Suffolk was lusting away between bids, and the Brighton lads were in doing their share. Our local dealers formed a crowd of sour faces in the corner. We were all mad about the Birmingham crowd turning up. They were here because of a small collection of Georgian commemorative medals, mostly mint. I knocked the collection down to them for a good price. Nothing else I could do but take the bids chucked at me, was there? The whole place was in a silent rage, except for the Brummie circus. A group of early Victorian garnet and gold pendants went cheap after that, though I sweated blood to get the bids going. A glittering piece of late Victorian church silver went to Devlin for five of our devalued paper pounds. I thought, what a bloody trade. If I knew Devvo he'd advertise it as an Edwardian ashtray. It hurts, especially when nerks like him are the ones with the groats, and deserving souls like me stay penniless.

So, in a cheery mood of good fellowship, while pedestrians hurried past outside in the rain and visitors sloshed up to the Castle Park to feed the ducks, in happy innocence I gave Tinker his signal to bid for the next item. My heart was thumping with pleasurable anticipation. It'd be mine soon, for maybe a quid.

'Item One Eighty,' I called. 'Small portable Japanese box. Maybe bamboo. Offers?'

'Showing here, sir!' Bedwell, the head miff, called from one of the cabinets.

I beamed around the place as the mob shuffled and coughed and muttered. There was very little interest. It'd go cheap.

'Anybody start me off?' I called brightly, gavelling

merrily like the over-confident idiot I am. 'A few pence to start?'

Tinker was drawing breath when the bird cheeped into action. 'Ten pounds,' she said to my horror, and we were off.

That's how the frightening trouble began. There was no way I could have stopped the evil that started then. And none of it was my fault. Honestly. Hand on my heart.

I'd be completely harmless if only people would leave me alone.

The crowd of bidders usually divides as soon as it's all over. Some throng the tea bar at the back of the dank warehouse and slurp Gimbert's horrible liquid, moaning about the prices of antiques. The rest surge into the Ship and sob in their beer, full of tales about missing a genuine Stradivarius (going for a couple of quid, of course) by a whisker last week. As I feared the big Yank collared me as I climbed down from the rostrum.

'Excuse me, sir.'

'Eh?'

The rotund weatherbeaten face of an outdoor man gazed reproachfully down at me. He was the size of a bus.

'You missed seeing my bid, sir. For Lord Nelson's father's letter. I've come a long way—'

I glanced about. Most of the mob had drifted—well, sprinted—pubwards so it was safe to speak. 'Look, mate. Nothing personal. But Nelson's dad snuffed it two years before that letter's date. And it began, "Dear Horatio". Wrong. He was called "Horace" by his own family.'

'You mean . . . ?'

'Forged? Aye. Go to the Rectory in Burnham Thorpe and have a butcher's—I mean a look—at his dad's handwriting. He got little Horace to witness the various wedding certificates sometimes. Always look at originals.'

His gaze cleared. 'I'm indebted—'

I had to be off. 'No charge, mate.'

He was eyeing me thoughtfully. 'If I may—'

But I shot out. The girl had vanished in the scrum. I was blazing. I collared Bedwell, miserable as sin among the tea-drinkers. He's a long thin nicotine-stained bloke. Funny shape, really. Miffs are usually sort of George III-shaped and sleek as a butcher's dog. Good living.

'Where is she, Welly?' I tapped his arm.

He grinned and nudged me suggestively. 'Always after skirt,' he cackled. Then he saw my face and went uneasy. 'Gawd knows, Lovejoy. Took that little basket and went.'

I groaned and bulleted into the yard. There's a side door into the tavern, but nobody's allowed to use it. Dolly intercepted me. Luckily she had her umbrella up against the drizzle or she'd have clouted me with it.

'Lovejoy! I knew you'd try to sneak off—'

'Oh, er, there you are, love,' I tried, grinning weakly.

'Don't give me that!' She stood there in a rage, shapely and expensively suited. Blonde hair in that costly new scruffy style. I glanced nervously about in case other dealers were witnessing my discomfiture. 'You've made me wait hours in this filthy hole!'

'Er, look, angel—'

'No. You look, Lovejoy.' She blocked my way. I danced with exasperation. I had to reach Tinker, get him to find the bird who'd got my beautiful antique bamboo cage. 'I'm thoroughly sick of your high-handed—'

'See you later, love.' I tried to shift her gently but she struggled and stayed put.

'That's just the point, Lovejoy! You won't see me at all. Do you seriously put me second to a cartload of junk?'

I stared, flabbergasted. Sometimes I just don't understand women. She actually meant antiques.

' 'Course,' I told her, puzzled.

Her aghast eyes opened wider. She gasped. 'Why, you

utter *swine*—' I saw her matching handbag swing but deflected it and she staggered. I held her up while her legs steadied.

'Listen, chuckie,' I said carefully. You have to be patient. 'Antiques are everything. Cheap or priceless, they're all that matters on earth. Do you follow?' Her horrified eyes unglazed but she was still stunned at all this. 'And *everybody* comes second. Not just you. Even me.' I straightened her up, gave her a quick peck to show I almost forgave her.

She recovered enough to start fuming again. 'Of all the . . .'

'Meet you tomorrow, love.' I let go and darted past.

This door leads to the back of the saloon bar. A chorus of insults rose from the solid wall of barflies as I emerged.

'Here he is, lads! Our auctioneer!'

Tinker was already half way into his first pint. I honestly don't know how he does it. He never stops from noon to midnight. I gave him the bent eye while Lily the barmaid scolded me for coming in the wrong way.

'Typical, Lovejoy.' She pushed me under the bar flap into the smoky bar to get me out of her way.

'Don't serve him, love,' the dealers shouted.

I'd nicked a bottle of brown ale on my way through so I didn't mind whether she did or not. Tinker's horrible aroma magically thinned the throng about us.

'Who was she, Tinker?' I breathed the words so the hubbub covered my interest.

'The bird with the big knockers?' He shook his head. 'She's new round here, Lovejoy. I didn't know whether to keep bidding or not—'

'Shut it,' I growled. She'd been so determined I'd knocked the precious One Eighty down to her, amid almost total silence. Dealers love a dedicated collector, especially a luscious bird intent on spending a fortune for a worthless wickerwork box. I was furious because it wasn't worthless at all. I'd hoped to get it for a song and make a month's profit. Instead I was broke again and the girl had vanished.

'Pint, Lil.' Tinker hardly muttered the words but Lily slammed a pint over. Tinker's ability to get served is legendary. I paid, this being my role in our partnership.

'Then why the hell aren't you out finding her, you idle burke?' I spat the insult at him, but kept smiling. Disagreements mustn't be obvious in our way of life, especially among friends.

'I am.' Tinker grinned a gummy grin. 'Lemuel's following her.'

I subsided at that and swilled my ale while he chuckled at my discomfiture. Lemuel's an old derelict who still wears his soldier's medals on his filthy old coat. He sleeps in our parks and church doorways and looks and pongs even worse than Tinker, which is going it somewhat. He has a nifty line in conning our wide-eyed and innocent social services ladies for every shekel they possess. Luckily for the nation's balance of payments, Lemuel recycles this colossal drain on sterling through the merry brewers of East Anglia and the sordid portals of our betting shops. He hasn't picked a winner since he was eight.

'Taking it up regular, Lovejoy?' Devlin's beloved voice boomed in my ear, getting a few laughs at my expense. Nobody hates auctioneers like a dealer.

'Maybe.' I gave the world my sunniest beam. 'You got a job yet, Devvo?' A laugh or two my side this time.

'I've a bone to pick with you, Lovejoy.' He loomed closer. He's a big bloke and never has less than two tame goons hovering behind his elbows. They follow his Rolls everywhere in a family saloon. They were there now, I saw with delight. It's at times like this that I'm fond of idiocy. It gives you something to hate. 'That Russian niello silver pendant. You didn't see my bid.'

'You bid late,' I said evenly. 'I'd already gavelled.'

'You bastard. You nelsonned it.' He meant I'd looked away deliberately—after Nelson's trick at Copenhagen—another illegal trick auctioneers sometimes use. The place had gone quiet suddenly. People started spacing out round us. Devlin became poisonously hearty. It's the way every burke of his sort gets. He prodded my chest.

'Don't do that, please,' I asked patiently.

'Gentlemen . . .' Lily pleaded into the sudden silence.

'I came especially for that pendant, Lovejoy.' Another prod. Thicker silence.

I sighed and put my bottle down regretfully. I've never really seen that whisky-in-the-face thing they do in cowboy pictures. Maybe one day. Helen moved, white-faced, as if to stand by me but Tinker drifted absently across to block her way, thank God. I didn't want her getting hurt.

'Ooooh! There's going to be *blood* everywhere!' That squeal could only be Patrick, our quaint—not to say decidedly odd—colleague in from the Arcade. He had his latest widow in tow to buy him pink gins from now till closing time. I saw one of Devlin's goons turn ominously to face the main saloon. The other neanderthal was grinning, standing beside his master with a hand fumbling in his pocket for his brass knuckles. You can't help smiling. Imagine chucking your weight about for a living. I despair of us sometimes. Where I come from, nerks like him would starve.

Good old Devlin dug my sternum again. 'I reckon you owe me a few quid, Lovejoy.'

'Don't do that, please,' I said again. 'Last warning, lads.'

The neanderthal mimicked me in a falsetto. 'Don't do that, please.' He laughed. 'Shivering, Jimmie?' A Glaswegian, if I wasn't mistaken. He reached out to prod me so I kneed him and broke his nose with my forehead as he doubled with a shrill gasp. He rocked blindly back, clutching himself, blood spattered across his cheeks and mouth. You can't blame him. It doesn't half hurt.

'You were saying, Devvo?' I said, but he'd backed away. His other goon glanced doubtfully from Devlin to me and then to his groaning mate. 'Look, girls,' I said, still pleasant. 'No fuss, eh? The auction's over with. And everybody knows you're too stupid to handle antique Russian silver, Devvo.'

I was honestly trying to cool it but for some reason he went berserk and took a swing at me. A table went over and some glasses nearby smashed. I snapped his left middle finger to stop him. It's easily done, but you must make sure to bend it rapidly back and upwards away from the palm—keep the finger in line with the forearm or it won't break, and you'll be left just holding the enemy's hand politely and feeling a fool. Devvo's face drained and he froze with the sudden pain.

'Well, comrade?' I was saying affably to the third nerk when the crowd abruptly lost interest and filtered away back to the booze. Sure enough, there he stood in the doorway, shrewdly sussing the scene out, the Old Bill we all know and love. Neat, polite, smoking a respectable pipe, thoroughly detestable.

'You again, Lovejoy?'

'Thank heaven you've come, Inspector!' I cried with relief, hoping I wasn't overacting because Maslow's a suspicious old sod. 'I've just separated these two.'

'Oh?' Sarcasm with it, I observed, and a uniformed constable in the doorway behind him.

'Some disagreement over an antique, Inspector, I believe,' I said smoothly, staring right into his piggy eyes with my clear innocent gaze. 'This man set upon Mr Devlin—'

Maslow asked, 'True, Lily?' She reddened and frantically started to polish a glass.

'Aye, Mr Maslow,' Tinker croaked. 'I seed it all, just

like Lovejoy says.' With his record that took courage.

Maslow swung on Tinker and pointed his pipe. 'Silence from you, Dill.'

'Perhaps I can help, Inspector.' Helen lit a cigarette, head back and casual. 'Lovejoy merely went to try to help Mr Devlin.'

'Are you positive, miss?' He sounded disappointed but kept his eyes on me. I blinked, all innocence.

She shrugged eloquently. 'Difficult to see clearly. It's so crowded.'

'Very well.' He jerked a thumb at Devvo's goons. 'Outside, you two.'

'Here, boss,' the uninjured nerk complained to Devlin in a panic. 'He's taking us in.'

'Be quiet.' Devlin was still clutching his swelling hand, pale as Belleek porcelain. 'I'll follow you down.'

Maslow turned to give me a long low stare as the heavies went out. He leant closer. 'One day, Lovejoy,' he breathed. 'One day.'

I went all offended. 'Surely, Inspector, you don't think—'

Maslow slammed out. Patrick shrilled, 'Ooooh! That *Lovejoy*! Isn't he absolutely *awful*?'

A relieved babble began. Devlin left for hospital a moment later, the constable delightedly piloting the Rolls. From the pub window I watched them go.

'Hear that, Tinker?' I demanded indignantly. 'Maslow didn't believe me.'

'Yon grouser's a swine,' Tinker agreed. Grouser's slang for an aggressive CID man.

'All clear, Lovejoy?' Lemuel ferreted between us and clawed my bottle out of my hand. His eyes swivelled nervously as he downed it in one.

'One day I'll get a bloody drink in here,' I grumbled, ordering replacements.

Lemuel wiped his mouth on his tattered sleeve.

'That's an omen,' he croaked excitedly. 'Blood Drinker, tomorrow's two o'clock race at—' It was becoming one of those days. I put my fist under Lemuel's nose. 'Ah,' he said, hastily remembering. 'That bint. I found her, Tinker.'

I glanced about, making sure we weren't being overheard, and met Helen's eyes along the bar. She raised her eyebrows in mute interrogation. Don Musgrave and his two barkers were with her. Don's antique pewter and English glass, and does a beano among tourists on North Hill. He's been after Helen for four years, but he's the kind of bumbling bear type of bloke that only makes women smile. Anyway, he hates cigarettes and Helen even smokes in bed. I gave her a brief nod of thanks and turned back towards the yeasty pong of my two sleuths. Owing women makes me edgy. They tend to cash in.

'Any chance of a bleedin' drink?' Lemuel croaked. 'I had to run like a frigging two-year-old.'

Irritably I shoved my latest pint at the old rogue. He absorbed it like an amoeba.

'She's a souper,' he said at last, wheezing and coughing froth at me. I tried not to inhale but being anaerobic's hard.

'Eh?' That couldn't be right.

'Straight up.' Lemuel nudged Tinker for support. 'I was right, Tinker.'

'Souper?' I couldn't believe it. Anybody less like your actual starry-eyed social worker was hard to imagine than that luscious leg-crosser. She'd seemed hard as nails.

'I got money from her for my auntie's bad back.'

'Which auntie?' I demanded suspiciously, knowing him. He grinned through anaemic gums.

'Got none.' He and Tinker fell about cackling at this evidence that the Chancellor too can be conned with the best of them. I banged Lemuel's back to stop the old lunatic from choking. All this hilarity was getting me down. Tinker spotted my exasperation as Lemuel's cyanosis faded into his normal puce.

'The Soup's down Headgate, Lovejoy.'

'Here.' I slipped Tinker three quid. That left me just enough for two pasties, my nosh for the day. 'Tell Helen I'll see her in the White Hart, tennish tonight.'

'Good luck, Lovejoy.' Tinker made his filthy mittens into suggestive bulbs. This witticism set the two old scroungers falling about some more. I slammed angrily out into the wet.

CHAPTER 2

The rain had stopped but town had filled up with people. I cut past the ruined abbey and across the Hole-in-the-Wall pub yard. Our town has a gruesome history which practically every street name reminds you of. Like I mean Head Gate isn't so called because it was our chief gateway in ancient days. I'd better not explain further because the spikes are still there, embedded in the ancient cement. The heads are missing nowadays. You get the message.

I hurried through St Peter's graveyard, envying the exquisite clock as it chimed the hour. These big church clocks you see on towers are almost invariably 'London-made' early nineteenth century, which actually means Lancashire made and London assembled. You can't help thinking what valuable antiques these venerable church timepieces are, so casually unprotected on our old buildings. The thought honestly never crossed my mind, but don't blame me if one dark night some hungry antique dealer comes stealing through the graveyard with climbing boots and a crowbar . . . I trotted guiltily on, out into the main street among the shoppers towards the social security dump.

You may think I was going to a lot of trouble over a modern bamboo box, and you'd be right. I wouldn't cross the road for a hundred as a gift. But for a genuine eighteenth-century Japanese bamboo firefly cage I'll go to a great deal of bother indeed.

A question burned in my brain: if scores of grasping citizens and greedy antique dealers can't recognize an *oiran*'s — star courtesan — firefly cage, then how come this bird can? And she had bid for it with a single-minded determination a dealer like me loves and admires — except when I want the item too. Of course I was mad as hell with the sexy woman, but puzzled as much as anything. I don't like odd things happening in the world of antiques. You can't blame me. It's the only world I have, and I'm entitled to stability.

You can't miss the Soup. Our civil servants have naturally commandeered the finest old house in Cross Wyre Street, a beautiful fifteenth-century shouldered house where real people should be living. I eyed it with displeasure as I crossed the road. The maniacs had probably knocked out a trillion walls inside there, true to the destructive instincts of their kind. The smoke-filled waiting-room held a dozen dishevelled occupants. I went to the desk that somebody had tried to label 'Enquiries' but spelled it wrong. This plump blonde was doing her nails.

'Yes?' She deigned to look up — not to say down — at me. I peered through a footage of sequinned spectacle trying to spot her eyes. I'm a great believer in contact.

'A young lady, one of your soupers — er, dole workers — '

She swelled angrily. 'Not *dole*! Elitist terminologies are utterly defunct. Sociology *does* advance, you know.'

First I'd heard of it. Elitist only means greedy and everybody's that. I'd more sense than to argue, and beamed, 'You're so right. I actually called because one of your, er . . .'

'Workers for the socially disadvantaged,' she prompted. One of the layabouts on the benches snickered, turned it into a cough.

I went all earnest. 'Er, quite. She dropped her purse at the auction an hour ago.'

'How kind.' The blonde smiled. 'Shall I take it?'

'Well, I feel responsible,' I said soulfully.

'I quite understand.' She went all misty at this proof that humanity was good deep down. 'I think I know who you mean. Maud Endacott.'

The bird hadn't looked at all like a Maud. The receptionist started phoning so I went to wait with the rest. George Clegg had just got in from the auction, and offered me a socially disadvantaged cigar. I accepted because I can't afford to smoke them often and tucked it away for after. He's a vannie, mover of furniture for us dealers. He labours—not too strong a term—for Jill who has a place in the antiques arcade in town. Jill too is a great believer in contact. She's mainly early mechanical toys, manuscripts, dress-items and men. Any order. George leant confidentially towards me, chuckling.

'That tart frogged you, eh, Lovejoy?'

I shrugged. He meant that she'd got what I wanted, which is one way of putting it. 'Don't know who you mean.' George was shrewder than I'd always supposed.

The phone dinged. 'Maud will see you now,' the receptionist announced, still Lady Bountiful. First names to prove nobody was patronizing anyone.

I gave her one of my looks in passing. She gave me one of hers. I leant on her counter.

'I wish I was socially disadvantaged,' I told her softly. She did the woman's trick of carefully not smiling. I waved to George and climbed the narrow stairs looking for the name on the door.

Sure enough the bird's room was crammed with radiators. I sat to wait, smouldering. The bloody fools had drilled the lovely ancient panelling full of holes for phone cables. Mind you, it was probably only oversight that had stopped our cack-handed town council flattening the lot into a carpark. I rose humbly as the bird entered. I noticed her stylish feminine clothes were now replaced by gungey tattered jeans and a dirty tee shirt. Back to the uniform, I supposed. She too was being humble—until she spotted who I was. Her concern dropped like a cloak.

'Oh. It's you.' She turned and slammed the door. 'I bought that box quite legally, so—'

'I know.' I thought, box? You don't call a precious antique firefly cage a *box*. Unless, that is, you don't know what the hell it is. Odderer and odderer.

'Then what are you here for?' She sat, legs and all. I watched her do her stuff with a gold lighter and cancer sticks. No offer of a cigarette, but she blew the carcinogens about for both of us to share.

Meekly I began, 'Er, I wondered about the box . . .' Her eyes were unrelenting stone, but it's always worth a go. I smiled desperately like the creep I am. 'I'm trying to make up a set,' I lied bravely. 'An auctioneer isn't allowed to bid for himself, you see.'

'And you want to buy it off me?' She shook her head even as I nodded. 'No, Lovejoy.'

'Perhaps a small profit . . .'

She crossed to pose by the window, cool as ice. 'I've heard about you, Lovejoy. The dealers were talking.'

'They were?' I said uneasily, feeling my brightness dwindle.

'If *you* want something it must be valuable.' She sounded surprised. '*Is* it?'

'I'm not sure.' Another lie. I gave as casual a shrug as I could manage, but my mind was demanding: *Then why the hell has she paid so much?* You can't do much with an antique firefly cage except keep fireflies in it.

'They say you're a . . . a divvie.' Oho. My heart sank. Here we go, I sighed to myself. She inhaled a trickle of smoke from her lips. Everything this bird did began to look like a sexy trick.

No use pretending now. 'That's my business.' I got up and headed for the door.

'Is it true, that you can tell genuine antiques just by feeling, intuition?'

I paused. Failure made me irritable. 'Why not? Women are supposed to do it all the time.'

She stared me up and down. I felt for sale.

'Then why are you in such a state?' she asked with calm insolence. 'Just look at you, Lovejoy. A skill like that should make you a fortune. But you're threadbare. You look as if you've not eaten for a week. You're shabbier than the layabouts we get here.'

I swallowed hard but kept control. Never let the sociologists grind you down, I always say. 'It's taxes to pay your wage, Maudie,' I cracked back and left, closing the door gently to prolong its life.

I was half way down the stairs when this harridan slammed out and yelled angrily after me from the landing. '*Lovejoy*!'

'What now?'

'You've turned the central heating off, Lovejoy! It's freezing.'

You have to be patient with these lunatics. 'Your door's the only one on the staircase that's original eighteenth-century English oak,' I said tiredly. 'Heat'll warp it. The others are Japanese or American oak copies and don't matter. Think of it,' I added nastily, 'as socially disadvantaged.'

'You're insane,' she fumed down at me.

For a moment I was tempted to explain about the rare and precious beauty in which she worked so blindly each day. About the brilliant madrigalist who once lived here,

and of his passionate lifelong love-affair with the Lady of
the Sealands. Of the delectable ancient Collyweston
stone-slated roof, unique in these part, which covered the
place. Of the fact that the cellar was still floored by the
genuine Roman mosaic and tiles of the oyster shop nearly
twenty centuries old. Then I gave up. There's no telling
some folks.

'Cheers, Maudie,' I said, and left it at that.

Downstairs George Clegg was whining at the grille for
his handout as I passed the main room. If he'd got a move
on I could have cadged a lift home in his new Lotus.

Pausing only to see if the Regency wrought-iron door
plates were still securely screwed in—regrettably they
were—I stepped boldly out on to the crowded pavement
and saw Devlin and his two burkes getting into their Rolls
outside the police station at the end of the street. Devvo's
hand was all strapped up. He saw me and paused,
glaring. He ignored my wave.

Oh, well. Anyway, it was time for my lesson.

CHAPTER 3

Buses to my village run about every hour, if there's not
much on telly in their drivers' hut at the bus station. I
waited uselessly by the post office over an hour, finally
getting a lift in Jacko's rackety old coal van. There's no
passenger seat. You just rattle about like a pea in a drum
and slither nastily forwards every time he zooms to a stop.
Jacko's an ancient reformed alcoholic who fancies himself
as a singer so you have to listen to gravelly renderings
from light opera while he drives. He can't drive too well,
just swings the wheel in the vague hope of guessing the
van's direction. He dropped me off on the main road.
The van stank to high heaven of bad cabbage.

There's a narrow footpath down the brook. It cuts off a good half-mile because the road has to run round the valley's north shoulder. I set off along the overgrown path, Lovejoy among the birds and flowers. Some people actually leave civilization to tramp our forests and fields, the poor loons. One couple I know do it every Saturday, when they could be among lovely smoky houses and deep in the beautiful grime of a town's antiques. No accounting for taste.

As I trudged I remembered Maud Endacott's face and got the oddest feeling. She'd been so determined, sure of herself. She'd paid over the true market value for a little cage — yet she didn't know what it was for, where it was from, its age or its value. And from the way she'd behaved she'd been prepared to pay every shekel she possessed to get her undeserving hands on it. None of it made sense.

For the last furlong I kept thinking about the exquisite Japanese masterpieces of the Utamaro school. His lovely woodblock prints don't look much at first, but with familiarity their dazzling eroticism blinds you. The truth is, Utamaro loved women. Women are everywhere, even — or maybe especially — in his *The Fantastic Print-Shop* series. You can't help chuckling to yourself. Of course he tried his hand at prostitutes, star courtesans and all as well. The point is that the brilliant lecher made lovely erotic art out of everything he saw. There's nobody else in the Ukiyoe School quite like him.

The reason the famous old Japanese prints kept haunting me as I walked was the fantastic lively detail they crammed in among all that sexy eroticism. One famous picture came into my mind's eye as I entered my long weed-crammed garden. Eishosai Choki's lovely silvered night painting, say 1785, give or take an hour. In it, a luscious courtesan holds a small cage on a cord. It's a firefly cage. And, straight out of that desirable print two centuries old, had come the little bamboo cage I'd auctioned off to Maud Endacott this morning.

My thoughts had gone full circle. I fumbled for my key, and found I wasn't smiling any more.

After swilling some coffee and chucking the birds a ton of diced cheese I felt a lot better. Rose the post-girl had called and pulled my leg about fancying Jeannie Henson who now runs old Mrs Weddell's grocer's shop, our village's one emporium. 'Make an honest woman of her,' Rose cracked merrily, shovelling a cascade of bills on to my porch. 'I would,' I gave back, sidefooting them aside for the dustbin, 'but her husband's a big bloke.' She mounted her bike and bounced suggestively on the saddle. 'That's never put you off before,' she said sweetly. 'Get on with you or I'll tan your bum,' was the best I could manage to that. 'Oooh, Lovejoy. When?' She pushed off down my gravel path to the non-existent gate. I waved as she pedalled up the lane, grinning. Funny how women have this knack of always getting the last word. Something they're born with. Usually it's irritating as hell. Today, though, it cheered me up and I went back in smiling.

I fried tomatoes for dinner, dipping them up with brown bread and margarine. They're all right but the actual eating's not a pretty sight. I had tried to make a jelly for pudding, only the bloody things never set for me. It's supposed to be easy, just pour water on these cubes and hang about for a few hours, but I've never had one set yet. I always finish up drinking them and they're not so good like that. By the time I'd washed up it was nearly time for Drummer. I'm always nervous at this stage, so I whiled away the time phoning a false advert to our local paper.

This is the commonest of all secondary tricks in the antiques game, and my favourite. I'm always at it. It creates a demand for something you want to sell, like this

Bible box I had. I had to cash it in urgently, my one remaining asset.

I dialled, putting my poshest voice on because I knew Elsie was today's newspaper adverts girl and she'd rumble my trick unless I was careful. I used to know her once.

'An advert for the Antiques column, miss,' I bleated in falsetto. 'Wanted urgently, English Bible box, oak preferred. Nineteenth century or older.'

'Address to send the bill, please?' Elsie put her poshest voice on too. Cheat. She's even commoner than me.

'Ah. Hang on, love.' I fumbled quickly through the phone book at random. Riffling the pages a name caught my eye. Oho. That posh address which kept getting burgled of its antiques, the careless burkes. Hall Lodge Manor in Lesser Cornard. Who deserved conning more? I read it out in full to Elsie, pleased at the idea of giving that snooty village something to talk about. 'And please include the name,' I added, still falsetto. 'Mrs Hepplestone. Send me the bill.' Damn the cost.

Happily I settled down with Hayward's book on antique fakery, pleased at having 'done a breader', as we dealers say. By tomorrow evening enough dealers would have read the advert, and my Bible box would be in great demand once I flashed it. Tough on poor old Mrs Hepplestone, though. Still, I thought indignantly, what was the cost of a grotty newspaper advert, for heaven's sake? And serve her right for being careless with her antiques. If I remembered right she'd been in the local papers at least three times for having her place done over. Paintings, ornaments and medallions had all gone in a steady stream. You'd think they'd learn.

The knocker clouted three times, bringing me back to earth. Drummer, I thought nervously. I got up to answer the door, my palms sticky like a kid at school meeting his teacher, and me the best antiques divvie in the business. I ask you.

*

'How do, son.' There he stood, looking like nothing on earth. Old tartan beret, scarf at the trail, battered clogs, shabby overcoat and enough stubble to thatch a roof. He lives down on the estuary with this donkey since he retired, giving rides to children. What a bloody waste of the world's last surviving handsilversmith. You'd think he'd live better in his old age, but he likes drunken idleness.

'Er, wotcher, Drummer.'

'Nice day.' Nervously I started to lead the way round the side of the cottage. 'How did it go, Lovejoy?'

'Er, not so good, Drummer,' I confessed nervously.

He smiled and paused to thumb a bushel of tarry tobacco into his pipe. 'Improving?'

'Well . . .' My throat had gone dry. I waited with nervous politeness while he did the fire magic.

The old man is gnome-sized, a mobile bookend. He's one of these blue-eyed Pennine men who are gnarled and grey-haired from birth. They seem a special breed, somehow, weirdly gifted and imaginative beyond the ordinary. They tend to speak in odd sentences which have most of the meaning in the breaths between. He looks dead average — until you see him at a benchful of raw silver. Then his rheumy old eyes spark and clear and his arthritic hands instantly become as tough as a wrestler's and graceful as a temple dancer's.

In a puff of grey tobacco smoke we walked into the back garden, Drummer's smile twinkling brighter at the unkempt state of it all. I ignored his silent criticism. Plants have enough troubles without me making their lives a misery.

My forge is actually a garage with a couple of brick structures — furnace and hot-sand table — erected near one wall. There's an end window opposite the up-and-over door. That's about it, except for a bench made out

of old packing cases for tools and any stray pieces of wood
I can cadge.

I offered Drummer the only stool. He sat and reached
across the bench for my gadroon. I stared. The instant
transformation in him gets me every time. It's remark-
able. From an old codger in clogs he becomes slick,
certain, completely in command. He hefted the heavy
steel plate about with casual ease. It cripples me just to
hold it upright.

'This it, Lovejoy?' he said at last, squinting along the
rim.

My heart sank. He actually meant: and you've brought
me here to see this travesty, Lovejoy, you useless burke?

'Er, yes, Drummer. That's it.'

He laid it down and smoked a bit. I looked dismally at
my gadroon and waited for the verdict while Drummer
gazed out on the bushes. It was honestly the best I could
do. My arms and elbows still creaked.

I'd better explain here about the Reverse Gadroon
because it's important.

I'd been lucky to find Drummer, lucky beyond belief.
He's the last of the real hammermen, a genuine
'flatworker'.

In days of yore silversmithing was silversmithing, every
task done by eye and hand. The polishers, modelmen,
finishers, all *did* their work. They actually *created*. And
of all these master craftsmen the greatest was the
hammerman, because he had the terrifying responsibility
of beating plain silver into a thing of miraculous beauty.
Without skill and love the final form would be piteous,
sterile. But with these two utterly human qualities the
luscious virgin silver catches fire. The design draws life
and love from its hammerman, finally glowing and
throbbing with a pulsating beauty of its own. This
explains why some silversmiths were superb, while some

silver—even good antique—is only moderately good.
There's a million designs, almost as many patterns as
silversmiths. But of them all, none is so difficult, risky
and beautiful as the Reverse Gadroon.

Drummer used to be an apprentice silversmith at
Gurrard's in the Haymarket. Now he's the last of the line.
I first realized who this old duffer was in a pub about a
year ago, and just couldn't believe my luck. I might have
missed it if I'd been casually gazing the other way.
Through the bar-room fug I saw this pair of crooked old
hands take a bent halfpenny from the Shove-Ha'penny
board and straighten it against the brass pub-rail with a
flick of a metal ashtray. Mesmerized, before I knew what
I was doing I'd pushed through the mob in a second and
collared the old scruff, and demanded, 'Can you do that
trick again?' Everybody laughed, thinking me sloshed.

'Aye, son,' he'd smiled. We were in people's way trying
to reach the bar. He took the coin and tapped once,
bending it literally like paper. Then straightened it
perfectly flat again with another tap on the rail. And all
the time he looked at me, smiling.

I'd cleared my throat, daring the question. 'Have you
ever heard of a Reverse Gadroon?'

His amusement lit with interest at the reverence in my
voice. 'I've done it, son. Now and then,' he said, by which
he meant for half a century.

And that was it. There and then I'd started learning
from him, twice a week in my homemade forge. I even
began exercises trying to strengthen my arms and
shoulders, with dismal results.

It sounds easy. You take a tray of solid silver and hold it
by the bottom edge over a patterned tool held in a vice.
The idea is to hammer the silver's perfect upper surface
over the die, thereby impressing the die's design. Then
you move the tray a fraction, and hammer again. Do this
all the way round, using even blows every time. If you've

held it right, judged every single blow to perfection, struck with the massive hammer at exactly the right spot and with the same force, if you've turned the silver exactly the same distance for every blow and never stopped until the whole piece is finished, and if you are possessed of Olympian strength, endless stamina and unerring judgement, then you've done a Reverse Gadroon. But make a fractional error, pause a split second or weaken, and you've ruined the whole solid chunk of precious silver. Nowadays machines do it all, without the slightest risk of a human error—or human love—creeping in. It's called progress.

Drummer's the last living original silversmith. I don't mind his eccentricities, that he's been made redundant by the onward rush of mechanization. I don't mind that for the past twenty years he's lived in a shack down on the estuary giving donkey-rides for a living. To me Drummer's a great man, a genius. But when he's gone, God forbid, I'm determined there'll still be somebody to pass on his priceless skill of the Reverse Gadroon.

Me.

Only at this particular moment I'd made another balls-up. Drummer gazed at me, puffing.

'Not so good, son, is it?'

'No,' I said miserably. The last time he told me off like this I felt suicidal, except living's hard enough as it is. I practise on thin steel sheet, cut in ovals. To take the weight I'd rigged up a wooden grip on a counterpoised cord. Old Drummer screwed his eyes at it.

'Look, son,' he said at last. 'Pretty soon you'll have the strength. After that it'll just be practice, direction and power.'

That sounded hopeful. 'And then I'll do a proper silver pattern?'

'No, son.' He rummaged for more tobacco. 'You're a

divvie, son. Stick to your trade.'

'Sooner or later I'll do a Reverse Gadroon,' I said doggedly.

'You're too immersed in antiques, lad. A new hammered silver's not antique. That's why you'll never do it, never in a million years.'

I ticked off on my fingers, narked at the old duckegg. 'Strength, Drummer. Practice. Direction. Level power,' I snapped. 'You said yourself I'll soon—'

'Give it up, son. Germoline could do better.'

Germoline is his donkey. I watched his match flare between puffs. 'Then what's missing?' I honestly couldn't see.

'Fire, son. In you.' He rose sadly and gave me the stool. 'Listen, Lovejoy. There's no such thing as weakness, getting tired, making a mistake. It does itself.' He opened the door. 'When you've got the fire in you, the Reverse Gadroon does itself.' He gave a slow grin. I was so mad I didn't smile back.

'But—'

'You've got it for antiques, son. Not for new things.' His gaze saddened me. 'Got a motif?'

I spoke without thinking. 'A firefly,' I said. Why I said that I'll never know.

'Fireflies? Never heard of a firefly gadroon, but why not?' He nodded and made to go. 'Might as well ruin a firefly pattern as any other, mate.'

We parted after that, still friends but me in low spirits.

'Look, Drummer,' I began at the gate. 'Er, I'm a bit strapped . . .'

He chuckled. 'The money? Forget it, Lovejoy.' I give him a quid every lesson when I can. I said I'd owe it. 'I don't need any fare. Joe's picking me up at the chapel.'

'Cheers, Drummer.'

He gets a lift from a chap called Joe Poges, our coastguard on Drummer's bit of coast, who comes into the village to see his sister. Her husband's one of these characters mad on racing pigeons. Drummer sets them free on the river and they fly home again. Have you ever heard of such wasted effort?

I stood until Drummer's small figure had vanished up the lane. Then I went back into the garage and tried and tried on a new sheet of iron. All I did was make it look like a clinker. After an hour I sagged to a stop, sweating and exhausted.

It had been a hell of a day. First losing the firefly cage like that. Then crossing Devlin and antagonizing Inspector Maslow. Then losing out with Maud. And last but not least getting the elbow from Drummer. Well, I thought in my cretinous innocence, it couldn't get much worse, could it?

I gave the day up and went back to reading Hayward on fakes.

CHAPTER 4

I'm not one of these constant blokes, urbane from cockshout to midnight. By the time the pubs opened I'd cheered up. Life is variation, after all, and I'm up and down with the best of them. Late that afternoon Tinker rang in with word of an inlaid early Victorian knifebox going cheap at Susan Palmer's antique shop on the wharf. And he'd sent Lemuel after a set of Shibayama knife-handles in Dedham but didn't sound very optimistic. Neither was I, to put it bluntly, because Lemuel knows more about astrophysics than antiques. Anyway, the horse-racing at York never finishes till five and I knew he'd lose the bus fare on some nag because he always does. The good sets are real ivory with inlays, the rare Shibayama being a composite of bronze and iridescent stones. (Always check that it is ivory and not synthetic ivorine; and the more varied the inlays — insects, birds, butterflies — the more pricey.)

'I'll bet,' I told him sardonically over the blower.

'Straight up, Lovejoy,' he croaked. 'Brad's going over tomorrow.'

Oho, I thought. Brad's mostly flintlock weapons and lately Japanese militaria, but he never goes anywhere without good reason.

I decided after a quick think. 'Okay, Tinker. Suss it.'

He caught me before I could hang up. 'Lovejoy, she come after you today.'

'She?'

'That sexy souper, the one with the big bristols.' He cackled evilly. 'You'll be all right with her, Lovejoy—'

'Shut it,' I told him. He did, but I could still feel his gappy grin down the wire. 'What did you tell her?'

'White Hart, eightish. That all right?'

I let him go, feeling much chirpier. Maybe she'd seen sense and wanted to sell me the firefly cage after all. Perhaps it wasn't what she'd expected. People commonly make this sort of mistake, assume some trinket box has secret compartments crammed with jewellery. You have to learn that the antiques game is one of dashed hopes.

Served her bloody well right.

Dusk was falling as I plodded up the lane. I have a lump of corrosion shaped like an old Austin Ruby somewhere in the long grass but its road licence ran out at an inconvenient moment of poverty. So until I strike a Rembrandt or two it waits, patiently oxidizing in the evening mists, and I walk everywhere. We have no street lights owing to the simple fact that we have no streets. Our three pubs are the only nightlife, except for a maniacal crowd of sweaty badminton players straining ligaments in the village hall, and a church choir murdering Palestrina twice weekly to the utter despair of our new choir mistress. The desirable Hepzibah Smith is a pneumatic young graduate from the Royal College of Music. She was attracted to our village not so much by an impressive musical tradition as the job we wangled for her bloke, a gigantic pear-shaped blacksmithing hulk called Claude who farriers horses on a local farm. Nobody laughs at his name, unlike mine. I could hear our choir from the path through the graveyard as they lumbered through the *Agnus Dei*. It came on to rain about then, heavenly retribution I suppose.

Most folk shun the Tile and the Queen's Head but the White Hart's always heaving like noodle soup by seven-thirty. It's here that local antique dealers congregate for nocturnal boasting about deals they haven't actually made, in order to make sure everybody else is mis-informed about deals they actually did pull off. Naturally our eternal wail is one of having sold the Crown Jewels too cheaply, of missing a cheap John Constable by a split second. The game is never to question the tales too deeply. They're all false. You'd only embarrass everybody by making some antique dealer admit that he couldn't have just snapped up Holman Hunt's *Light of the World* from a bloke in the flea-market. Just go along nodding and tut-tutting with sympathy. You can even make up a few tales of your own. The sober truth is that deep down in all the smoke and crap of the taproom every single dealer has had his hands on at least a few precious glowing beautiful antiques in the past few hours. Except me, that is, I thought, standing dripping in the doorway. And even I have a Bible box.

After the silence of the dark hedgerows outside the cacophony from the crowd dinned my ears. I'm always blinded for a minute while the light and the smoke tear at my eyes. Then my lungs adjust to the taproom smog and I push in, aiming for the bar.

'Hello, Lovejoy,' came from all sides.

'Watch your women, lads,' from some wit. 'It's our favourite auctioneer.'

'Make much profit, Lovejoy?' That was Joe Lampton, antique musical instruments and books.

I grinned. 'I charged Cuthbertson commission, Joe.' I got a few approving laughs.

Tinker was among the boozy crowd. I slid into the space his noxious vapours kept clear. Lemuel was over by the fireplace unerringly selecting cripples from tomorrow's Newmarket line-ups. Joe Lampton followed, pulling a first edition of Anne Cobbett's housekeeping handbook from his pocket. My chest clanged from lust, but I kept a calm face.

'This any good, Lovejoy?'

While Ted the barman got round to me I felt the book gently. In her day Anne Cobbett was as famous as Mrs Beeton. Be careful, though, because good modern photo-lithographic productions exist of many old books including *The English Housekeeper* — the paper and binding give them away. Any genuine old item, though, will scream its genuine character as soon as you get in reach. Joe's book was genuine all right. I told him so and valued it for him, loving the touch of the pages and the thick spine.

'Thanks, Lovejoy.'

I carefully wiped my hands down my trousers a few times as he merged happily with the mob. As I'd opened the book a fine chalky powder had fallen out. Doubtless some diligent housemaid had wished to protect an important household asset against bookworm by powdering the flyleaves with mortared white lead in a muslin bag. It's poisonous to *Homo sapiens* as well as to bookworms. Don't forget this when bookshop browsing.

Tinker was complaining. 'Here, Lovejoy. You could have charged Joe for pricing that bloody book. You always do it bleedin' free.' He was only worried where the next pint was coming from.

I shrugged and paid my pasty money over for a pint for him. I got the half. Mercifully Lemuel was still absorbed with the horses.

'Shut it,' I said. 'Run round.' Dealers' slang: summarize the main antique business of anyone knocking about. He slurped a gill and wiped his mouth on his oily sleeve before beginning. Sometimes I wish he wasn't so horrible. People are always on at me at the state he's in, as if it's my fault.

Helen wasn't in yet, I observed, but through the mirrors I could see Olive and Bill Tatum deep in an alcove, probably plotting their new stall in the town Arcade. That's the glass-roofed monstrosity which ruins the High Street. Bill hasn't much go in him, but Olive's fierce determination to out-Sotheby the rest of us spurs him on to a greater glory than his handbarrow of disintegrating trinkets in the Castle Yard.

'Olive and Bill mortgaged again,' Tinker croaked in a whisper seeing my glance. 'They bought that Staffordshire collection Jill got from Colchester.'

I nodded to show I'd heard him and swallowed my sudden hard anger. We were leaning on the bar, apparently chatting affably. In reality we were reckoning the chances of leaching anything we could out. That was important news about the Tatums. They'd now be desperate to sell rather than buy for the next month or two. Jill on the other hand would be a keen buyer—always assuming she could spare a few minutes from her latest young seaman. I could see her snappy poodle in the grip of a bewildered youth at the other end of the bar while Jill saw to her lipstick. She has one sailor after the other. Never the same twice. Tinker says they get danger money for just putting in to East Anglia.

I prompted Tinker, spotting a familiar cropped head

against the far wall. 'Jason?'

'You saw him buy, Lovejoy.'

Jason, once a regular army officer, now goes straight as an antique dealer in silver and furniture. A surprising success in the Arcade. He'd successfully bid high for a satinwood commode today, to the annoyance of the Birmingham crowd.

'And Tom Haslam's started ferrying.' Tinker's beer had gone. He gazed forlornly into the glass while I tried not to notice.

'A lot?' Tom's one of the wealthier dealers so this was important too.

'Almost every stick. And running it.'

Roughly translated, Tinker was reporting that Tom had decided to start exporting antiques wholesale to Continental buyers, and illegally at that. It's really smuggling in reverse. Hereabouts it's simple enough. We have too many small inlets for the coastguards' peace of mind. Ferrying gives a profit that's fast but 'flat', as we say — you tend to get as much profit this month as the next. If you think about it, this implies you're being underpaid for the better quality antiques. Curiously, dealers who ferry are regarded with a mild sympathy by the rest of us. They should worry.

I asked about Patrick, now busy shrieking at Deirdre — his latest widow I told you about — for doing his pink gin wrong. Tinker eyed the battle with distaste.

'But, darling . . .' Deirdre was expostulating. She inherited a fruit farm down on the estuary and is bent on reforming Patrick with the proceeds, which is a laugh. A sad one.

'And your *hat*!' Patrick screeched viciously. I honestly don't know why she puts up with him.

Tinker snorted. 'He bought three finger jades today—'

'Japanese or Chinese?'

'Dunno, Lovejoy. Does it matter?'

Today's accent certainly was eastern. I thought a bit as the far door swung open and Maud Endacott stepped inside. I decided it did matter. 'Yes. Find out who he sells to.'

Lemuel saw us just then and weaved foggily towards the bar. To my relief Maud Endacott advanced, through a shoal of ribald remarks. Oddly enough Big Frank from Suffolk was with her. Big Frank says he has wives like other folk have 'flu, time after time and every virus different. He paused to chat with Olive and Bill. Maud came on like the Light Brigade.

'Lovejoy.' She stood facing me, trouble all over. Tinker began to edge away. So did Lemuel, and so did I. I'd lost both rounds so far. There seemed no point in a third.

'Sorry, love,' I said. 'Just going.'

'Three pints, please,' she said over my shoulder. Tinker and Lemuel reappeared like magic, trapping me against the bar but avoiding my eye. Loyalty, I thought bitterly. She got a complicated vodka thing for herself and paid up with a flash of notes that momentarily quietened the pub into reverence. I hadn't known sociologists got a percentage.

'And again, please,' she told Ted. He was hovering handily, ogling. Tinker and Lemuel cackled and slurped frantically, ready for another.

I made sure I spoke softly. 'What's the game, Maud?'

'Want a job, Lovejoy?' She gazed at me over the rim of her glass. 'Antiques.'

'For . . . ?'

'For me.' She squeezed my arm but I've had tea-ladies before. A tea-lady's our slang for a bird who teases a knowledgeable bloke on until she's learned all he knows in his own particular field—say, Georgian manuscripts. Then she'll ditch him and take up somebody else and repeat the process. Lucrative, but definitely one-way.

I shook my head. 'No, love.' Tinker nudged me

desperately. I gave him the bent eye, implying that
barkers do as they're told or get a thick ear. He ducked
back into his beer.

She smiled sweetly. 'I understand there's a fee,
Lovejoy.' And the world shivered to a quivering halt right
there in the pub's unbreathable air. Money's nothing in
itself, not really. But it's the golden ladder you climb to
reach antiques. My resolution faded. Maybe I could eat
again, something except fried tomatoes.

'Er, well . . .'

'See you outside in a minute.'

'Er . . .' But she'd already crossed over to Big Frank.
They seemed very, very friendly.

'For Christ's sake charge her, Lovejoy,' Tinker croaked
urgently in my ear. 'Sod that little box.'

'Lemuel,' I asked. 'That Shibayama set?'

'Oh.' He got into his whining crouch. 'Sorry, Lovejoy.
Never reached Dedham. Lost the bus fare. My pocket.
Must be a hole . . .'

Typical. I told the two of them to be in the Arcade
tomorrow noon. Helen would be narked that I'd missed
her, but Tinker was right. I'd have to get a groat from
somewhere or I'd starve. But why me? Big Frank's as good
a dealer as they come, which admittedly is really pretty
mediocre. Maybe he'd failed her in some way, I thought
unpleasantly.

Anyway, wisely or not I pushed my way to the pub door
and out in a mood of total hope, which only goes to show
how really thick I can be. My judgement in antiques is
great. In everything else it's just the opposite.

Outside was pitch black and drizzling. A car swished by,
all lights and aggro. A few people slammed in and out of
the public bar. I waited under a tree in the bitter cold like
a duckegg. The way Maud spoke back there it looked like
she wasn't going to let the firefly cage go. I wondered idly

about Maud and Big Frank. Headlights turned in to the forecourt and blinded me.

'Lovejoy?'

'Hello, Dolly.'

The motor's lights dowsed. Only the shrouded pub lanterns showed her standing gleaming in the darkness. Maybe men like blondes because they're easier to find in the dark. I'd never thought of that before. We dithered before I lost as usual and had to speak first.

'Look, love,' I got out after clearing my throat a million times. 'I've a job on just now. And, er, sorry about today—'

'You're an outrage, Lovejoy.' Her voice was quiet, flat. She stepped closer and slowly lit a cigarette. 'I don't know what's got into me, Lovejoy.'

What can you say to this sort of stuff? 'Er, well, love—'

'Don't invent excuses.' She seemed without emotion. 'I must be insane.'

Women make me nervous when they're in these odd moods. I wish they'd stay fair-minded and reasonable like me. Life would be a hell of a sight easier.

'I'm not a . . . slag, Lovejoy.' Her voice was unchanged. 'Is that the word?'

'I know you're not.'

'Don't bother even saying it.' She sounded tired, resigned. Her eyes lit in a passing motor's beam. We waited politely until the distant noise faded, as if the countryside's belly had rumbled. 'You always were . . . eccentric.' I drew breath but she went on in the same level voice, 'I have a busy husband, nice home, good furniture. Funny that I never rated you till we met again. Are you broke?'

'No.' I lied defiantly. 'I've this job on . . .'

A voice called. 'This way, Lovejoy.' Good old Maud, goose-stepping out right on time. 'Where the hell are you?'

'Mmmmh,' Dolly said. '*That's* the job, I suppose?'

'Yes,' I said eagerly. 'She's got this antique . . .'

Dolly put her hand on my face. 'Shhh. See you tomorrow.'

Then she'd gone, clipping off among the cars. She never even glanced towards Maud's voice. Maud was working on her mouth with lipstick by pencil light when I finally found her midget car. How did Big Frank get in, I wondered. I made it, finding joints I never knew I had. She watched another motor's headlights sweep the trees.

'I suppose that cow's your fat blonde?' Dolly's not fat, but women hate each other on sight. No telling why. A man's stupid to join in, so I ignored the crack.

'Where are we going?'

'Yours,' she said curtly. 'Direct me.'

So I did.

'Jesus Christ. What a *dump*.'

I said nothing, but was secretly pretty narked. I think my cottage looks really quite good, thatched roof and all that. It's just a bit dog-eared because I don't get much time to tidy it. I heard her derisive snort at the faded wooden sign against one of the apple trees: 'Lovejoy Antiques, Inc.'

'Leave it further up the drive, please,' I asked.

'Drive? This is a frigging swamp with gravel, Lovejoy.' She drove in anyway.

Charming. I got out and felt for the keys. If I forget to switch the alarm off before opening the front door our village's vigilant bobby infarcts. He's always moaning about it.

'Cut the lights, please,' I asked. 'Er, the hedgehogs don't like them . . .' She ignored that and drummed her foot impatiently. 'Come in.' I held the door. She waited while I put some lights on, then pushed through the little hall.

'You actually *live* here? I wouldn't have come if I'd known.'

I shrugged and made a feeble pass at clearing some books for her to sit on the divan. It unfolds into my bed. There's quite a lot of space in the living-room, really, but it never seems to be as available as it might be. Maud walked past the space I'd prepared and moved about the room, flicking aside the curtain to inspect the kitchen alcove with distaste. I noticed the grime on the windows.

'It's a shithouse, Lovejoy.'

I was red-faced, shovelling things aside on the low table for her handbag. She sat at last. I know I don't create much of an impression as a high-powered antique dealer but she needn't be quite so blunt.

'Can't you get anything better?' she demanded. 'We ought to condemn it.'

'It keeps me in antiques,' I explained. The trouble is that when I'm embarrassed I go defensive, as if everything's my fault.

'You're really into this antiques crap, aren't you?' For the first time some gleam of curiosity showed. 'Here. Open this.' And she pulled out the bamboo firefly cage.

You have to smile at some antiques. This little cage stood jauntily on my table, cockily aware of its undoubted elegance. Its side and top netting had frayed, of course, but the little half-door at the bottom was intact and the side and bottom struts of bamboo were perfect. It was no taller than a few matchboxes.

'What's so funny, Lovejoy?' Maud gazed from me to the cage and back.

Still smiling, I took the lovely intricate cage. Light as a feather. The ancient maker would have searched for days to find the right bamboo. Then he would have seasoned it, exposing it to sun, laid it in the right direction, talked to it, encouraging the pieces to become accustomed to a new life. Then slicing, and balancing on his outstretched finger to ensure an even lightness. At last, the incredible detailed jigsaw assembling, and the delicate net windows to retain the fireflies. Then the *oirans*, those lovely women, the star courtesans so dedicated to feminine elegance, would take it, wandering in the gardens of the Green Houses. Among the night-blooming flowers they would catch fireflies until the little cage would glow with a soft nebulous splendour. And at the Hour of the Rat, about midnight, the first-rank lady courtesan would finally lie reclining in love with her ardent suitor by the seductive glow of its gentle but brilliant emanation, perhaps watched through the screens by her *shinzo*, invariably so eager to learn the breathlessly inventive techniques with which the *oiran's* erotic skills lifted her soul to her lover's as they soared—

'You're a fucking nut, Lovejoy.' Maud was still looking at my face. 'Get on with it.'

Crump. I breathed a deep breath and opened its door carefully.

Maud watched, puzzled. 'Is that it?'

'Yes.'

'Nothing inside? No other places?'

I sighed. She had the secret-compartment syndrome I told you about. I examined it carefully. 'No.'

'What the hell *is* it?'

I looked at her sitting there. Aggressive. Trendy. Impatient, full of certainty. Clueless as the rest of them. Everything that everybody is nowadays. And a sociologist to boot. I thought, what's the use?

'Just a box.' I said a mental apology to it. 'Was that the job you mentioned? You could have opened it yourself.'

'No. I just wanted to see you do it. *This* is the problem.' And she pulled out another.

I stared. Another firefly cage? Exactly the same, a small rectangular tower on four round stumpy legs. A front part-door. Side and top netting. But all black as

Newgate's knocker and glittering with an extraordinary dark lustre I'd never seen before. I reached over and picked it up. Heavy and cold. I looked at one top corner of the little door where it had been chipped by some lunatic trying to lever it open. Good old Big Frank. It's a wonder he hadn't used a hammer. I inspected it with a hand lens a long while before the penny dropped. *It was made of coal.* And I mean real coal, the sort you burn in a grate. The netting over the windows, the door and its handle, even the minuscule hinges. The entire thing was coal. Somebody, perhaps the maker, had covered it with black lacquer, presumably to keep it from smudging things, maybe to strengthen it. Coal carvings are occasionally still done, but this small fragile cage was superb, far higher quality than most. Yet it felt modern.

I readjusted my face. A gaping expert's unconvincing to a customer.

'Who made it?'

'Just open it, Lovejoy.' That cold determination again. 'And give me a cigarette.'

I glanced at her as I felt at the exquisite little cage of living coal. She sat there almost quivering, her eyes fixed on the object with an eagerness that could only be called lust. I realized she'd bought the bamboo firefly cage hoping it would reveal the way this copy opened. And it hadn't.

She snapped her fingers at me impatiently. 'I said cigarette.'

If I was putting up with her for the price of a pasty I sure as hell had no fags. 'I'll tell your mother you smoke.'

'Sod it.' She rose and paced among the clutter. 'This place is bleeding perishing, Lovejoy. Light the fire.'

I ignored her and attended to the cage. The coal version had something the bamboo antique had not. If you ran your fingers down its length there was a faint step just palpable halfway. Squinting sideways you couldn't see it. Another use for the coat of lacquer, to conceal a carved line round the cage? I took a pin from a drawer and slit the lacquer along the line, feeling my way in fractions. So the carver had copied the bamboo cage exactly the same but different, so to speak. It could easily be lacquered again.

'Is there likely to be anything inside?' I asked.

'How the hell should I know?' She was sulking furiously now. Our relationship was going downhill. I wouldn't have minded except she was the one with the money.

It seemed worth looking at the cage from all angles. The box was slightly smaller at the top than the bottom, like to bits of a telescope. I pressed the top down gently. After a faint pause it slid easily into the bottom half a little way and the door swung open. The whole thing was its own key. Clever.

That stopped the sulks. Her lust came back, force nine. 'Give it here, Lovejoy!'

'Hang on.' I deflected her hand and peered in at the little space. Empty. I'd guessed that.

Now, I thought. If a box was meticulously designed to conceal its own hollow emptiness, whatever needed hiding had to be in the walls, right? And since there was no other key . . . I held the little door ajar and pressed the box's top half down again. I was wrong. Not the walls. It was in the legs. One was hollow.

The corner of the box floor tilted leaving a triangular hole. Keeping the cage firm I switched the lights off and got my pencil torch to peer down inside the hollow stumpy leg. Nothing except faint spiralling down the wall of the hollow. For a moment I caught a brief flash of mauve, or thought I did. I looked again but only saw the black interior of the hollow cut deep into the leg. I showed Maud.

Just my luck. 'Whatever was in there's gone.'

'Shit.' She snatched the cage before I could move. She

peered into the minuscule hollow leg of the coal cage and glared at me in disgust. 'Useless.' She put the lights on and halted, staring at me. 'What's up, Lovejoy?'

'Nowt.' But I was clammy and cold for no reason. You feel stupid when that happens.

'You're white.' Maud pulled her coat round her. 'No wonder, living in this gunge. It's freezing in here.'

It had been the shadow. Maud's firefly cage had cast a shadow in the dark room. The pencil torch had thrown a curious blunt dark patch on my wall, very fleeting. I'd only caught it with the corner of my eye for an instant before it vanished as Maud bent to look in the cage. I was shaking like a frightened colt.

I'm honestly not the imaginative sort. No, honestly. After all what's more stupid than letting yourself get scared of nothing? And a shadow's nothing. I mean to say, a grown man, for God's sake. I mopped my face with my sleeve, cold and hot all at once.

A motor-horn sounded twice outside. I started towards the window but Maud snorted.

'Keep calm. It's only my gig.' She was still mad at not finding anything, but what had she expected? She'd still got two glorious works of art, one a genuine antique, the other a brilliant modern copy in a unique material.

'Gig?' I nodded wisely thinking, what's a gig? Must be some sort of motor car.

She rammed both firefly cages into her handbag and snapped it shut. My stomach turned at the risk the two beautiful little objects were running, living with good old Maud. I suppose my face changed because she was suddenly amused.

'These things really turn you on, don't they?' She paused suddenly in the hall on the way to the door. 'Do you want them?'

'Eh?' There must be a catch in it. Birds like Maud don't become instant Sweet Charity for nothing. 'Well, yes. But

I'm a bit short . . .'

'Your pay for opening the cage,' she said. There was a
pause full of significance. The hall's only narrow. She
came even closer and slowly put her hand round me
under my shirt and squeezed with steady insistence.

'Er, well,' I said hoarsely. 'I, er, usually charge, er—'

She lifted my hand on to her breast. Tinker had been
right about her. She really was luscious. 'Which is it,
Lovejoy?' Her voice went into a husky whisper. 'You can
have the cages. Or you can be tonight's gig. Which?'

Well, I'd already got a motor. A motionless one, but
definitely a horseless carriage. 'The cages.'

She yelped and pushed me back. 'You *bastard*!' I fell
over the carpet.

By the time I'd got up she'd stormed off, taking the
cages with her. I went to the door and saw Big Frank's
car. It was rolling backwards out of my garden, being
followed by Maud's bubble car, and the penny finally
dropped. So that's a gig, I thought. A gig's a bloke or a
bird, or any combination of the two. Well, well. That
seemed the end of Maud and me, and the end of
my—well, her—lovely firefly cages. A woman scorned
and all that. I shut the door as the phone rang.

'Lovejoy! Where have you been?' Helen.

'Hello, love. Look. Can you come round urgently,
please?'

'I thought you'd never ask.' My voice must have
sounded odd because she said, 'What's the matter?'

'Something for you. Be quick.'

'What is it?'

'A gig,' I said, casually as I could. 'Oh, love. Can you
bring a pasty?'

CHAPTER 5

You must admit, sometimes women deserve gratitude. Like I mean even with Helen staying I woke sweating and shivering now and then throughout the night.

Next morning she brewed up in the alcove and fetched the cups across. I could feel her looking interrogatively at me, but pretended to be reading Kelly on restoring oil paintings.

'Lovejoy.'

'Mmmm?' I turned a page carelessly but she took the book away to see my face.

'You spent a terrible night.' She said it like an accusation, but who the hell has nightmares deliberately? No wonder women peeve you.

I said tut-tut. 'Did I?'

'Muttering and threshing all night long.'

I lowered my eyes innocently. 'I'm not used to having company in bed. Makes me restless.'

She choked laughing and nearly drenched herself in instant coffee. 'Lovejoy! You're preposterous!'

I watched her fall about. Women are lovely in the morning, faintly dishevelled but warm and soft. Morning women aren't half so vicious as the night sort. I always find they're more fond of me. You can get away with more after a night's closeness. Odd, but true. Helen's no exception. She always wears my threadbare dressing-gown to slop about in. It makes no difference to the allure you feel, just seeing her sit on the edge of the bed lost inside the tattered garment. After rolling in the aisles some more she sobered and asked me about shadows.

'The one you got up to draw on the wall.'

'Eh? I did no such thing.'

She pointed to the wall near the mantelpiece. I'd thought she was asleep when I did it. And there was me tiptoeing about like a fool with my torch half the night, which shows how treacherous women are, deep down. She'd been watching all the time.

'You should have been kipping,' I said coldly.

Helen was at the pencilled outline, head tilted. 'What's it a shadow of, Lovejoy? A leaning castle? A window? A book, end on?'

'Dunno.'

If she hadn't been an antique dealer I might have told her what was on my mind. The lines showed the firefly cage's silhouette almost exactly as I'd cast the shadow last night when Maud called. There's this old iron grate in my living-room with a cornish above and a brass rail about head high. A painting I did years ago of the Roman road at Bradwell hangs nearby. Then there's a space where I used to have my Wellington chest before I flogged it for bread six months back. Then there's a tatty reddish curtain busily festering in whatever feeble sunlight totters through the window's grime, and that's about it. The shadow had stretched obliquely up from the black grate's mantelpiece almost as far as the corner. Climbing up there to mark it in the darkness had been really difficult. I'd nearly broken my bloody neck. I had the odd feeling I wouldn't have been so frightened of the odd lopsided shape if it had stayed exactly like the firefly cage. It was the skewed slanting weirdness of it on the wall that was so petrifying. But why? I closed my eyes. Maybe I was going off my nut. I'd gone clammy again.

Helen came back and put her arms round me. 'Don't be scared, love.'

That really got me. I broke away, annoyed. 'Who's scared?' Some women really nark me, always jumping to stupid conclusions with no reason. 'It's a . . . a scientific problem, you daft burke.'

' 'Course it is, love,' she said, not turning a hair. 'You're right. Sorry, sweetheart. I meant . . . preoccupied.'

That mollified me a bit. 'Well, all right then.' But my eyes kept getting dragged to the grotesque quadrilateral on the wall. I'd used crayon and charcoal to thicken the outline here and there. I've been scared of some real things before, but never a bloody shadow.

'What do you want for breakfast, love?'

'Er, I'm not hungry . . .'

Her eyes narrowed. She went searching.

'Ferreting in people's cupboards is very rude,' I reprimanded.

She started to slam about, flinging some clothes on. 'There's *nothing* here, Lovejoy! Not a single thing to eat.'

'Isn't there? Good heavens! I forgot to call in—'

She had wet eyes when she finally stood over me, arms akimbo. 'What am I to do with you, Lovejoy?'

You feel such a twerp lying down starkers when everybody else is up. Socially disadvantaged. 'Look, love,' I said uncomfortably, but she swept her coat and handbag up and slammed into the hall. The outside door shook the cottage to its foundations. I sighed. Unless you count Tinker, that meant I'd alienated practically all mankind, and even Tinker was narked because I hadn't charged Joe Lampton over divvying his book. Anyway, what is grub to do with Helen? She only eats yoghurt. I lay there listening and thinking, aren't people a lot of trouble. Helen's car started and scuffed away.

The shape scared me. All right, I admit it. Somehow it made my scalp moisten and my palms run. Somewhere it had scared me even worse than now, not as a mere scraped outline done in a wobbly hand during the dark hours, but in a solid terrifying reality, with the great oblique rectangle . . . *I'd seen it before*.

I was in the garden in my pyjamas when Helen

returned. There's this unfinished decorative wall I keep meaning to brick to an end when I get a minute. It's a sitting and thinking wall. She drew the car up. You could tell she was still mad from the way it slithered.

'What are you doing out here, Lovejoy? You'll catch your death.'

'Oh, just watching the birds.' They walk about on my grass being boring. What a life. Nearly as successful as mine. Helen's eyes left me and observed the open cottage door behind me. I was frigging freezing. It was an airy fresh morning and the grass wet through.

'Come back in with me.' She got out, her arms full of brown bags. 'Let's feed you up before we do anything else. I'll go in first.'

'Caviare and chips, please,' I joked, following her. My bum was frozen from the wall. Helen didn't smile. I always think that's the trouble with women. No sense of humour.

About Helen: she is reserved, in charge of herself and usually boss of everybody in arm's reach. She isn't like Angela, say, or Jill or Patrick, who couldn't have made it as antique dealers without considerable fortunes from interested donors. She's a careful blue-eyed cigarette-smoker you don't take for granted. And there's no doubt about her dealing skills, so precisely focused on oriental art, fairings and African ethnology. Helen's not an instant warm like Dolly. More of a slow burn.

While she made breakfast and I shaved I couldn't help thinking about her. Antique oriental art. We'd been close when she first hove in from one of the coastal fishing villages. Eventually she bought a little terraced house in the ancient Dutch quarter near the antiques Arcade, and she'd arrived. Now, I thought, politely passing the marmalade, why are we suddenly so friendly again? It haunted me all the way into town, because antique

oriental art includes Japanese firefly cages of the Edo
period, right?

Sadly, I'm afraid this next chunk is about that terrible
stuff called money and those precious delectables we call
antiques. You've probably got cartloads of both. But if
you are penniless please read on and save yourself a bob
or two.

Helen dropped me in the Arcade. This is a long glass-
covered pavement walk with minute alcoves leading off.
Each is no more than a single room-sized shop with a
recess at the back. It doesn't sound a lot but costs the
earth in rates. That's why we dealers regard possession of
a drum in the Arcade as a sign that you're one of the elite.
Woody's Bar perfumes the place with an aroma of
charred grease. We all meet there for nosh because it's
the cheapest known source of cholesterol-riddled pasties
and we can all watch Lisa undulate between tables. She's
a tall willowy PhD archæologist temporarily forced into
useful employment by the research cutbacks—the only
known benefit of any postwar government. Woody keeps
messages for barkers like Tinker while serving up grilled
typhoid. I always pop in to Woody's for a cup of outfall
first, to suss out the day's scene.

'Wotcher, Woody!' I called breezily. 'Tea and an
archæologist, please.'

'It's arrived, lads,' Woody croaked. He's a corpulent
moustache in a greasy apron. 'Chain it down.'

'Here, Lovejoy.' That was Brad beckoning through the
acrid fumes. He'd only want to moan about the
scandalous prices flintlocks were bringing. He couldn't be
more upset about it than me, so I pretended not to see
him for the smoke.

A few mutters of greeting and glances from bloodshot
eyeballs acknowledged my arrival. My public. Pilsen was
in, a half-crazy religious kite collector who lives down on

the Lexton fields somewhere. Devlin was absent, which mercifully postponed the next war. Harry Bateman was in the far corner still trying to buy a complete early Worcester dining set for a dud shilling, and Jason our ex-army man was still shaking his head. What puzzles me is that Harry—a typical antique dealer, never paid a good price for anything in his life—thinks other people are unreasonable. Liz Sandwell waved, smiling. She's high class, a youngish bird with her own shop in Dragonsdale village. Her own bloke's a rugby player, but I'd never seen the geezer she had with her now. She had three pieces of Russian niello jewellery pendants on the table between them—think of silver delicately ingrained with black. One was the pendant Devlin had complained to me about. I crossed ever so casually near her but Liz stopped talking so I couldn't hear the prices. Wise lass. That way I landed Pilsen.

'Wotcher, Pilsen. Get rid of your scroll?'

'A blessing from the Lord upon thy morning,' Pilsen intoned, hand raised.

'Er, ta, Pilsen.' I sat gingerly opposite while his head bowed in prayer.

'May heaven bring its grace upon Lovejoy and our holy meeting.'

'Tea, Lovejoy.' Lisa plonked a cup down. She always ruffles my thatch. 'Money, please. Woody says no credit for the likes of you.'

'Ruined any good antiques lately?' We're always arguing. I've not forgiven Lisa for what the professional archaeologists did to the Roman graves at Stanway, bloody grave-robbers.

'Don't start.' She edged away. 'And keep your hands off my leg.'

'Oh God. Forgive thy erring servant Lovejoy his wickedness . . .'

'Shut up praying, Pilsen.' Religion's bad for the soul.

'That Ethiopian amulet scroll. What's your price?'

'A Cantonese ceremonial dragon kite,' he said instantly. 'Or no sale.'

I sighed. I'd been trying to get that Ethiopian scroll for months. There are literally thousands knocking about, but Pilsen's was special. They are passed down in families which festoon their donkeys, sometimes as many as three dozen dripping from a single beast's neck to protect them on the road. Richer people had silver filigree containers as long as your finger to hold one. Others put them in horn cylinders or leather boxes. At the time of that appalling drought, dealers went over and shipped them on to the antiques markets of the world literally by the hundredweight. St Michael's a popular figure, usually the main one of five pictures separated longitudinally by calligraphed passages from Gospels. The eyes will prove them genuine. Nobody can paint those eyes with only a stick like the old Copts. Those and the delectable glowing brick-orange of the dyes. Pilsen's was the oldest and best-preserved scroll I'd ever seen, and he wanted the impossible.

'A Bible box?' I offered resignedly.

'Get knotted,' said this holy paragon. He gave me a quick blessing and shot out of the door, having been waved at through Woody's window by Maud. Now there's a thing, I thought. Pilsen and Maud. Well, well. Maud took his arm and they strolled off down the Arcade. She was being her beautiful best, suited and high-heeled. The slop of her social worker set was gone. She looked straight off a fashion page. Odderer still. I decided to follow. Lily tried flagging me down from her table but I hurtled past.

'See you in the White Hart, love.'

'But Tinker said . . .'

I dithered frantically, then resigned myself and screeched to a stop. Just as I'm Tinker's only source of income, so Tinker's messages are my only lifeline. Lily hopefully pushed the tissue paper bundles across the table as I plumped down.

'. . . you'll have these.'

That sounded a bit high-handed for Tinker. Lily was risking a bowl of Woody's opaque gelatinous soup. She used to be with Patrick until the Widow Deirdre homed in on him. Now she miserably endures her pleasant husband and all the comforts of home and affluence. Looking across at her I despaired of women. Some just seem to need to carry a heavy crucifix, and I'll bet crucifixes don't come any heavier than Patrick. Yet since losing him she'd been at a low ebb. The trouble is I'm too soft.

'Right, love.' I slipped them into my pocket, nodding. Pilsen and Maud would be in the High Street by now. 'Settle up later tonight?'

Lily was relieved. 'Thanks, Lovejoy. They're not perfect.'

'Who is, love?' I cracked, bussed her and shot out into Arcade, managing to ignore Woody's howl for his tea money, impudent burke. Gelt, for that swill. I ask you.

And Pilsen and Maud had gone. Great. I darted frantically among the shoppers for a few minutes hoping to see them but kept falling over pushchairs and dogs. Margaret was at the door of her shop. She'd seen me streak past.

She curtsied. 'Can I help you, sir?'

I went in resignedly. 'Wotcher, Margaret. Still got the Norfolk lanterns?'

'Special price for you, Lovejoy.'

Gazing about the interior of her enclosure depressed me more. Practically all of her stuff was priced and labelled by me because we're, er, close. Margaret's one of those older women who are clever dressers, interesting and bonny; she has a slight limp from some marriage campaign. Nobody asks about her bloke, whoever he was.

His dressing-gown fits me, though.

'Put them to one side for me, love.'

You'll see a thousand reproduction Norfolk lamps for every genuine antique one, and a real antique pair is so rare that . . . well, it's no good going on. Imagine you took an ordinary earthenware drinking mug, complete with handle, then bored assorted holes in the side. You'd have made a Norfolk lantern. They were used with oil and a perforating wick or, more usually, a candle stump. The holes are often arranged in cruciform patterns. Margaret got them from an old farmhouse. Well, I thought, I owe everybody else. Why not admit Margaret to my famous payment-by-deficit scheme?

'Did Lily catch you with her coal carvings?'

Coal carvings? 'Eh?'

'What's the matter?'

I sat on a reed-bottomed Suffolk chair and fumbled the tissue paper bundles out. There were three. It's difficult not having a lap so I unwrapped them one by one. A little cart, crudely done, an even more imperfect donkey, and a little hut of some sort. All very poor quality, each chipped and frayed. But definitely coal. Miners everywhere have tried a hand at carving the 'black diamond', but there was a world of difference between the lovely firefly cage and these. These were crude rubbish, the most inept carvings I'd ever seen. Modern crap. I wrapped them, thinking hard.

'Are you in trouble?'

'Not yet.'

I had to catch Lily and find where she'd got them, though this isn't the sort of thing one antique dealer ever dares ask another. Oddly, they reminded me of something or somebody . . . I looked up. The alcove had suddenly darkened and there was this chauffeur, resplendent in uniform. I stared. He looked as though he'd left a thoroughbred nag tethered to the traffic lights.

'You Lovejoy?' he snapped, all crisp.

'Yes.'

'Come on.' Clearly not a man to be trifled with.

'Clear off.' I stayed on the Suffolk chair.

'You've to come with me,' he said, amazed. 'Mrs Hepplestone instructs.'

Oho. So my newspaper advert had gone full circle. I'd throttle Elsie for turning me in, especially to a serf like this.

'Sorry, mate.'

He reached over and hauled me to my feet. 'Don't muck me about,' he was saying threateningly when his voice cut off owing to me taking reprisals. I had to be careful because Margaret always has a lovely display of porcelain in, and never enough reliable shelves to show the pieces off properly. He gasped for air while I leant him against the door jamb.

Margaret hastily put the 'Closed' notice up. 'Lovejoy! Stop it this instant!'

'He started it!' Honestly, I thought, narked. It's no good. Even trying to stay innocent I get the blame. There's no justice.

'I saw you!' she accused. 'You fisted him in the abdomen.'

A couple of potential browsers peered in, smiling, then reeled hurriedly away at the scene in the shop. Time I went. No way of winning here for the moment.

'See you, love.'

'But this poor man . . .'

'Chance of a quick sale.' I grinned and left him wheezing.

Lily had gone when I reached Woody's again. I asked Lisa where to but nobody knew. It was one of those days. Thinking hard about the three crummy coal carvings, I wandered disconsolately along the Arcade, exchanging the odd word here and there with the lads and lassies. A

kid could have carved better. Yet they were a clue, if I
could only think.

Jane Felsham saw me shambling past and hauled me
in — well, beckoned imperiously. I've a soft spot for Jane.
She's thirtyish and shapely, mainly English watercolours
and Georgian silver. She sports a mile-long fag-holder to
keep us riff-raff at bay.

'Your big moment to help, Lovejoy,' she told me airily.
'To work.'

Remembering Tinker's admonition to fix a price for
my services first, I drew breath. Then Jane showed me the
plate. It was wriggle-work, genuine wriggle-work. My
mind went blank and I was into her place like a flash. All
was suddenly peace and light. Pewter's the most
notoriously difficult collecting field, but some pieces just
leap at you. This was a William III plate, with a crowned
portrait bust of the King centred in a rim decorated by
engraved wriggles. It screamed originality. Many don't
care for pewter, but its value should ease any artistic
qualms you have. Weight for weight it can be more
precious than silver. It had the right pewter sheen, like
reflection from a low sun on our sea marshes. Modern
copies don't have it, though heaven knows some are great.
Jane was poking me.

'Lovejoy. I asked is it original?'

'Luscious,' I confessed brokenly. 'Just feel its beat.'

She was delighted. While I priced and labelled it
correctly my eyes lit upon a genuine old Sphairistike
racquet. I couldn't block my involuntary exclamation.
Jane looked puzzled.

'That? I thought it was just an old tennis racket —'

I sighed. People really hurt my feelings sometimes.
'Once upon a time, love, a retired major invented a game
for playing on the croquet lawn. He invented a name,
too. Sphairistike. It's called tennis now.'

That pewter sheen lured my eyes back but it would cost

my cottage. I asked her if she had any coal carvings. She said no without emitting a single bleep.

I left and did a bit more divvying for the goons in the Arcade, seeing I was unemployed and had passed up the only chance I had of improving matters. Anyhow, I reasoned, Josiah Wedgwood's famous 'Fourteenth Commandment' was 'Thou shalt not be idle,' so who am I to quibble? I asked everywhere about coal carvings. Harry Bateman caught my interest with an old countryman's dove-feeder, genuine eighteenth-century. They make reproductions in country potteries now, but the shape's the same—a big stoneware bottle siamesed to a smaller one, with half of the side scooped from the titch to let the bird drink. Jenny thought she had a priceless item—a King Alfred hammered silver penny.

'It's been mounted, love.' I showed her the plug where somebody had sealed the pendant attachment. Mounts or holes in a coin don't quite make it worthless but my advice is to simply move on.

'Does it matter?' she asked, poor soul. 'That only proves it's real, though, doesn't it?'

'It would have been worth a year's takings. Now . . .' I saw her eyes fill at the disappointment and scarpered. I had enough problems without taking on psychotherapy. And neither Harry nor Jenny had seen a coal carving in months.

Dig Mason was waiting for me and dragged me across the Arcade. He's the wealthiest dealer in the Arcade. I quite like Dig, though he has more money than sense. Like now.

'You didn't buy *that*, Dig?'

'Sure.'

Fairings are so-called 'amusing' pottery figures you used to win at fairs for roll-a-penny or chucking balls into buckets. They were made in Germany between 1860 and 1890, and were given away as worthless in junk shops when I was a kid. Now, things being the way they are, they cost the earth—well, at least a full week's wages for one.

'Hong Kong, Dig,' I said sadly. 'Made this month. That dirt's soot from an open oil-wick.'

'You're kidding—'

It was a ceramic of a man washing himself and stopping a lady from entering. This 'Modesty' figure is one of the rarest, but the commonest (a couple getting into bed, in the form of a candleholder) is also forged.

'I've no time even for the originals either, Dig,' I told him, but he was mortified.

'You must be wrong, Lovejoy—'

He too hadn't seen any coal carvings lately, so I pushed on. All fairings are ugly to me. Hong Kong will make you a gross of the wretched things, properly decorated and meticulously copied, for two quid or even less. A couple of dozen of these forgeries will keep you in idle affluence a year or so—if you're unscrupulous, that is.

As poor as I arrived, I borrowed a coin from Lisa and telephoned the White Hart. By a strange stroke of luck Tinker was in there getting kaylied. He didn't know where Lily had got the three carvings from, either. I slammed the phone down in a temper. A harassed woman was waiting for the phone. She had this little girl with eyes like blue saucers.

'I'm so sorry to ask you,' she said to me. 'But could you watch Bernice while I phone? I'll only be a second—'

Feeling a right nerk, I sat on the pedestrian railing holding this little girl's hand outside the phone-box. Brad happened by on his way to viewing day at the auction. Seeing me there looking daft he drew breath to guffaw but I raised a warning finger and he soberly crossed over looking everywhere but at me. Bernice was about three, and obviously a real traffic lover. She kept trying to crawl under everybody's feet into the motor-car maelstrom. She told me about her toy, a wooden donkey pulling a cart. And the cart was full of seashells. I thought about it a lot. Pewter sheen, like sun on an estuary. Donkey. Cart. Seashells. And a little hut. I showed her my coal carvings, trying to keep my legs out of everybody's way.

Bernice's mother came out, breathlessly dropping parcels like they do. 'Thank you so much. Was she good? It's the traffic I'm worried about . . .'

'My pleasure,' I said. And I meant it.

If I'd had time I might have chatted the bird up. As it was, the baby's toy donkey-cart full of seashells had reminded me that down in the estuary Drummer and Germoline, pride of the seaside sands, make an honest if precarious living. I tore up the streets looking for a lift and saw Dolly's car by the war memorial.

CHAPTER 6

Dolly ran me down to the estuary going on for three o'clock. Our whole coast hereabouts is indented by creeks, inlets, tidal mudflats and marshes. As you approach the sealands you notice that the trees become less enthusiastic, stunted and leaning away from gales on the low skyline. They have a buttoned-up look about them even on the mildest day. Then the sea marshes show between the long runs of banks and dykes. You see the masts foresting thinly among the dunes' tufted undulations. Anglers abound, sitting gawping at their strings in all weathers. A few blokes can be seen digging in the marsh flats among the weeds. Well, whatever turns you on, but it's a hell of a hobby in a rainstorm. A lot of visitors come to lurk among the reeds with binoculars when they could be holidaying in a lovely smokey town among the antique shops, which only goes to show what a rum lot people are.

'Head for the staithe, Dolly.'

'I must be *mad* in this weather, Lovejoy.'

The birds are different, too, sort of runners and shovellers instead of the bouncy peckers that raise Cain in my patch if you're slow with their morning cheese.

There seemed a lot of fresh air about. The wind was whipping up as Dolly's motor lurched us down the gravel path between the sea dykes, blowing in gusts and hurtling white clouds low over the water. A staithe is a wharf alongside a creek where boats can come and lie tilted on sands at low water. You tie them to buoys or these iron rings and leave them just to hang about. Tides come and go, and the boats float or sag as the case may be. The main river's estuary's littered with the wretched things.

'There's *nobody* here, Lovejoy.' Accusations again.

'Drummer's bound to be.'

'I should have brought an extra cardigan.'

We got out. The wind whipped my hair across to blind me and roared in my ears. The force of it was literally staggering. For a moment I wondered what the terrible racket was. It sounded like a thousand crystal chandeliers tinkling in weird cacophony. Then I realized. The masts. They're not wood any more. They're some tin stuff, hollow all the way down. And the wind was jerking the ropes and wires, thrashing every one against its mast. There's never less than a hundred boats at least, either drawn up or slumped on the flats at low water. Say three taps a second, that's three hundred musical chimes every pulse beat, which in one hour makes—

'Lovejoy. For heaven's *sake*!'

Dolly had gathered her camelhair coat tight about her, clutching the collar at her chin. Her hair was lashing about her face. I'd never consciously noticed before, but women in high heels bend one leg and lean the foot outwards when they're standing still. In a rising wind they exaggerate the posture. Odd, that. She was on the seaward side of me, caught against the pale scudding sky. She looked perished and had to shout over the racket of the gale and the musical masts.

'What's the matter?' she shrieked. 'Lovejoy. Stop daydreaming. We could be home, with a fire . . .'

'You're beautiful, Dolly.'

Her face changed. She can't have heard but saw my lips move. She stepped to me, letting go of her coat which snapped open and almost tugged her off her feet. We reached for each other, all misty, and this bloody donkey came between us. Its wet nose ploshed horribly into my palm.

'*Christ!*' I leapt a mile. We'd found Germoline.

' 'Morning, Lovejoy. Miss.'

My heart was thumping while I wiped my hand on my sleeve. It had frightened me to death. Dolly was livid. Normally she'd have scurried about for some bread, or whatever you give donkeys, but just now I could tell she could have cheerfully crippled it. She muttered under her breath and concentrated on not getting blown out to sea.

'Wotcher, Drummer.' He had his estuary gear on, the tartan beret with its bedraggled tuft. Still the battered sand-stained clogs and the scarf trailing across the mud, the frayed cuffs and battledress khaki turn-ups. His donkey looked smaller if anything. I wondered vaguely if they shrank.

'Say hello to Germoline, then.' He grinned at Dolly. 'She loves Lovejoy.'

Dolly managed a distant pat. Germoline stepped closer and leant on me. This sounds graceful but isn't. She wears a collar made from an old tyre with spherical jingle-bells, the sort that adorn reindeer so elegantly. Usually you can hear her for miles. The din of the boats had submerged her approach. Add to that the problem of her two-wheeled cart — it holds four children on little side benches—and even the friendliest lean becomes a threat. Anyhow I leant back feeling a right pillock.

'Want a ride?' Every time Drummer grins his false teeth fall together with a clash. Whatever folk say about our estuary, I'll bet it's the noisiest estuary in the business.

'A word,' I bawled.

'My house, then.'

I scanned the estuary without ecstasy. Over the reedbanks stands Drummer's shed, looking impossible to reach across dunes and snaking rivulets that join the sea a couple of furlongs off. A row of proper houses stands back behind the wharf where the pathway joins the main road, aloof from the seaside rabble. The tallest of them is a coastguard station. It's not much to look at but it has those masts and a proper flagpole and everything. Joe Poges was on his white-railed balcony with binoculars. He waved. Joe's one of life's merry jokers, but all the same I quite like him. His missus gives Drummer dinner now and then. Knowing how much I would be hating all this horrible fresh air, Joe did a quick knees-bend exercise and beat his chest like Tarzan. It was too far to see his grin but I knew he'd fall about for days at his witticism and tell everybody they should have seen my face. I waved and the distant figure saluted.

'That's Joe, Miss,' Drummer explained, his teeth crashing punctuation. 'Home, Germoline.'

Dolly tried clinging to my arm on the way over but I shook her off. I was in enough trouble. There was no real path, just patches of vaguely darker weeds showing where the mud would hold. Twice I heard Dolly yelp and a quick splash. Life's tough and I didn't wait. I was too anxious to put my feet where Germoline put hers. Half way across the sea marsh Germoline turned of her own accord facing me and waited while Drummer unhitched the cart. I swear she was grinning as we set off again. Her hooves were covered in the sticky mud. Drummer always ties blue and white ribbons to her tail, his football team's colours.

We made it. He's laid a small tiled area near the shed door. Germoline jongled her way to a lean-to and started eating from a manger inside. Dolly arrived gasping and wind-tousled.

'Lovejoy,' she wheezed. 'You horrid—'

'Keep Germoline company a minute, please, love,' I said. Drummer went in to brew up.

It took a second for her to realize. Then she exploded. 'Stay out *here*?' She tried to push me aside. 'In *this*? Of all the—'

I shoved her out and slammed the door. It has to be first things first. She banged and squawked but I dropped the bolt. 'Sorry, Drummer.'

Drummer was grinning through crashes of pottery teeth. 'Still the same old Lovejoy. Here, son. Wash them cups.'

I pumped the ancient handle while Drummer lit an oil lamp. There are scores of freshwater springs hereabouts, and some even emerge in the sea. Old sailors still fill up with fresh water miles off the North Sea coast where the freshwater 'pipes', as they're called, ascend to the ocean's surface. They say you can tell where a pipe is from the sort of fish that knock around. Drummer chucked some driftwood into his iron stove. There's not a lot of space, just a camp bed, a table and a chair or two, shelves and a picture of Lord Kitchener and a blue glass vase with dried flowers. A few clothes hung behind the door with Germoline's spare harness.

'Coal carvings, Drummer.' I'd checked Dolly couldn't hear. 'Know anything?'

'Ar,' he answered, nodding when I looked round enquiringly from the sink because locally the same word can mean no as well as yes. 'It's getting the right sort of tar coal nowadays.'

'Much call for them?'

'Ar,' with a headshake. 'I sold three this week.'

I sat at his rickety old table and pulled out the three carvings. 'Drummer,' I said sadly, 'they're horrible.'

'What d'you expect, Lovejoy?' he demanded indignantly. 'Anyway, people needn't buy them. And they aren't bad as all that.'

True. But if these three monstrosities were Drummer's idea of art, then sure as God sends Sunday he'd never carved the lovely firefly cage.

'Just suppose a bloke saw a coal carving,' I got in when his teeth plummeted and shut him up, 'so intricate and clever it blew his mind. Where would he look for whoever did it? Think, Drummer.'

'I already know. My mate Bill.' Drummer inhaled a ton of snuff from a tea-caddy and voomed like a landmine. The shed misted with his contaminating droplets. 'That's better—'

'Who?'

'Bill Hepplestone. Me and him was mates—till he married up this rich young tart. Farm and all. Not far from here.' He pointed to show me the kettle was boiling. 'Stopped coming over at the finish. Too posh. Always trouble, posh women are. Never take up with posh, Lovejoy.'

'*Hepplestone?*' The name's not all that common. I filled the kettle. 'Any idea where he lives?'

'Dead, son. Poor old Bill. Used to be inland, place called Lesser Cornard in a bleeding great manor house.'

'Right, Drummer. Ta.' I rose to open the door, finger to my lips. 'Not a word. I owe you a quid, right?'

Dolly fell in, blue from the wind. Germoline gave me the bent eye as I shut the door again. It didn't look as if they'd exactly got on. I beamed at Dolly but all I could think was, great. That's what I need, to go spitting in the face of fortune. Some uniformed burke of a chauffeur wants to take me right to the bloody place I'm searching for, and I thump him senseless. Really great. Sometimes I'm just thick. Mrs Hepplestone of Hall Lodge Manor. Widow of Bill the coal carver.

Meanwhile Dolly was tottering towards the glowing stove, whining miserably.

'Ah! You're *there*, Dolly!' I tried to beam but she stayed mad.

'I'll kill you, Lovejoy.'

'Now, Dolly . . .'

'We're done, Lovejoy.' She swung at me, blazing hatred. 'Finished! Do you hear? I've taken my last insult from you. I've put up with you long enough—'

I shrugged at Drummer who was enjoying it all, chuckling as he poured the tea out. Women are an unreasonable lot. Now I'd have to find the bloody chauffeur and say I'd made a terrible mistake. What a life.

The next half-hour was the longest I'd ever spent. Dolly sat there in front of the stove with her back speaking volumes of annoyance. She ignored the tea I took her even though I'd given her Drummer's only saucer.

We left when Dolly had warmed enough to move. Drummer came out with us to lead us over the salt marshes.

'Tide's turning,' he remarked brightly, pointing. It looked the same to me, just a few scattered folk among the boats slanting on the mud, though I noticed one or two boats were floating now.

Looking seaward, I saw two vaguely familiar figures. I paused to focus better with my streaming eyes peering into the cold north wind. A man and a girl. They were over among the oyster-beds and seemed to be buying some. A fisher lad was hauling on a rope while the man pointed and the girl crouched to peer down into the water. Neither turned to look our way, not even when

Germoline brayed and tried to catch Dolly's heel with her hoof. Odd, that, I thought. The fisher lad heard our donkey, though, and turned to wave, laughing. He takes care of them, the very same oyster beds that the Romans established twenty centuries ago. I waved and we moved on.

We splashed our way across the precarious muddy shore. It was riskier than before. Puddles were now ponds, and small rivulets had become streams flowing swiftly inland. Once-placid dinghies now tugged irritably at mooring ropes. The almost imperceptible path was untraceable. In several places Germoline's hoofprints were immersed in the mud and Drummer led us in a detour. We were almost back on the foreshore before I realized. Maud. Only Maud, our beloved social worker, could be that scruffy, hair uncombed and patched jeans frayed, quite at home among a straggle of estuary people hooked on boating. And the neatly dressed bloke, yachting cap, blazer and white flannels, giving orders to an oyster lad as if to the manner born—who else but good old Devlin, doubtless calling for a few dozen oysters to have with his champers at the hunt ball. I could even spot his bandaged hand from here. I prayed he hadn't seen us, and hurried on after Germoline and the others.

Drummer fastened Germoline's cart on and Dolly was given a free ride. By the time we reached the small crumbling wharf the estuary was filling with unnerving speed and the tangle of wrinkled sea marsh was ironed out into a single choppy flood. Joe waved from his coastguard balcony and mimed frantic applause at our feet reaching land, the burke. Drummer handed Dolly down to the firm ground.

As we left the staithe I couldn't help glancing down towards the oyster beds. The oyster lad was still working there but Maud and Devvo had disappeared, a hell of a trick on a series of exposed mudflats and marshes. You can see for miles, all the way out to the old World War gun platforms standing miles offshore. Unless they'd gone for a swim, and they hadn't looked ready for that, especially in this cold.

'Lovejoy. For heaven's *sake!*' Dolly was tugging me up the path.

I winked at Germoline and said goodbye to Drummer. He clogged off chuckling with a clash of teeth. Three children were waiting by Drummer's flag for a last ride in Germoline's cart, so somebody was in luck even if I wasn't.

Dolly didn't speak all the way back to my cottage. There she dumped me unceremoniously and did an angry Grand Prix start, though I asked if she'd see me tomorrow at the Castle pond. Half my gravel went whizzing across the grass from the spinning tyres, I saw with annoyance. It would take me hours shovelling that lot back, if I got round to it.

I went in thinking of the estuary, and Devvo and Maud's disappearing trick. She seemed to be going through us antique dealers at a rate of knots. One thing was sure, though. I'd not be included.

CHAPTER 7

Next morning was a red-letter morning, notable for the start of cerebral activity at Lovejoy Antiques, Inc. Not all that brilliant, but a few definite synapses. My threadbare carpet conceals a flagstone inset with an iron ring. Lift it, and you can descend the eight wooden steps into a flag-floor cellar by the light of a candle. It was constructed by loving hands four centuries before this age of jerry-built tat, doubtless serving as some sort of storage place for herbs and harvested stuff. Now it's ideal for antiques—should any ever happen my way by some freak accident. Down there I have boxes of newspaper cuttings and notes to keep track of deals and auction sales.

Hall Lodge Manor had had a rough time. From my cuttings our local papers seemed to give it reverential sympathy whenever antique thieves struck—which happened once every few months. Despite 'elaborate safety precautions' windows were forced, locks picked, alarm circuits were blistered and guard dogs distracted with almost monotonous regularity. And every time a few choice items were nicked. Not a lot, just a few. A Norwich School harbour scene attributed to Cotman went missing in its frame the same night a nineteenth-century tribal figure of Guinea ivory vanished from among a display of similar carvings in a bureau. Nothing else seems to have gone on that occasion. Then a matching pair of Gouthière firehearth bronzes went, and with them a diminutive wood carving described as 'Adoration of the Magi'. Four months later a gang struck again . . .

I poison myself with one of those little Dutch cigars on occasions like this. I went back upstairs and sat in the open air for a think. How strange. Nothing has boomed in value like Norwich School paintings, those reflective dark lustrous oils that find a ready market any-where—and which are very, very hard to identify with precision when you have only a description to go by. And the ivory piece was strange too, because the one type of ivory which all collectors love is the hard best-quality ivory from Guinea, whereas much Ivory Coast, Senegal and Sudanese ivory is semi-soft greyish rubbish. And Gouthière's bronzes may not look much, but they won their way into Marie-Antoinette's boudoir. The wood carving sounded suspiciously like a South German piece, from the novice reporter's bumbling narrative. Pictorial woodwork has never surpassed the brilliant German Renaissance craftsmen like Tilman Riemenschneider.

Round the stalls I'd heard rumours about such a piece for a year or more.

It was the same throughout the whole list. Everything pinched fell into the same category—highly prized, collectable and valuable. *And quite small.* Still, an antiques thief naturally goes for what's valuable and what he can carry, doesn't he?

Hall Lodge Manor had been burgled six times, the last a couple of months before Bill Hepplestone had died. Since then, nothing. I'm not a suspicious-minded bloke but you can't help thinking.

I became worried in case this old bird had me pinned for the robberies from her place. Maslow would believe the worst, suspicion being his thing. I'd have to go and calm her down, make her see reason.

I caught Jacko's van at the chapel and emerged in town two arias later with shellshock and a pong of decaying fish about my person from his latest cargo.

On a hunch I walked down to the pond in Castle Park. Dolly was there, watching children boating, and feeding ducks.

I came chattily up. 'Hello, love. I'm glad you—'

'Shut up, Lovejoy.' She took a deep sobering breath and linked my arm. 'I must be off my head. Come on.'

She stood us both nosh at the bandstand café, asking questions which I did my best to evade. Her odd mood began to evaporate and at the finish she was prattling happily. Eventually I got her to agree to giving me a lift to Mrs Hepplestone's at Lesser Cornard, lucky lass. Needless to say this got her mad again. She kept up a tirade of abuse and reproach all the blinking way.

'And the risks I take for you, Lovejoy.' This was because her husband had been in a few days before when I phoned in my posh voice pretending to explain she'd forgotten her library book at the hairdresser's. She said I didn't sound like a hairdresser's assistant. I tried saying that's not my fault but got nowhere.

We took an hour driving the eleven miles, owing to pulling into a lay-by to—er—lay by for a minute or two. Maybe it was our dishevelled mental state which made us so unprepared for the splendour of Mrs Hepplestone's cranny when we finally drove in to Lesser Cornard. It was palatial, straight Inigo Jones set in a Capability Brown landscape. Dolly was overawed at the trees, the curving rose-beds and the score of minions beavering among the yews.

'I'd better not stay, Lovejoy,' she said nervously as we came in sight of the mansion.

'How will I get home?'

'Er, a taxi, dear? They might let you phone.'

I knew what it was—she was worried her skirt and twin set weren't exactly right for meeting the landed gentry. I caught her patting her hair and fingering her artificial pearl necklace as she drove. She normally saves one hand for stopping me mauling her thighs while her eyes are on the traffic. Mind you, the scene which greeted us was daunting. The house was glorious, a long frontage and vintage doorways. All authentic, every brick. I gave Mrs Hepplestone top marks for defying the lemming rush of demented modern architects and leaving well alone.

Dolly didn't even cut the engine. With a quick wave of her hand she was gone, a flash of red lights showing as she turned past the rhodedendrons. I was alone in an acre of gravel in front of Hall Lodge Manor. I looked quickly about for the chauffeur because I've read my Chandler, but no. None of the gardeners bothered even to look up.

The hall door was open. I dithered like any respectful serf, trying to find nerve. You can feel antiques, actually sense the pulses beating out of a place so strongly it becomes hard to breathe. My chest was bonging like a firebell. And inside the hall there was this suit of armour.

I swear it was original sixteenth-century. Never mind anything else—just look at the fall-away part of the 'sparrow-beak' visor from the side. If it's *concave* and the whole suit feels genuine rush out and sell your house, send your missus down the mines and get your idle infants out doing hard labour. Then buy it. Even if you finish up out in the streets and destitute you'll be one of the few owners of a Greenwich suit of sixteenth-century armour.

So there I was in the porchway being mesmerized and broken-hearted when I suddenly felt watched.

'Lovejoy?'

A lady was sitting under this tree about thirty yards away. Slightly greying but smiling and being amused at a shabby intruder. She was knitting, cleverly not checking what the needles were up to.

I plodded over. 'Mrs Hepplestone?'

'You're younger than I thought,' she commented. 'I expected an old reprobate.'

'How did you find out?'

'The advertisement?' She laughed and made me a space on the tree seat. 'I had a word with the proprietors.'

Funny, but you don't normally think of dailies having proprietors. I'd always thought of them like churches, vaguely existing without belonging. I'd have to watch out—and make my displeasure known to Elsie, gabby cow. She'd no business divulging truth just to save her own crummy neck.

There seemed no way out of this. 'Er, an unfortunate slip,' I stammered uneasily. I suppose it would be fraud or something. Breach of the peace at the very least.

'Nonsense,' she said firmly. Odd, but she was still smiling. My spirits bottomed out. 'It was quite deliberate, Lovejoy. Admit it. Now, before we go any further, sherry?'

Dolly had guessed right, with a woman's sixth sense for social encounters. This was no Woody's Bar. A man dressed like the Prime Minister came out with a lovely gadrooned tray, only Edwardian and therefore not properly antique but it brought tears to my eyes.

'Is he a butler?' I whispered as the bloke receded. He'd left the tray for us on a wrought-iron garden table.

'Yes,' she whispered, amused.

I was impressed. I'd never seen one before. I'd felt like kneeling. The sherry was in a sherry decanter, too. I'd never seen that before, either. And a silver tray really used, not just salted away for investment. No wonder Dolly had scarpered. Maybe I should have stayed with her and had another snog in a lay-by.

Forces seemed suddenly too large to handle. Out of control, I asked dejectedly, 'Will you turn me in?'

'Certainly not.' She invited me to pour while I thought, thank God for that. The glasses were modern, but the silver-mounted decanter screamed London and genuine. Typical work of the Lias family, now prohibitively priced. They're easy to spot because there seem so many letter 'L's in the hallmark. John and Henry Lias were right characters . . . Mrs Hepplestone caught me smiling and joined in.

'Er, nice decanter,' I said feebly.

'Thank you.' She was doing the woman's trick of seeming cool while secretly screaming with laughter. I could tell.

A gardener had lit a bonfire nearby. You can smell wood smoke even upwind. Odd, that. I glanced covertly at the bird while the fire crackled. Stylish, forty-five give or take an hour. Still knitting. Maybe I was expected to make conversation.

'Er, sorry about your, er, chauffeur, missus,' I tried.

'Think nothing of it, Lovejoy. I quite understand.'

Then what was I here for? 'You going to tell me off?'

'No.' Knitting down now, loins girded for the crunch.

'You'll have to forgive me, Lovejoy. I'm unused to . . . your circle.'

Well, I was unused to hers. I forgave.

'The fact is that I was extremely discountenanced when I learned of your — *deception* — over the advertisement. As discountenanced as you probably felt on being exposed.' She smiled to take the sting out of her remark. I'd felt discountenanced all right, whatever that meant. 'But you are very clearly a professional at your trade.'

'Well . . .' I shrugged.

'Everybody seems to know you, Lovejoy.'

'They do?' This conversation was getting out of hand, like the gardener's fire over among the bushes. Too dry. Not enough rain.

'I made enquiries, Lovejoy.' She invited me to pour more sherry for myself. 'So I shall forgive you the chauffeur and the advertisement, and you shall do a simple task for me.'

Typical of a woman, that bit. I gazed about. Beyond the gardens a pair of huge lumbering horses were trotting, trailing an iron thing while two blokes marked the ground with white-painted pegs. Tractors clattered in the background. Maybe she wanted me to drive a tractor a day or two.

She laughed and shook her head. 'No. Nothing to do with my driving teams, Lovejoy.' She made a face. Something rankled with her, and out it came. 'Mind you, you couldn't possibly do worse than my own men. We lose the competition every year to the Wainwrights — ever since that new blacksmith joined them, wretched man.' Probably Claude, from our village.

'Then how simple?' I asked shrewdly, not wanting to get involved in the county set's social wars.

'For an antiques divvie — is that the word? — elementary.'

I brightened. Antiques. 'A valuation?'

'No. I want you to open a little cage for me, please.'
She saw my expression go a bit odd because she cut in
hastily, 'Not a true antique, I must confess. My husband
made it. Rather curious, really. It's a little cage carved in
coal.' She took my silence for puzzlement, which it almost
was. 'A rather strange hobby, but I understand not
altogether unique. I don't want the cage damaged.'

I cleared my throat nervously. This was where I came
in, being asked to undo a coal carving. 'Where is it, love?'
Maybe there were hundreds of the damned things.

A voice said, 'It's here, Aunt Maisie.'

And it was—held by good old Maud, together with its
antique bamboo partner. Today's outfit was a subdued
bottle green with sensible shoes, swagger bag, hair neat
and chiffon scarf just right. Crisp little modern brooch
and all. Just right to go visiting a rich auntie. Maud was
beginning to seem like a chameleon. I glanced around,
and sure enough there was another antique dealer in the
background—also different, as usual. It was Don
Musgrave this time, all tweed and hornrims. I began to
suspect Maud chose her blokes like an accessory. From
the doting grin on Don's face he apparently had other,
less decorative, tasks to perform. Maud was using us all
up at a rate of knots.

'Good heavens, Maud!' Mrs Hepplestone gestured for
more chairs and the Prime Minister strode gravely forth
to do his stuff. 'How ever did you—?'

'I borrowed it.' Maud's tone was quite cool and
detached.

'But why, dear?' Mrs Hepplestone was in command but
Maud was not going to be put under. 'You knew I was
seeking an expert to open it—'

'I see you've found one.'

I went red. Bitterness from women always makes me do
that. I wish I knew how to get myself cured. 'I opened it
for you,' I said defiantly.

Maud's eyes glinted. 'So you did, Lovejoy. But the question is, did you detect some compartment that you are keeping quiet about?'

'Don't be daft.' I rose, reaching for the cages, intending to show Mrs Hepplestone. 'It's too small—'

'Then you won't mind if I do this, will you, Lovejoy?' Maud stepped the few paces to the fire and threw the cages on, watching my face. The crime took a split second. Don reached out for her, sensing quicker than me what she intended, but the cages were among the flames.

'You stupid . . .' I was scrabbling dementedly in the fire but Don and the gardener dragged me back. I ran round to windward, eyes streaming smoke and coughing like a veteran. The serf ran with me and rummaged with a rake but the heat pushed us off. The fire was one of those steady garden fires, hot centre and lopsided flames. Two gardeners were holding me still after a minute. I think I could just see the outline of the coal cage beginning to lick with flames and glowing. There was a curious sparking flash of colour, one single brilliant flash from it. Then it sank into the red hot core. Gone. The antique bamboo firefly cage must have burned instantly.

'Well,' Maud was saying sullenly to Mrs Hepplestone when I came to. 'If Uncle's box had nothing inside . . .'

'It was a keepsake, Maud,' her auntie was reprimanding frostily. 'You had no right—'

'Some keepsake! A piece of *coal*!' with scorn.

'That's not the point, Maud, dear. And look how you've upset Lovejoy. He's white as a sheet.' Mrs Hepplestone's hand took my elbow. 'Do sit down. You're quite shocked—'

I pulled away. No good staring at a bonfire all day, is it? Maud and Don were standing there so I stared at them instead. Don knows I can get nasty. He stepped back uncertainly. 'That was none of my doing, Lovejoy.'

'What's all the fuss?' The crazy bitch was actually

sneering at Don. I admit he's not much of a dealer but he'd never have done what she had. 'You're scared of him! Of *Lovejoy*!' She pealed laughter.

'You burned a genuine antique,' I managed to croak at last.

'It was mine,' she said, ice. 'None of your business.'

'Oh, but it is.' I try not to let my voice shake but it always does when white rage takes hold. I never sound convincing. 'Antiques are everybody's business.'

She laughed again. How I didn't chuck her on the bloody fire I'll never know, iron willpower I suppose. 'Then I'll hire you to buy Aunt Maisie a replacement, seeing you're practically penniless. On commission, of course.'

I gazed at her, appalled. Some people just have no idea.

'Maudie,' I said into her eyes, 'I wouldn't piss on you in hell.' And I turned away. Now that both cages were gone, literally in a flash, they could all get on with it.

I was plodding a mile on the road out of Lesser Cornard village when the familiar black Rolls came alongside. The chauffeur said nothing. I climbed in and got carried home silently but in style, to find the electricity and telephone were cut off for non-payment of bills. That's our bloody government for you, selfish swines. But in my mind was wonder at a mob of antique thieves who hit Mrs Hepplestone's manor house time and time again, but who missed a precious glittering suit of armour — worth a fortune — in the hallway.

I spent the last hours of daylight furiously trying to do the Reverse Gadroon on sheets of tin and finished up in a blind mania hammering the whole bloody lot into an unrecognizable mass, finally slinging the hammer against the wall in a temper. Then I went in and read by candlelight till so many shadows loomed on the walls that I snuffed it out and went to bed fast.

End of a perfect day.

And it really was—compared to the blood-soaked days that came after, though I didn't know it then.

CHAPTER 8

Remember where I said I'm resilient, never miserable for very long? Well, I take it back. I'd never felt so down. Maybe I sensed it was going to be one of the worst days of my life.

I deliver morning newspapers for Jeannie Henson when I'm broke. Not far, only round the village and pedalling like a lunatic to get round before my back tyre goes flat again. It isn't as boring as it sounds. You'd be surprised how many people are up before cockshout. Farm men off to the fields, lads driving cows, women clustering for our first dozy bus, a gasping jogger or two. And, I thought jealously, people in well-lit warm-looking cottage kitchens making lovely meals for each other, seeing they could afford those luxuries.

Doing a paper lad's job is embarrassing but it helps to keep me in the antiques game. I called on my way back for some bread and a tin of beans with my wages. The luscious Jeannie Henson was adding it up when our post-girl Rose came in for a packet of tea.

'Fancy meeting you, Lovejoy!' Rose said, mischievously glancing from Jeannie to me and back. She's a pest.

' 'Morning, Rose.'

'I mean, *rising* so early to *serve* Jeannie!' I went red and mumbled something while Rose fell about at her sparkling wit. She put the money on Jeannie's counter.

'That'll do, Rose.' Jeannie was a bit red, too. 'Time you finished your letters.'

'I like your skirt, Jeannie. New, isn't it?'

'Get on with you!'

Rose slung up her postbag and went, grinning. 'Make sure Jeannie pays you *in full*, Lovejoy. Andy'll be back soon.'

I loaded my stuff while the doorbell clanked to silence.

Jeannie smiled apologetically. 'That Rose. Your change, Lovejoy.'

I gazed at the money thinking, one paper round isn't worth all that. 'Er . . .'

'No.' She pushed the money in my pocket. 'Lovejoy. Andy's been on about an extra hand in the shop lately. Don't misunderstand.'

'Oh, I don't.' We assured each other of this for a minute or two. 'Thanks, Jeannie. But it's antiques, you see.'

'I know.' She pushed a wisp of hair off her forehead. 'Well, look. They're firing Wainwright's fields today. It's good money. Andy and Claude are helping. You'd get there in time.'

I thanked her, promising to do a free paper round.

'When you get round to it,' she added with a crooked smile that puzzled me. That explains how dawn found me pedalling along the river dykes between the fens while a blustery wind tried to blow me into the surrounding marshes. It's not my scene, but a few hours' work would keep me for a week, at my high rate of living.

I got to Wainwright's fields and found where the straw lines lay. A small cluster of folk were already huddling on the farm's rise, ready for firing the fields before the ploughing. Everybody helps out in some way hereabouts, harvest in East Anglia being no time for differences. Even penniless antique dealers have been known to lend a hand, I thought bitterly. Andy and Claude the blacksmith were putting people's names down and allocating us bits of the fields.

' 'Morning, Lovejoy.'

'Wotcher, Claude, Andy.' I slung my bike under the hedge and joined them. The lovely Hepzibah Smith our choir mistress was there in her headscarf and gardening gloves, with three or four choristers in tow. They looked as glum as I felt. Wainwright was in the distance on an enthusiastic horse, ready to signal. Wainwright's our local lord of the manor, a cheery, beery bloke I'm rather fond of. He's famous for doing the exact opposite of what the government says. 'Can't go far wrong doing what they tell you not to,' he often remarks in the pub when people ask what he's playing at. Like when the Minister advised all East Anglia to automate and share combine harvesters, Wainwright sold all his that week. Now he uses these huge horses like in the olden days. 'Saved my neck in the energy crisis,' he told me, laughing. I wish there were more like him. A couple of stragglers arrived while we stamped and tried to keep from freezing to death. A whistle sounded somewhere signalling the start of the day's jollity.

'Glad you could come, Lovejoy.' Claude grinned. He knows what I think of the countryside.

'Men on the high fields,' Andy called. 'Women on the low. Places everybody. Get ready.'

Hepzibah gave me a long smile at my hatred of it all and we thinned out, one of us at two-stetch intervals across the harvested fields. I watched with some reluctance as the women went while Claude saw we lined up right and the distant mounted figure of Wainwright checked us in a slow wave. I made the traditional corn dolly, folding the straws into a nice thick handle and sheaving its head up lovely and loose. There was a lad next in line to me, new to field work but vaguely familiar. I made his dolly and showed him the trick of coiling the bottom of the handle so you don't get your hands burnt to blazes. People collect them as endearing knick-knacks but they have a grim history best not gone into. Antique examples are very costly — and unbelievably rare.

I asked the lad, 'You're Joe Poges' youngest, aren't you?'

'Yes, mister. Alan.' He waved the torch experimentally. 'You're Lovejoy. Saw you with Drummer. Dad said I could come as long as I did what the blacksmith says.' I grinned. Catch any of us disobeying Claude, I thought.

'Shouldn't you be helping your brother Eddie with the oysters?'

'Yes,' he said, quite unabashed. 'He has a big order today for the party on Mr Devlin's boat.' To go with the caviare and champagne, no doubt. That explained Devvo's disappearing trick with Maud. They hadn't vanished into thin air, just got on to a boat. I was about to enlarge on Devvo's many charms when a horn blew and Andy came haring along with his torch flaring.

'See you don't go slow like last time, Lovejoy,' Andy panted as I took fire from his torch.

'Okay, okay.' I'd deliberately let my lines of stubble take their time burning last year to give the rabbits and voles an extra escape route. So Wainwright had noticed after all, the shrewd old sod. You have to scuffle your feet about to make sure your straw lines don't ignite before the rest from your torch's drips or your name's mud with the other burners.

Two blasts of the horn came now, and the whole line of us bent on the run touching torches to the straw lines. Smoke rose in an ugly cloud, greyish white. It's a desperate business because the flames take hold and sprint ahead of you. Joe's lad got into difficulties and I had to run across and help him now and then. The great thing is to keep an eye across the other fields and see the wind's not done the dirty by veering. The village women wear showy coloured headscarves easily seen but we've not the sense. The great trick is to look for bobbing torches where the other men are. Women keep in better lines, calling if one of them gets behind.

I don't know if you've ever helped with field burning, but it's a filthy game. It's supposed to clean the fields for ploughing. A real laugh. You start clean at one end of lovely golden parallel piles of straw stretching over domed fields, and finish up kippered in acres of charred ash.

The odd thing was I wasn't excited by it all even though it's an exciting happening. Maybe I was in an odd mood. I don't know. But the running fires caught my attention then as never before. They are erratic, sometimes pausing and seeming likely never to move, the next minute flinging flames along your rows until everybody's yelling you are out of line. I kept looking at the flames, bright reds and golds against black soot. When Maud had chucked that marvellous little cage of carved coal into her aunt's bonfire I had caught a flash of bright green so brilliant it had stayed on my retina a whole minute afterwards. But coal burns red and gold or smoky. Whoever heard of a piece of burning coal flashing green? Yet when I'd opened the cage and shone the pencil torch into the aperture there had been a distinct bluish *mauve* gleam at the bottom. No green. I caught Alan laughing at me.

'Chucking earth won't put it out, Lovejoy,' he shouted.

'Shut up, you cheeky little sod.'

He'd seen me dropping handfuls of pebbles into my burning rows. I tried twigs, a couple of buttons which had strayed on to my jacket, saliva, soil, various stones, a hankie, half a shoelace and anything else I could rip off me and stay respectable. No greens. Assorted colours, but no greens. No mauve. Odd.

All that day we scurried on among the flaming rows of stubble. By the end of the afternoon I was knackered. A great pall of smoke was swirling seawards from the fields. I'd run miles up and down my rows, leaping the rushing fires which splattered and crackled. We did well. The women had been slow for once and came in for a good deal of ribbing when we assembled for teatime nosh. Wainwright fetches grub on a farm wagon. The women bring baskets and add to it. Andy and Claude take over while us burners rest. By a sheer accident I found myself sharing Hepzibah's pie. I'm happy to report that Claude was half a mile off.

'I hear you've been at Mrs Hepplestone's, Lovejoy,' she said innocently.

'Me?' I asked, wide-eyed. I can be innocent as her any day of the week.

'With Maud, wasn't it?' she pressed.

'Signed on for her ploughing team?' Wainwright put in, to general hilarity.

I joined the chuckles though they were at my expense, assuming Wainwright meant that time I'd overturned one of his tractors years ago.

'Claude will win again,' Wainwright continued confidently, taking a chunk of cheese flan. 'Best in East Anglia.' He smiled at Hepzibah.

One of the sooty men spoke up with a headshake. 'Ar; but only since Gulliver left the farms.'

'Aye. Gulliver was a great champion ploughman.' Wainwright rose to tap the cider barrel. 'Word is he's gone to the dogs.'

I listened to the idle country banter. These casual gossip sessions are fascinating if you've time, but I was beginning to feel decidedly odd, and it wasn't Hepzibah's pie. The smoke was ascending seawards. I turned to watch it. It would be hazing the estuary. Maybe it was the unaccustomed effort of the morning but I was uneasy. Or maybe it was the terrible night's dreaming of shadows. Or being so close to Hepzibah's lovely shape yet daunted by thoughts of being beaten senseless by her giant blacksmith. Maybe it was the pall of smoke. Fire. Perhaps the little firefly cage and its coal copy which Maud chucked on the bonfire seemed some sort of omen. I found I was on my feet heading for my bike.

'Where you off to, Lovejoy?' somebody called.

I shouted back, 'Take my fire lines, Alan.'

They shouted after me but I was running between the charred streaks towards the hedge where I'd left my bike. I just didn't think, merely tore away in a blind panic. We were three miles from my village. Then, say four miles to the estuary.

Oh Jesus, I panted desperately as I dashed, sick to my soul. Please let Drummer be alive. Please. Or at least let me be in time to help.

CHAPTER 9

Looking back now, I could have saved Drummer.

If only I'd confessed my fears to Wainwright he would have done something. I'm sure of it. He's a decent old stick. Or if I'd explained to Hepzibah; she might have got Claude to leave the field-burning. And Claude is a good ally—nobody gets in his way when he's moving. Or if only I'd just had the sense to ask for a lift, or gone to telephone Dolly or Helen to run me down to the staithe . . . If only. Some epitaph.

I pedalled off like a maniac leaving Wainwright's farm and shot like a bullet on to the Bercolta road. Not even the wit to save my strength in the early stages. I went like the wind, cranking my old bike dementedly up and down the low folding roads until I was knackered. Soon I was waggling my arms frantically at overtaking motorists begging a lift but they only hooted angrily back thinking I was abusing them for bad driving. I collapsed in the first phone-box I saw after realizing I was reduced to a snail's pace. I could hardly stand, let alone dial. Unsuspected muscles throbbed feebly as I tried to move me about.

'Get Inspector Maslow,' I gasped, coming to my senses.

'Fire-police-ambulance?' the girl's voice chimed.

'Police, you stupid bitch!' I screamed. 'Police.'

It took a full minute for Inspector Maslow to come on, me shaking and dripping sweat and fuming at the bloody phone.

'Thank God.' I tried to swallow and be plausible. 'Inspector. Look, this'll sound unusual—'

'Who is it, please?'

'Lovejoy. You know, the—'

'Antique dealer.' His voice went funny. 'Yes, I know.'

'Listen, Maslow. Get help to Drummer. Please. Now. You've got radios in your cars, haven't you? A squad car or something—'

'Take it easy.'

'No, for Christ's sake!' I screeched, almost weeping. If he'd been here I'd have strangled the thick bastard. 'Help Drummer.' I began to babble. 'Please, Maslow. Just send one copper. Now.'

'What *is* this, Lovejoy? Are you pissed?'

'No. Honestly.' I struggled for control. 'Please, Inspector. A squad car.'

'Drummer's that old donkeyman, isn't he? Where are you?'

I told him. 'I'm still three miles off. I've only got my bike. Hurry, for God's—'

'Hold it.' The terrifying tones of smug incompetence oozed over the wire. 'On what evidence are you asking me to send a squad car out?'

'Because I'm sure they're doing Drummer!' I yelled, dancing with rage.

'Who?'

'I don't know!'

'Has somebody asked you to pass this message on?'

'No.'

'Then where is Drummer now?'

'Where he always is.' It was too much. 'On the sands.' I said again brokenly, 'Please, Maslow. I'll do anything—'

'Let's get this straight, Lovejoy.' He was enjoying himself, I realized with horror. Actually enjoying playing with me like a cat with a mouse. 'You are miles away. Yet suddenly you take it in your head to summon police assistance, alleging that a senile sand pedlar is being assaulted by persons unknown, on no evidence at all?' The seconds ticked away while the burke gave me all this crap.

'Please, Inspector.' I even tried to smile. Pathetic. 'Please. It'll only take you a couple of seconds—'

'Not for wildgoose chases, Lovejoy—'

'I'll pay for the fucking petrol!' I yelled.

'Look, Lovejoy,' the creep said. I recognized the boot in his tone. 'Why not pedal over there and have a chat with old Drummer? Then phone in and—'

I gave up. 'Maslow,' I said brokenly. 'Remember this call, that's all. Write it down. Time, place, date.'

I dropped the receiver and hurtled off again. My chest was sore and my legs felt cased in tin but I made fair speed. The trouble was I felt late, late, too late by days.

Autumn had really come to the estuary. Boats were laid up all along the hard and there was hardly a soul on the staithe, a young couple strolling home and a lounger or two. Joe's other lad was nowhere to be seen near his oyster beds. Just my luck. The tide was on the turn from low. A couple of boats were already stirring on the mudflats. The sailing club's light was still not on, so their bar was still shut. Not yet five. And only four cars on the club forecourt, nobody about. No help there.

'Seen Drummer?' I called out to one old bloke sitting with his dog on a bench.

'Eh?'

I ignored the gormless old fool and pedalled on, down the gravel as long as I could keep going, then jumped off when it turned to sticky mud and stumbled across the sea-marsh towards Drummer's hut. It hadn't seemed so far off the other day. I took no notice of the wet but kept going in a straight line as near as possible, occasionally floundering on my knees and having to push myself up with my hands. Once I glanced over to Joe Poges's look-out point but the idle sod wasn't there when he was needed.

I reached Drummer's hut like a monster from the deep, breathlessly slithering up the slight bank to Germoline's shelter. No sign of either of them. The hut inside was the same as the other day except for a pile of green samphire on the rickety table. It's a sea-marsh plant East Anglians nosh as a vegetable. Maybe Drummer had gone collecting samphire. I knew he sometimes took sacks of the stuff to market.

'Drummer!' I bawled, like a fool. I could see for miles, much further than I can shout.

Outside, the marshes looked dead. Wainwright's smoke was smudging the whole sky to the north, looming out to sea. Looking inland towards the main staithe you could see tracks where I'd chased across. I leaned against the hut, sweating and panting, wondering if Maslow was right but knowing he wasn't. Tracks. If I'd left tracks maybe Drummer and Germoline did too. A donkey can't tiptoe, that's for sure. But the sea was coming in and sea covers footprints in mud.

I clambered up the side of Germoline's lean-to shelter and, shuddering in every shagged muscle, pulled myself on the shed roof. Like an idiot, I grasped the iron chimney for steadiness and burnt my hand on the hot metal. It made me squawk. Wobbling, I rose flat-footed and gazed over the sea marshes. The roof creaked. If I so much as moved I would go through into the hut below.

It's surprising the difference a few feet in height makes to what you can see. Facing me was the staithe, several small inlets now running with the rising tide and the boats foresting the main estuary. The whole of the foreshore was now empty of people, only a couple of birds shovelling in the mud. The most seaward of the oyster beds was now almost under water. Breathlessly I wobbled flat-footed through ninety degrees and balanced feebly, arms out, while I took in that quarter. I was now looking south along the coast. A trio of distant sails showed where the last of the yachts raced on the incoming tide for the Blackwater's swollen inlet a few miles off. A tanker's flat line lay on the sea horizon. And that was all, apart from two small lads digging for sand worms a mile away where some bungalow gardens came down to the shallows.

Another dithering shuffle round on the frail roof in a quarter turn to face directly out to sea. A spready wobble and I straightened up slowly—and saw Drummer on the dunes maybe a quarter of a mile away.

'Drummer,' I bawled.

He was huddled in a mound. If I hadn't caught sight of Germoline standing forlornly with her painted cart I might have missed him even then. From the hut, the bare muddy promontory, laced by scores of small tidal rivulets, extends into the elbow of one of the sea's curved reaches beyond which is this muddy dune. It stands quite off-shore, and is only slightly domed. Most tides cover it. Germoline was over the low hump. Somebody had left her on the seaward side, sure that Drummer wouldn't get up and come home. An ugly thought. I yelled again.

'Help! Joe Poges!' I almost bawled my lungs up. What the hell was that panicky message they always shout on the pictures? 'Mayday! Mayday!' I howled. A seagull rose and hung, swirling gently in the air above me. It didn't even glance my way, the rotten pig. Surely to God, I

prayed desperately, those drunken slobs in the yacht club
would have their bloody bar open by now. It must be
already gone five o'clock. Who the hell ever heard of a
sailors' bar opening late?

I slid down the sloping roof and tumbled on the flat bit
of ground. Now I was practically at sea level I could no
longer see Drummer or Germoline. The clever bastards, I
thought as I started running towards the water's edge.
Cleverer than me, because I'd forgotten to take some
mark to guide me exactly towards Drummer. I glanced
despairingly round, then waded into the cold sea now
flooding into the creek, and hoping I was going to land up
reasonably near where Drummer lay. I waded with arms
out like a scarecrow's for balance and going a bit sideways
on against the force of the running sea.

It was probably only a few minutes but I seemed to be
wading for hours. I kept shouting, 'Drummer, Drummer!
it's Lovejoy. I'm coming,' but in the finish I gave up
and concentrated on making landfall—well, dunefall.
Eventually I managed to pull myself on to a dune heaped
with thin spiky grass and gasped a bit before compelling
my legs to move again. There wasn't much time. At high
tide there would be only a tuft or two of grass above the
water. All the rest would be horribly immersed, deep
below the North frigging Sea, with me and Drummer and
Germoline swirling deep underneath if I didn't watch it.
Moaning with terror, I scrabbled to the central mound
and almost tumbled over Drummer, right on him.
Germoline gave a brief bray, maybe of alarm at the sight
of this dishevelled hulk looming from the sea. I'm never
very presentable at the best of times. At the moment I
could have put the fear of God into anyone.

'Drummer.' I flopped down and tried to turn him over.
'It's me. Lovejoy.'

Somebody had knocked him about, rough and dirty.
There was dirty blood, brownish, on the sand. His tatty

garb was covered in blotches of blood to which sand clung. He still clutched a handful of samphire. Germoline's cart was half full of the stuff. I heard him exhale.

'Lovejoy? It were Dev . . .'

'Oh Christ, Drummer.'

I rose and yelled for help again towards the shore. Nobody stirred. The yacht club's bar was lit now — it bloody well would be now it was out of reach. And Joe's beacon lamp was blinking, but I couldn't recall if it always did that anyway. 'Mayday,' I bawled, incoherent with impotent rage.

I asked stupidly, 'Drummer. Can you walk?' He lay motionless, unconscious. What first aid do you do for a going-over? I'd learned the drowning bit at school, but what's the use? The sea reach was spreading. When I'd started out the biggest dune had been all of a couple of hundred yards long, and maybe half that wide. Now it had shrunk ominously to about thirty wide and eighty long. 'Oh Jesus,' I moaned. 'We're goners.' I'd have to swim for it. The channel between us and the promontory looked too deep to wade now. Germoline would drown before we'd got half way. For a second I stood helplessly watching the spreading black-green rising waters. Its speed was incredible. From a quiet calm reach it had swelled into a fast-flowing mass pouring inland. Within minutes the whole chain of sandbanks lying along the coast would be engulfed. If only I had a torch to signal. Maybe the old geezer with the dog was alerting helicopters and frogmen. I glared wildly out to sea. Maybe the Royal Navy was already proudly mobilizing its one remaining coracle . . .

It would have to be on my own. Even the yachts from the Blackwater were gone now and the sky was fading swiftly into dusk. Great. Why hadn't one yacht at least kept a proper lookout . . . ?

A yacht. A boat. A *boat*! *That's* how you cross an estuary full of grotty sea! And the place was heaving with the bloody things. I rushed to the top of my dune and looked across the estuary. The nearest craft was one of those sea-going power boats with a plasticky roof and silver knobs. It was facing the open sea but rocking sideways on to me. A hundred and fifty yards, maybe more. Certainly not less. It had a chain thing and kept tugging almost as if it were alive and raring to go.

'Look, Germoline,' I said, hauling off my shoes and starting to chuck my clothes into a heap near Drummer. 'Hold the fort, eh? I'll be back. Somehow I'll be back. Promise.'

I went over and patted her head. I'm not much good at it but maybe she got the idea. Down to my underpants, I waded in, gasping and jumping at the water's chill. It was frigging freezing. Panting in small spurts, I flailed into the water, as much to stop perishing as to get anywhere. The sea race pulled me to the left. I floundered right, doing an uncoordinated mixture of crawl and sidestroke. At last I steadied and began to take markers on the darkening shore. The trouble was I kept losing them. I would belt along like a drunk for as long as I could, then tread water, checking if I'd made any progress. It was more trial and error, and a lot of the latter. Proper swimmers count their strokes but I was so panic-stricken that I finally swam slap into the hull with a sickening thump that dazed me before I even saw it. A minute or two clinging on the anchor chain for breath and I edged up it towards the deck.

They are always bigger when you are on board. No time to go exploring. I clambered on to the transparent roof and checked Germoline and Drummer were still there. The sandbank had shrunk, a bare forty yards long now. How daft — I'd not thought to shift Drummer and Germoline to the highest bit. Cursing and blinding, I blundered to the pointed end. The chain looked thin and promised no trouble, but I had a hell of a time pulling it up. Some kind of a small winch stood on the deck for whoever knew how to work it. The anchor came free and the boat began to move. I staggered back into the cockpit carrying the anchor and, bracing a leg against the driver's seat, smashed the slimy anchor against the glossy wood panel of the dashboard. While the boat drifted in the tide race I chewed the wires through, twined the exposed flex and thankfully heard the roar of an engine.

Now it was dusk all along the estuary. I'd zoom aground if I wasn't careful. Lights were showing, greens, reds and yellows. What the hell did they all mean? Red for going forwards, something like that. I flicked switches experimentally. No light, nothing except the engine beating comfortably under my feet. Well, what the hell. I moved the steering-wheel and fiddled with the controls. It seemed simple enough. A throttle but no brakes. How do you stop a boat? Still, you can't look a gift horse in the mouth. I got her front end pointed seawards and took her forward motion off gradually so she gradually drifted backwards towards the dune.

Looking over my shoulder I spotted Germoline, now braying anxiously trying to encourage the motionless Drummer to get them to safety. I shouted I was coming but stopped that when Germoline took a few eager paces towards me. If she wandered off or panicked now it was hopeless. Handling the boat was difficult. The best way I found after several false goes was to keep the engine slow ahead and putting the wheel over inch by inch so the square end moved closer to the dune. I lodged aground with a horrible grinding noise and fell over. I had the wit to shove the gear into neutral as soon as I got vertical again. No good drifting with the propellers broken into smithereens.

'Okay, Germoline,' I said, shivering with cold yet

delighted at one success. Now I only had to work out how
you get a donkey to climb aboard a boat from a sand
dune. And the dune was now low down. The donkey cart
was wheel deep and Germoline was stamping in alarm as
the waves climbed her legs. Drummer was still dry.

The trouble is, everything on a boat takes time. I
clambered to the front with the anchor and slung it over,
then rushed about searching. No planks or boardwalks.
Nothing for it. I found this harpoon thing under the side
of the cockpit and used it to stove in the cabin door. As
long as it was insured. More vandalism, and two planks
from the bunks. I slung the rear anchor over the side,
hurling it as far as my knackered condition allowed. It
was the best I could do.

I flopped the planks between the gunwale and the
dune's top. It would be a steep climb, and my improvised
bridge wobbled like hell. Germoline would just have to be
a good balancer.

Drummer was easier than I expected though I had to
drag him all the way. Then there was nowhere to lay him
down except the cabin floor, so I dragged him in there
with Germoline braying and screaming like a demented
thing. I scrabbled back to her, just undid the straps under
her belly and left the bloody cart there. By then the sea
was over the wheels and the cart was tilting with every
wave. The samphire was floating off, and most of my
clothes were gone. I got my jacket which had lodged on a
dune tuft.

Getting Germoline on the boat was a real shambles.
Twice the planks tipped us off. I only got her to trust me
by lugging Drummer up and showing her he was already
aboard. Then she streaked up the planks on her own and
stood, drenched and shivering, half in and half out of the
cockpit and coughing like an old sweat.

Drummer seemed to be breathing but I couldn't be
sure. The cabin interior was dark. Dusk had practically

fallen. I found a length of rope and tied Germoline up to the struts of the cockpit. The trouble was I kept retching, probably reaction from fright, practically getting myself drowned and having to exert my atheromatous frame in an unwonted manner. And I'd swallowed half the bloody North Sea.

I covered Drummer with one of the blankets just as he was because I was scared of trying to straighten him, and bundled a pillow under his head. Then I ripped a hole in another blanket and stuck my head through like a poncho. That left a sheet for Germoline. She didn't like it very much but I wasn't having any backchat from a temperamental donkey at this bloody stage and bullied her into being draped with it. Then I cast off, if that's the phrase, moving us cautiously into the main estuary with the throttle a bit forward. I still couldn't find any light switches. Maybe I'd stoved them in.

The boat must have moved about half a mile when Joe's tower started flashing us. He drove me out of my mind, beaming a light right into my eyes so I could hardly see where I was going. 'You're too sodding late, you useless burke!' I bawled at the light. I cut the throttle so there was hardly any movement, which was just as well because Joe's barmy light made me run into a sankbank. Putting into neutral — I couldn't get reverse — and trusting to the sea's velocity rocked us off and we recovered the midchannel after some time. At least there was a red and a green light up ahead and the yacht club bar's glowing windows. Everywhere else was in gloom now except for the lone red lights topping the old gun platforms miles out to sea.

I made the middle of the staithe by a miracle of brilliant navigation, though to be honest the tide was slower there and only one channel heads that way. The reflections from Joe's daft searchlight even helped me a bit. If I knew how to semaphore I would have signalled what I thought of him, stupid sod.

I don't know how long it took us to get anywhere near the stone wharf but it put years on me. Rocking boats moored in the main reach kept looming out of the darkness and they all seemed to be pointed angrily at us, but by now I didn't care if I sank a few here and there. I was past worrying about details. If the flaming owners couldn't be bothered to get up off their fat arses when I'm shouting that Mayday thing and floundering stark bollock naked in the briny they didn't deserve to own bloody boats in the first place. It was the yacht club lights that saved me from driving straight at the stone wharf. When I saw them nearly in line I put the engine into neutral, left the cockpit controls and dashed forward to chuck the anchor over. Then I did the same at the back end and cut the engine. As I did my elbow caught on a protruding button. A klaxon horn blared for an instant from the front of the cockpit. Now I find it, I thought bitterly. No lights, but a horn at last. Enough to wake the dead, or so I told myself then. I leaned my head wearily on the control panel.

'Help's coming,' I said to Drummer. 'We made it. Hold on, Germoline.'

I reached for the button and kept my hand there for what seemed hours. The horn blared and blared and blared.

CHAPTER 10

They got a quack whose surgery stood across from the staithe proper. I can still see Drummer's body on the yacht club's new carpet. In the dreadful glare of the strip lights you could see what the bastards had done to him. He was in an appalling mess. His face was practically unrecognizable. His arms were deformed, bent the way no arms were ever meant to. Blood caked his nostrils and his stubbly chin. He must have tried to fend the blows off. It was too painful even to think about, the old bloke vainly attempting to evade the maniacal battering on the dunes . . . Somebody gave me a brandy which I fetched up, then some gin thinned out with minty stuff which I kept down.

I've never had much time for club people, especially golfers and these yohoho boat characters. You can never tell what they're saying, for a start. They have private languages. But this crowd was really kind. They'd come out at a rush to our boat and ferried us off, calling their nautical terms in the night with gusto. They carried Drummer on a makeshift stretcher and cleared their posh bar for him, ignoring the muddy filth which trailed from Drummer and me. I asked somebody to please look after Germoline and was told she was safe ashore—the first time I've been called 'Old Sport' and not got mad.

The doctor gave Drummer a good cautious examination in total silence while the amateur sailors sipped rums and glanced ominously at each other. I wouldn't go and lie down. I'd never seen so many polo neck sweaters in my life. Everybody was very friendly in an awkward embarrassed way. One or two patted my shoulder in sympathy before the doctor rose, folded her tube thing and told us Drummer was dead. 'I'm sorry,' was how she put it. In better times I'd have chatted her up because she was a cracker, especially for a quack, but now all I could think of was Maslow's maddening voice. Joe was seeing to the boat I'd nicked.

They lent me some clobber, trousers, socks, oddly a pair of running shoes and the inevitable woolly sweater. I even got a crested yachting cap. People said things but I could manage nothing back. I think I got out a few words about sandbanks.

An hour or so afterwards they took me to Joe's house. His wife Alice was still up and his two lads, Alan back from Wainwright's and Eddie from the oyster beds, the three of them pale and quiet. I couldn't eat the hot soupy stuff Alice gave me and just went to lie on the couch in their living-room.

All night long I lay there listening to the sound of the sea. It seemed the shortest night on record, though I was sure I never slept.

Joe never rested that night. He worked like a dog, and looked worse than me at breakfast. He and two helpers had gone around all the households on the wharves knocking folk up and asking what they had seen that evening. The local school teacher hit on the bright idea of taking small portable cassette tape-recorders along. They gave the completed tapes to the bobby about six, but people had seen nothing significant, or so they said. Everybody was eager to please. Nothing like Drummer's death had ever happened before in Barncaster Staithe, and Drummer was a favourite among the colourful characters living locally.

I was summoned to Dr Meakin's surgery after breakfast to make a formal indentification of Drummer. I felt stupid because there wasn't anybody for miles around who could mistake Drummer. Anyhow I stood there, muttered my piece, and signed the policeman's paper. Doc Meakin said how sorry she was and thanks for having tried to save him anyway. Drummer was cleaned and brushed down. He lay on a roller stretcher covered with a sheet. A few of the yachtsmen were there signing statements.

The police car brought Inspector Maslow after we'd finished the formalities. By then Drummer had been something over twelve hours dead. In Maslow came, bossy and thick. I watched him arrive with complete detachment, almost as if he were a celluloid image straight off a screen. He had a quick chat with the Staithe policeman, then asked us to clear off, all except one. Guess who. Dr Meakin went with the others after glancing at me. She was worried. I wasn't, not any more.

Maslow crooked a finger at me, chancing his luck. 'A word with you, Lovejoy.' We stood like two bookends in the surgery with Drummer lying to one side. 'Lovejoy,' said the burke. 'What do you know about all this?'

'Only what I told you.' My voice was somebody else's. 'Before it happened, you will recall.'

'Never mind that,' he snapped, puffing up. 'The implications are you know plenty. Are you concealing evidence?'

'No,' I said. I was mild as a duck pond. 'But you did.' My head felt hot and light.

'*Me?*'

'Yes. I notified you of a crime in good time to prevent it. And you suppressed my notification.'

He decided on attack. His sort honestly get to me worse even than traffic wardens. 'You stole an ocean-going motorized luxury launch, Lovejoy.'

That shut me up. Well, I had. Then this big familiar-looking bloke cut in. He'd thoughtfully dallied in the hallway while the rest shuffled outside to stand around the garden lighting pipes. I recognized him as the Yank I'd saved from buying that crummy forgery of Nelson's letter at the auction. It seemed æons ago. He looked all nautical, which was why I'd not recognized him earlier.

'Excuse me, Inspector,' he said. 'Not steal exactly. It's my boat. Name of Naismith.'

'And you gave him permission, sir?' I could see Maslow was going to be stubborn.

The bloke hesitated. 'Not exactly. But I would have, if I'd been here.'

We all thought hard. There was some New World logic

in there somewhere. To me it seemed preferable to that
relentless Old World stuff you can never argue with.

'Thanks, mate,' I told him.

'You're welcome.' He ducked out again. A big bloke,
he kept having to mind the low oaken beams. I noticed he
again idled in the hallway, gazing absently at a seascape
hanging by the stairs. Don't say I've an ally at last, I
hoped in disbelief. Unless he turned out yet another
friend of Maud's. They'd been near each other at that
same auction . . . Maslow was apoplectic but trying to
stay calm.

'All right, Lovejoy,' he said at last. 'You can go. But
watch it, that's all. I'll want you down at the station
later—'

'Maslow,' I said, grinning like I'd never done before.
'Piss off.' There was only one witness, though I like now to
think Drummer was watching too.

Maslow rounded on me, finger raised in warning. We
were as pale as each other. 'Look here, Lovejoy—'

I hit him then, sweet as a nut. He folded with a whoosh
and crumpled to the floor. Lovely. I decided to save some
of Maslow's punishment for later. The big Yank hadn't
even turned round, though he must have heard.

'So long, Drummer,' I said to the sheet. 'I'll do you the
gadroon. You see.'

Maslow, trying to stand, crumpled in agony again and
fell between me and the door. I kneed him ever so gently
on his back, still folded and grasping his belly. 'Out of the
way, Maslow. There's justice to be done.' The law has no
sense of what's right.

I passed the big bloke in the hall. He was still frowning
at the seascape.

'Be careful, Mr Naismith,' I said. 'That's a
reproduction.'

'Is that right!' he said affably to the seascape. 'Well,
thanks.'

I went out by the back door to avoid Doc Meakin and the others. There was a feeling I'd see more of the big Yank called Naismith.

Before I left the Staithe I went over to Joe's house at the end of the staithe. I asked Joe if I could look at the sea reach between the promontory and the big sandbar where I'd found Drummer and Germoline.

'Can we look from your coastguard place?'

'If you like.' He tried grinning and failed. 'It's only the same sea, Lovejoy.'

Joe's lad Alan ran ahead of us and started explaining about his dad's telescope and instruments. The lookout space was recessed back from a balcony, with walls covered by charts of isobars and whatnot.

'Don't fool me, Joe,' I said, trying my best. 'You never get the weather right.'

'That's the Meteorological Office,' he cracked back fast. 'We're coastguards.'

I looked out. And it *was* the same sea, same estuary. The reach looked narrower, hardly a stone's throw, but then the tide was lowish. And the same dunes. And Drummer's pathetic ramshackle hut, just the same. And the distant old gun platforms low down and miles off. The ocean-going ships on the horizon. The same gaggle of tiny yachts already racing from the Blackwater. Yet . . .

'Something's missing, Joe.'

'Eh?' He scanned the outside world, puzzled. 'No. Same as always.'

'No, Joe. Something's odd.'

I kept looking at one place. Wherever I tried to look, my eyes kept coming back to it. It was the dune, the big mounded dune where I'd found Drummer. Its top just touched the horizon for what seemed an inch or two when seen from here. But so what? And they'd done Drummer on the far side *where they wouldn't be seen from Joe's place*. If I hadn't stood on Drummer's hut roof I'd never have seen him and Germoline, from that different angle.

Joe tried kindness again. 'Go home and have a rest, Lovejoy. Do as Doc says—'

'Lovejoy's right, Dad.'

Joe looked at me, then at Alan. 'Show me what you mean, son.'

Alan pulled at us both, jubilant. We followed him in silence out on to the balcony, as far left as the railing let him. 'Lean out, Dad.' Alan was proud as Punch. '*Now* look at the sea.'

And suddenly I knew. Even before looking I *knew*, knew it all—or most of it.

'Good lad,' I told Alan. I was downstairs and walking off when Joe and Alan came running after me.

'Lovejoy. You didn't even look.' Joe didn't know whether to be annoyed at himself or pleased with Alan's observation. 'It's—'

'I know,' I said. 'The gun platforms.'

'That's right.' Alan was grinning as we walked out, chuffed at being one up over everybody. 'From almost everywhere else you can see three gun platforms. From Dad's lookout you can only see two, because—'

'That big dune obscures it.' I stopped and waved to Alice at her window. 'I'll get the clothes back when I can get a minute.'

'You're welcome, Lovejoy. Here. What's so special about the old gunfort?'

'Nothing, Joe. Forget it. Thanks for everything.' We stood about being embarrassed. I decided to thumb a lift back from the road.

'Cheers,' Joe said. Alan said the same, a bit self-consciously. 'Er, Lovejoy,' Joe called. 'Don't forget Germoline.'

Germoline and her cart were tied at the railing of the

yacht club. A few members were having coffee in the bay of their verandah, clearing throats and studiously reading papers.

'We got the cart and did it up,' Joe added. 'She's been fed, only . . . well, she'll be a bit lost . . . and she likes you . . .'

The cart was spotless. Somebody had laboured most of the night on it. I bet it was the yacht club people now so preoccupied. Germoline's harness was gleaming and her coat was brushed to a fine dark sheen. Even her hooves shone. She looked really posh. Broken-hearted, but posh.

I managed to say after a bit, 'Tell them thanks, Joe.'

'Get in. It won't hurt her.'

I did as I was told. The shafts rocked a bit but Germoline shuffled expertly and we balanced up.

'It's a long way to my cottage,' I said anxiously. Now I had a bloody donkey to worry about.

'She likes work,' Joe informed me. Alice was smiling and nodding from her steps. 'It's Germoline's trade, like antiques are yours.'

I sat there like a lemon holding these straps while everybody avoided looking.

'Er . . . ?' I got out at last, quite lost.

'You say, Gee up, Germoline,' Alan prompted.

'Gee up, Germoline,' I commanded apologetically. 'Please.'

And I rolled home at a slow stroll to the sound of Germoline's harness bells.

One donkeypower. Well, I thought helplessly, it's more than I'm accustomed to.

CHAPTER 11

Countryside never stops being astonishing. When you think of it, it's only a collection of villages dotted thinly among trees and estuaries and other boring pastoral crud. So you'd think news has a difficult time getting itself spread about. Nothing is further from the truth. An hour after I reached the cottage a silent pale Dolly arrived with a hot meal, sat me down to eat and moved about tidying up. Several times she bravely answered the door but didn't let anybody in.

I don't know much about donkeys but I'm sure Germoline knew what was up. After her terrifying experience she'd be daft if she didn't. I was scared the journey home was too much for her but Dolly said she was probably glad of a job, take her mind off things. We went out to her about fiveish just as Tinker arrived stinking of fish meal, Jacko's flavour of the month, and carrying a dirty sack. Dolly linked her arm with mine defensively and recoiled as Tinker came plodding up the gravel.

'Had to walk bleeding miles, Lovejoy,' he whined indignantly.

'Get it?' I'd phoned him from the box by the chapel to bring Germoline some grub.

'Aye. You owe Lemuel for it.' Tinker slung the bag on the grass disgustedly. 'He says it's enough for two days.' He hawked deep and spat messily on the gravel.

'Show us how to feed her, Tinker.'

Germoline was standing forlornly in the garden. She had a half-hearted go at chewing a bit of grass, then sobbed a few heart-breaking donkey sobs. Naturally Tinker grumbled but did it, threading a rope through the sack some way and hanging it over Germoline's face. It

looked a dicey business to me, though Germoline got the
hang of it smartish. And it stopped her crying, thank
God.

'You really need Lemuel for this,' Tinker groused. 'He's
a natural with nags.'

'I've heard—from the bookies,' I said sardonically.
'There's a beer indoors, Tinker.'

'Should I fetch it out?' Dolly suggested brightly,
thinking of her cleaning, but Tinker had streaked off.

A car screeched to a stop in the lane.

'Lovejoy! You poor, poor *creature*!' Patrick descended,
grand with grief in his orange suit and blue wedge heels.

I'd put a couple of planks across the gap in the hedge to
show Germoline her territory. Patrick momentarily shed
his unmitigated sorrow to curse this arrangement while he
stepped gingerly over. Lily followed lovingly. Oho, I
thought, where are the widows of yesteryear? Lily's
husband was in a cold bed again.

'Wotcher, Patrick, Lily.'

Patrick posed on the gravel, orange trilby tilted and
hands clasped to show the depths of his emotion.
'Lovejoy! We've all heard and we're positively *distrait*!' He
was going to enlarge further but got bored and decided to
notice Dolly. 'Ooooh!' he squealed. '*Love* your pearls,
dear! False, though, aren't they?'

You have to take Patrick with a pinch of salt. He's not
as daft as he looks. On average he pulls a high-priced deal
in minor master paintings once a year, which shuts his
critics up for quite a while.

I introduced them all, Dolly as an old school friend.

'No *need* to apologize, Lovejoy.' Patrick fluttered his
eyes at Dolly roguishly. 'We won't say a single *mot* about
you and Lovejoy rutting the way you do.'

This was getting out of hand. I cut in. 'Patrick, do me a
favour. Ask Brad about a boat.' Brad's brother Terry has
a boatshed.

'How old, dear? There's only those old sailing barges—'

'Not antique. One that goes.'

If he was surprised at this non-antiques enquiry he concealed it well. 'For you, *anything*! But why, Lovejoy?'

Anxious not to reveal too much, I turned the chat to antiques for a minute or two. Clearly Patrick was disappointed at not finding me moribund. His enthusiasm for the visit weakened visibly when Tinker reappeared from the cottage swigging ale from a bottle.

'We'll go. In case we get *covered* in *fleas*,' he hissed. 'One thing, Lovejoy.' He pulled me aside and whispered, '*Do* tell that sweet Dolly there's a *limit* to how much tan a bottle-green twinset can *bear*. Promise?'

They departed, Patrick abusing Lily for bad driving as she made eight noisy attempts to turn their car. 'You're giving me a headache!' he was screeching. Neither remembered to wave.

'Frigging queer,' Tinker growled after them. 'What's this about a boat, Lovejoy?'

'We need one for a couple of days.'

'That'll cost us,' he grumbled.

Dolly took my arm gently. 'Come in, love. I'm chilly now the nights are drawing in.' I was glad to call it a day.

That day all I could think of was where to get some money. Dolly has a car and her husband has a good job, but could I tap her for a boat's hire, deposit and all? Probably not. And how much is a boat anyway? While she was running Tinker back to town, Helen dropped by to ask if it was all true about Drummer. It was a curiously stilted visit, her standing in the doorway saying, no thanks she wouldn't come in just now. I told Helen thanks for visiting and I was fine but Drummer was killed. She said politely how she quite understood and turned on her heel and zoomed off in her red saloon. I think she sensed Dolly. I went and sat on the grass near Germoline to think.

Devlin, of course, killed poor old Drummer—the only pair of eyes looking seaward at a precise spot on the ocean, from the dune. And I knew roughly why. It was the gun platform, one of the sea forts, as people call them here. Thanks to young Alan, I knew which one.

They stand some miles offshore. Our people built them during the war as flak batteries against enemy raiders. Soldiers were posted there for only limited periods because of the constant risk. It was no rest cure. Between bomber raiders there was the constant fear that every warship was an enemy until proved otherwise. Apart from that there were only the terrifying storms which tried to shove the gun tower over into the deep ocean. And the blizzards. And the fogs, when you began to wonder if the rest of the world had simply vanished . . .

Drummer was dead. It would be me next. I forced myself to think of shadows. A few years ago I unintentionally went sailing, with a bloke who lived on a cabin cruiser. Still does. He had some nautical gadgets for sale, a sextant, two old ship logbooks and a navigator's table from sailing days. I wouldn't even have gone on board but it was one of those fine calm summers when our estuaries are crowded with holidaymakers. It seemed safe as houses. Doug, an old mate of mine, laughed at my fears.

We had a drink or three while we haggled. It was only early Victorian, none the less desirable. I knew I had plenty of keen customers for his stuff. We were both fairly well pickled when I noticed I couldn't see the shore any longer through the cabin window. While we'd been fixing the deal a dense fog had fallen. In fact we couldn't see a damned thing, not even another boat.

Doug laughed again, but this time less convincingly because it seemed we were drifting. Doug's bloody carelessness with his anchor had put us in the most dangerous position you can ever be on water—drifting in a fog.

Naturally by then Doug was too sloshed to think straight. Terror sobered me, but I know nothing about boats. Naturally the nerk's engine wouldn't go, and to cap it all his famous electronic gear failed to bleep. He kept saying, 'We're fine, great,' the lunatic.

About half an hour later foghorns began booming. The most mournful sound in the world except for a sobbing donkey. The trouble is you can't really tell which direction they are coming from. Fog does weird things to sounds. I was sure they were trying to tell us something, but of course Doug was singing nautical gibberish and unable to do anything even if he knew what was going on. We had another drink or two. Not much else we could do for the moment.

Scared as I was, I must have nodded off. I'd been swigging Doug's filthy homebrew since clambering aboard. Anyhow the next thing I remember of this holiday cruise was coming to, still befuddled and grinning with Doug snoring loudly in the cockpit. I sat in the well area peering blindly around at the grey fog. The sea heaved its unpleasant oily surface against the boat. No need to worry, though. Doug, that experienced sailor, said so—sloshed out of his mind but undoubtedly experienced. He'd told me we'd just float in the estuary till the fog lifted.

'Hey, Doug,' I remember bawling from my reclining posture. 'I can see a roof.'

'Eh?' He came to and yawned extravagantly. 'Impossible. You're drunk, Lovejoy.'

But I could, a tilted dark mass exactly like a pointed roof. And there was a noise, an intermittent sucking and slurping. Doug came staggering up from the cabin, stretching and scratching. I pointed. The mass seemed to be hardening and growing fast.

Doug froze. *'Jesus!'* It wasn't even a shout. It was a moan. 'The *gun fort!*' he screamed.

At that moment a faint gust thinned the fog. I gaped at the appalling sight, nearly peeing in sheer terror. We were floating fifty yards off the most colossal thing I'd ever seen. An immense looming black concrete rectangle filled the sky hundreds of feet above us. Vast cylindrical pillars plunged from its flat belly into the sea. They were horribly stained by weed and begrimed by rims of discharged oil. The sea sloshed on them with that gruesome sickening slurp I now realized I'd been hearing for some time. With the erratic sloshing of the greeny-black oily sea around its legs the horrible bloody thing seemed to be wading towards us like a huge uncoordinated giant bent on our destruction.

'Get us away from it!' I screeched. 'Get the fucking boat —'

'We're drifting for it!' Doug yelled. He attacked the stupid engine controls on the dashboard, kicking and blaspheming, while I subsided into an aghast silence as the great malevolent mass seemed to plod its mad way nearer and nearer. To my shame I hid my head between my hands in the cabin, too terrified to do anything, though Doug was screaming for me to come out and help. He called me all the abusive names he knew but I didn't budge. The one glance I gave nearly made me faint. We'd drifted between the tower's obese legs, about forty feet off to either side, and above, the grotesque soiled dripping underbelly of the gun fort filled the whole world, a mass of slanting shadow.

Doug did well from then on, all on his own. I stayed in the cabin mute with terror even when the engine mercifully roared into action. I couldn't bear to look out until Doug yelled that we were clear. Doug became quite chirpy as we puttered home through the lessening fog. I recognized the anecdote syndrome. This would be the basis of one of his famous nautical tales in the pubs along the coast. How I Escaped The Sea Drift In The Worst

Fog . . . He could have the glory any time, I thought fervently. All I wanted was to stand on solid ground and never get off.

Doug assumed I'd been too seasick to help him near the sea fort. I didn't disillusion him. I said, what the hell could you expect from that homebrewed plonk he kept offering me, which gave him a good laugh. I joined in — once we stepped ashore.

That was my shadow. Until now I'd made myself forget. Now I made myself remember.

And I'd done something even more stupid. I'd forgotten to look at a map. I went in and got out my one-inch-scale Ordnance Survey.

Immediately I found another missing link. Mrs Hepplestone's fields ran down to the sea marshes at the estuary's northern shore. Exactly opposite, a small crossed square was printed on the map's blue ocean. 'Platform (dis)', it said.

It fitted into an unpleasant scheme. Old Hepplestone had copied a firefly cage, carving it beautifully in coal. But he had made the legs and base exactly like those of the gun platform — no harm in that, surely? After all, he'd seen it often enough from his wife's lovely estate. Yet there was this irksome little secret hollow leg with the shiny bottom. Empty, but undoubtedly a hell of a lot of time and trouble to make. How odd, to work so cleverly merely to draw attention to an empty hole. *Unless he was drawing attention to something on the sea fort itself?*

A steady stream of nicked antiques had vanished and never been recovered. Now the point is, that the gun platforms aren't just planks on a trestle. Each was a compact fortress garrisoned by a whole artillery company, and capable of resisting assault and blockade. Plenty of room out there for stolen antiques to wait in solitude for eventual collection by night boats.

Dolly came back as I folded the map away. I was glad

to see her. The beautiful woman had brought a portable battery television set and a bottle of wine. I gave her a real heroine's welcome. She might not know it, I swore fervently, but she's going to stay here tonight if I have to rope her to the sink. She seemed delighted at her reception.

CHAPTER 12

I needed a boat.

For a whole thirty-six hours I worked like, well, a donkey. My old Bible box got the full treatment.

If money was needed — seeing wealthy Mrs Hepplestone had scotched my phoney advert — I had to sacrifice a lifetime of principles and make it look the best preserved antique in the kingdom.

Oak fades with age to a displeasing dry pallor, so it's a unique problem. Normally I hate tricks with antiques. I've had more fights and spilled more pints over this evil than any other kind of sin, but it's so common nowadays that antique dealers — and even real people — think it's perfectly proper. And 'restoring' the surface patina invariably ups the value — to the unknowing. Some burkes in our trade have so little sense they'll sandblast and varnish anything that stops still long enough.

A Bible box is anything up to three feet long, usually oak, with a simple plain desk-type lid. If it had been teak the wood's own natural oils would have preserved it. So a gentle rub with a little trichlorethylene (open the windows or your liver rots), then a little teak oil and it comes up lovely. 'Cheap and easy,' we dealers say of teak. I'm really fond of anything that looks after itself like that. Oak can't. In fact it evolves different acids which spoil bronzes, medallions and even some pewter so you have to be careful what you use oak furniture for.

While Dolly went home to win her badges back, I set to. Germoline came to listen while I explained. Some Victorian swinger eager for a bit more gloom had painted it a filthy brown. I began scraping the paint off with broken glass. Some French restorers even use corrosive chemicals and a hose-pipe. I once saw a bloke in a filthy Rouen garage, hosing down a long-suffering bureau as if it was modern gunge. Scraping with a piece of broken glass sounds worse but it's the kindest method. I never use gloves. If my fingers start bleeding it serves me right for pressing too hard. After all, doctors still use plate glass fragments for cutting the thinnest possible sections for electron microscopes, which only goes to show something or other.

The trouble is that 'restoring' isn't restoring at all. It's pretence, a sort of underhand trick. That's why I hate it. You remove all traces of that lovely human warmth, that precious care lavished on a piece of furniture for centuries, that priceless chance of contact with your ancestors. Then you replace it with a splash from a tin. It's a disgusting process.

You need to wash furniture that has 'slid', as we say. I use a little gentle detergent in warm water and a soft shoebrush, with a painter's Rowney S240 nylon brush for the crannies. A careful wipe with some old underpants, then air it on a towel in the open.

I had something to tell Germoline and this was the right moment. 'Coffee break, Germoline.' She plodded round the back after me.

I got her a bucket of water and brewed up for myself. Donkeys drinking are really quite interesting. Germoline's nostrils seemed to go under the surface but not so she spluttered. We rested on the grass beside the Bible box.

'Look, pal,' I said after a few hesitations. 'Devlin did Drummer over, and left you both on the dunes, right? It's something to do with that old gun fort, the one you can see from your dune but not from Joe's lookout. You and Drummer saw Devlin's boat up to something.'

Nobody in their right mind would bury anything on the dunes, because our dunes shift and erode. So it had to be the old sea fort.

'But whereabouts in it?' I asked Germoline softly, giving her a handful of grass. 'It'd take a month to search a place that huge. It'd be like searching a whole ship. Useless . . .'

Germoline stopped noshing and looked at me. I looked back.

'Unless that cage told us exactly *where* and *how*.'

We went back to work, thinking of all those break-ins at Mrs Hepplestone's.

The next bit's unpleasant. You use potassium hydroxide — caustic potash — and all the care in the world because it's dangerous to eyes, skin and everything else you've got. It is necessary to wash the caustic solution off, and this has to be done fast. You need the caustic to alter the oak's colour. Don't wait to see it darken — the oak knows what to do. A swift (five to ten seconds) application and then wash it *all* off, or crystals of the horrible stuff will 'flower' out in ugly little encrustations just when you think you've finished a marvellous job and you'll have to start all over again. Remember all woods are different. Spanish chestnut, for example, goes a rich red under this treatment.

Germoline gave me a nudge just as I'd ended this phase. Eight or nine children were carrying books up the lane to meet the library van. Germoline was doubtless wanting to get down to some hard slog carrying them about like she normally did on the sands.

'Bloody pest,' I reprimanded angrily, but downed tools.

'We aren't to fetch you any more books, Lovejoy.' That

was Ginny, a prim seven-year-old, getting her spanner in first as I came out. 'Miss Smith says you don't return them on time.'

'Miss Smith can get knotted,' I said. I wasn't going to be lectured to by a bossy infant. 'Come and see my donkey.'

They were disbelieving at first but crowded excitedly in. Germoline was a fantastic success.

'A saddle!'

'And a *cart*!'

I took the opportunity of exercising authority, my first and only time, and said sternly, 'Germoline is a specially trained sand-donkey. She's an expert, so do exactly as she lets you. Proper turns.'

'Please, Lovejoy. How do we strap her in?' Trust Ginny.

'Er—'

'You don't know, Lovejoy.' That was Dobber, her scornful little cousin, a two-catapult psychopath of considerable local fame.

I rammed my fist under his nose and threatened to knock his emerging teeth back into his gums. 'I'm not telling you how. It's a test, see? The one who fastens the straps right gets first go.'

They fell about laughing, to my annoyance, while I skulked back to my restoration and let them get on with it.

If you wax antique oak furniture immediately after stripping, something grotty happens. The oak becomes utterly dull, finishing up a miserable grey colour that will never polish up for the rest of its gloomy life. You have to 'lift' it, as we say. Hydrogen peroxide lifts quickly, but the necessary strength (120 volumes is about right) will bleach you as well as every stitch you wear, so watch out. Oxalates are fast too, but need a ghastly pantomime with kettles of hot water. I advise dilute hydrochloric acid and copious washing. It's moderately safe as long as you mind your eyes. My rule is to know where every drop goes, and to wash a million times afterwards.

I locked the workshop door. Actually the oak looked little different even after its acid and water washes when I took it out for its second dry.

Germoline was happily trundling her cartload of children round the garden. Ginny had decided a rider in addition was too much, so a queue had formed. Two at a time rode inside, or one on the saddle.

'We're careful about your pram, Lovejoy,' Gwen called. She meant my ancient little Ruby, overgrown in the long grass. 'Ginny stopped Dobber from lighting its candles.'

'Great.' I wrung a promise out of the mob not to chop my box into firewood while I went in the kitchen for a spirit burner.

With the children's excited racket as background I put a small pan of water over the burner and stood a pot in it. Five ounces of beeswax to a pint of turpentine and stir every three minutes. When I did this first, everything caught fire. Now I have an old dustbin lid and some sacks on hand in case. Make sure the oak is absolutely dry, then brush the wax on with a one-inch decorator's brush, missing no part out, and dry it again. The next bit is really murder unless you know how. I keep a fantail burner blowlamp to get a good spread of flame on the solid beeswax. A local beekeeper gives me that. One pass of the waxblock through the flame, and then you rub it hard on the oak. Every so often you whisk the flame over where you've rubbed. Don't for heaven's sake plonk a block on and just melt it or it'll take ages to clean the great molten mass of crud off. Patiently ease the beeswax in, using the flame as a gentle nudge, remembering that a hell of a lot of bees have a vested interest in your progress. Once done, a stiff carpenter's flatbrush removes the excess wax. The edges are shined up by a small mahogany burnisher. (Just cut the edge of a piece of mahogany at a 50-degree angle, then give the edge two or three soft rubs using grade 100 glass paper. The world's best burnisher. It will last you years and gives a shine nothing else can impart.) Then out into fresh air.

Done.

I sat back on my heels looking at the box. 'Sorry, mate,' I said apologetically. 'But it had to be. I need some money to murder someone.'

'*What* did you say, Lovejoy?'

Oho. Hepzibah Smith, sexy blonde choirmistress and volunteer librarian for the travelling van which brings culture to our midst. I cursed myself for carelessness, rising sheepishly to say hello. 'Hello, you flaxen Saxon.' I grinned with false heartiness.

'Please, miss. Lovejoy was only talking to his box,' Dobber explained.

'I hurt it,' I said, feeling the embarrassment of having restored it.

'Aw,' the children chorused sympathetically.

'It's beautiful, Lovejoy,' little Ginny said.

And it was. We were in a circle, the box on its towel in the centre. It emitted a lustrous honey-gold iridescence. With the natural brilliance any antique acquires from its centuries of love and life, it dazzled us all. I swear even the flinty Miss Smith caught her breath in the momentary silence. Hepzibah broke the spell.

'Yes, well,' she said critically. 'Anybody who talks to a box is silly.'

'Lovejoy has a donkey,' little Dobber pointed out, eyes narrowed for argument.

'And you haven't,' I told Hepzibah maddeningly.

She broke through the rising chorus of explanations. 'That doesn't explain why you children failed to bring your books to the library van. You've made us late for Dragonsdale. Come along, all of you, this instant.'

'Dragonsdale?' We all trooped down to the lane. I had a brainwave. 'If you see Mrs Hepplestone there, tell her I'll drive for her in the ploughing match.'

She laughed, giving me an odd look. 'Are you serious, Lovejoy? I didn't know you could.'

'Saturday, isn't it?' I said airily, blowing on my fingernails to show I moved in high society. 'Been driving for years.'

I was waving them off as Dolly's car swung in.

She climbed out with a bag of shopping. 'What on earth's been happening here, Lovejoy?'

'Oh, nothing. Giving some children donkey rides.'

She fell about at that. 'How very pastoral, Lovejoy.'

I let her go on laughing as we went in. Well, I couldn't tell her I'd spent the peaceful hours working out how to kill Devlin, could I?

He now stood accused, tried and convicted. Being a law-abiding sort of bloke, I would first let Maslow know the result of my mental trial.

Then the execution.

CHAPTER 13

There was no question where I'd sell my precious Bible box to some undeserving swine. Once a week there's a gathering of antique dealers called Ye Olde Antiques Fayre in the Red Lion. The only antique you can be sure of, though, is the Red Lion itself, this being well documented since the Romans first brewed up on the site. I was sad to be harnessing Germoline up that morning, but I had other reasons for going.

I had to create a disturbance, to draw Devvo out, now Devlin and I both knew the game. And I was eager to see which dealer Maud had in tow, as she worked her way through us, so to speak, in her blundering attempts to unravel the mystery her old uncle had left. My Bible box went easily into an old pillowcase. No sign of rain. I asked Germoline to gee up please and we hit the road. At the chapel crossroads our bobbie George Jilks was nodding off, vigilant as ever on the chapel bench. I woke him after asking Germoline politely to hold it a second.

'Sorry, George.' I gave him a moment to splutter awake. 'But supposing I knew who killed somebody?'

'Eh?' His eyes cleared, focused. 'What the hell you up to, Lovejoy?'

I gave up. No use explaining to a nerk like George. 'Tell Maslow from me that Devlin killed Drummer. Cheers.'

I invited Germoline to proceed, George trotting after us frantically trying to scribble in his notebook. As if he can write.

'Maslow knows where, when and how, George,' was all I would say. 'Just tell him.'

He dashed in to phone as we passed his house. I was glad. I felt conspicuous enough driving a donkey cart without having the Keystone Kops making matters worse.

I whistled all the way to town. My personal disturbance was nicely under way.

Town was agog, or what passes for agog in dozy East Anglia. Lots of cars and folk, a small autumn fair in the park and a shirt-sleeved band parping away. The flea-market was in the coaching yard. Margaret blew a kiss, looking unhappily frozen in about six coats as I arrived to a chorus of catcalls. Helen gave me a distant nod. Wrong again. Oh, well. Patrick yoohooed. Lily had forked out for the best patch in the yard for him, facing the main gateway. Lucky old Patrick.

'Don't bring that *beast* in here, Lovejoy,' he screamed, doing a theatrical swoon.

'Get stuffed. Whoa, please.'

Eddie Trasker came over sheepishly as I climbed down. 'Stall money, mate.'

'Don't want one, Eddie. This cart's my stall.'

'Er . . .' Eddie's quite good on late Georgian furniture but weak on donkey parking law. He's a jaunty chequer-suited extrovert everybody likes, so he gets all the rotten jobs like collecting dues.

I turned Germoline round but secretly I was worried about the cart. How do you keep it still? Germoline has no brakes. 'Stay!' I ordered. 'Please.' A good fifty customers were in among the twenty or so antique stalls. Don Musgrave and Margaret were already wrapping stuff for happy customers and Jason had sold a good walnut Canterbury to a bloke who was wreaking havoc backing his car to load up.

Tinker hove in, tattered and bloodshot, instantly all over the Bible box.

'Restored it, Lovejoy? How much we asking?'

'Don't breathe on it,' I cracked. 'You'll strip it again with that breath.' Tinker received the price I quoted for him without surprise and drifted off to put the whisper round.

Within ten minutes I'd sold the box to Jason for a really good mark-up, though not without a pang of genuine grief. He took it off reverently in its protective pillow-case. I gave Tinker his back commission, which made him thirsty and reminded him it was opening time. I could see the nondescript figure of Lemuel feverishly beckoning this news from the pub window.

I shrugged. 'All right, you can go. But find me a set of personal cruets, Tinker. Eighteen-thirties.' This always happens, money burning my pocket when it's earmarked for other purposes.

'Eh? What's a personal cruet?'

'Noshing wasn't always sharing the same sauce bottle

like in Woody's,' I told him caustically. Once upon a time, elegance dictated that guests should be given individual silver pepper and salt-cellars at dinner. I've always wanted a cased set.

He grinned farewell and was off like a ferret. By nightfall the job would be done, deserving a tipsy celebration in the White Hart. A hand tapped my shoulder. Honestly, I was actually smiling as I turned. Here we go, I thought cheerfully. Personal disturbance Part Two. I'm always at my best when hate shows the way.

' 'Morning, Inspector,' I beamed. 'Isn't shopping hell?'

'In there, Lovejoy.' He hadn't brought an army, which was a pity. I wanted spectators, mayhem, blood all round the frigging town. The mob of dealers and customers thronged to a standstill.

'No,' I said, being poisonously cheerful. When you're being pushed about by the Old Bill happiness is big medicine.

'You passed on a message—'

'Pigeon reached you, did it?' At least three customers were still focused on Margaret's early Stonebridge ware. I yelled, 'Pay attention, everybody.'

Maslow started sweating, conscious that the good old public was all ears and him not exactly bobby-dazzling. He went for pomp, silly fool. 'Conduct liable to cause a breach of the peace—'

I boomed heartily, 'Devlin killed Drummer. That's k-i-double-l-e-d. I warned you before it happened. Where and when. So like I mean, sod off.'

Nearby the band played erratically on. Cars and noise filled the High Street. But inside the coachyard you could have sliced the appalled silence with a blunt shovel. I leant forward to him confidentially. The crowd leaned with me, breathless to catch the next bit.

'I could sell you a lovely Georgian pendant, a bargain—'

He went then, pushed through the frozen mob.

I bawled after him, 'I'll not let you forget, Maslow. I've posted the details to the Chief Constable —' No good. He vanished among the shoppers across the street. Margaret came by me apprehensively but I was grinning like a fiend.

'What on *earth*, Lovejoy?'

'It's my new image.' I felt on top of the world — money in my pocket, antiques nearby and vengeance at hand.

'You'll get yourself arrested, Lovejoy,' Jason prophesied. Jenny Bateman ruefully shook a warning finger. All this made me notice the silver eggcase Jason was busily overpricing on his stall. Staring intently at it with my Bible box money corroding my jacket made me notice the early seventeenth-century stumpwork box next to it. Which made me spot a dazzling Queen Anne baby-walker — basically a walnut wood ring, just big enough for a toddler's waist, held between four finialled wooden balls separated by brilliantly turned 'stretchers' or rods. Which made me notice, sweating with excitement, a pile of old theatrical playbills. These currently average no more than half a day's wages, and they're rocketing. Feeling great, I paused for a fatal second. It'd do no harm just to look . . .

Of course I should have first collared Brad about hiring a boat, or phoned Joe Poges at Barncaster Staithe, or maybe the glamorous Doc Meakin — she had a million nautical patients and was bound to have some idea. Instead I finished up an hour later with the stumpwork box — it's a kind of embroidery in which ornamented scenes are fetched out in relief. You get religious scenes, pastoral motifs or moral exhortations on jewellery boxes or vanity purses. Sequins, pearls and occasionally coloured glass beads are worked into the design which, I warn you, isn't to everybody's taste. But the value of stumpwork has soared because three centuries ago women couldn't resist showing little scenes of domestic and other worthwhile labour.

I'm making excuses. All right. I bought it from Jason for about half its value. And the collection of old theatre playbills. And gave Jenny Bateman a deposit on a carved beechwood chair of the Great Civil War period, the first time cane-bottomed chairs made sitting almost comfortable. I got it for half its true value. (A tip, learned the hard way: never forget that the 'true' value is what you can sell something for *the same day you buy it*.)

But it wasn't all self-indulgence. During those two hours I collected gossip about thirty-one antiques nicked in the past three months, about half from my mates. Naturally only the honest dealers had reported the thefts, which meant Margaret — no antique dealer welcomes investigations round his doorstep. Taxmen have long ears. I was impressed by Devvo's industry. No wonder he was our most regular attender at local auctions. How else could he gather reliable information about who had what? It was then I had my one stroke of luck.

A raucous shout made me turn with interest. Mannie, large as life. He is a youth who showed up two years ago as a tourist — a real one — off a coach. He took one look at our antiques arcade and bade a delighted farewell to his astonished coach party. Tell Mum not to cry and everything. He stayed and became one of us. I pushed my way through to where he lounged with this long-case clock.

'For you, Lovejoy,' he greeted me straight off, 'ten per cent discount.'

Mannie has two styles of dress — the new straggly filth look, or a multicoloured caftan thing with bells and a striped pointed cap. Never anything on his feet. It looked like the Dalai Llama had hit town.

'You'll catch your death, Mannie.'

'I've not mucked about with the white face, Lovejoy,' Mannie said earnestly. 'Notice it?'

'Good heavens!' My pretence was a bit theatrical because nobody in their right mind can miss a genuine white-faced long-caser. Especially Mannie. He was half asleep. 'Go back to bed, Mannie. You're knackered.'

He gave a rueful grin. 'Daren't. Left this bird there. I had to fight my way to the door.' He plucked me closer while I examined his clock. 'Here. Know anything about Japanese boxes?' He fumbled in his clothes to a jingle of prayer bells, smoothed the crumbled paper he somehow managed to find. A crude outline sketch of a firefly cage on ordinary notepaper. So Maud had found time for something else during the night besides romping with Mannie.

'Search me.' I hardly glanced at it, ducking the mystery for the moment. The clock was dazzling me anyway.

Nowadays 'grandfather' (properly called long-case) clocks have become something rather special. Twenty years ago they were a space problem, a polishing problem, a servicing difficulty and a plague to keep looking just right. You couldn't give them away. I remember as a lad seeing our auctioneer begging anybody to take two pianos and a derelict long-caser for half a crown. Nowadays everybody's crazy for them, and they cost you the earth.

'No good, Mannie,' I lied. 'No gold tracery decoration.'
'Doesn't matter, does it?'

Long-case clocks are a whole new area of ignorance. If you see a dial embellished with gold tracery you're on to a rare pre-1800 model, such as Thomas Crawshaw made in Rotherham about 1792. The actual dials were sub-contracted out, mostly to Birmingham craftsmen of the calibre of Osbourne or Byrne. Mannie's antique was brilliant, a genuine Samuel Deacon masterpiece. Sam was a merry soul from Barton in Leicestershire who bought his dials from James Wilson, again a Birmingham dialler and who was Osbourne's partner until they had words in

1777. Wilson became a front runner in the fashion of japanning. Remember that the name you see displayed on the dial is the clockmaker's, not the dialler's. It's important—a dial from a prominent dialler makes a wrecked long-case clock worth twice as much as even the best superbly preserved specimen. Always look behind for the iron 'falseplate' on the dial's back. The dialler's name is often engraved there.

'Sorry, Mannie. I need a brassfacer.'

'Never seen one, Lovejoy.'

The first long-case clocks before 1770 had brass faces. Some modern fakers even get the silvered engraving right, so watch out. The white dial fashion is what people want nowadays, though. Don't make the mistake Margaret did. She once turned down a 'porcelain china' dial clock because the dial was neither porcelain nor china. Those terms were only descriptive—the process is a kind of so-called 'japanning', stove-hardening of repeated layers of paint (usually white) applied to iron sheeting. Word is that Osbourne and Wilson were the first-ever dial makers to do it. I have my doubts, though they claimed this to their dying day.

Mannie had dozed off in all this excitement, people all round grinning at him. I kicked him awake and we fixed a price. With the long-case loaded on Germoline's cart, I gave him what I had left for deposit and promised the rest of the money by weekend, may heaven forgive honest liars. Helen found me an old car blanket.

I had a sudden thought. 'Here, Mannie. That Japanese box . . .'

He grinned sheepishly. 'Just a bird who wants to see one. I don't suppose there'd be much in it. Anyway,' he dismissed the matter, 'she said it has to be before Sunday.'

I was hitching Germoline when Brad drifted over and showed me the price of hiring a boat. His relative Terry had written it down. 'Eh?' I'd never seen so many noughts. 'For a bloody battleship maybe—'

He got narked. 'Look, Lovejoy. I passed Patrick's message to my brother. He's quoted a reasonable price . . .'

I reeled off, broken, realizing my stupidity. I now hadn't enough money left for an hour's hire, let alone the three days I'd need to search the sea fort. I'd finished up with antiques but no money. Therefore no boat and no chance of one.

And Mannie had said *before* Sunday.

I felt ill but kept my air of bright friendliness up almost to the bottom of North Hill. There I had to stop and have a shaky half pint in the Sun yard. I'd have had a whole one but Germoline scraped her hoof, so I had to stand like a fool while she slurped the rest.

Sometimes I despise myself. Germoline's stony stare tipped me off why she was mad at me. 'I couldn't help it.' I muttered it under my breath so people wouldn't think I'd gone loony talking to a donkey. 'I didn't know how much a neffie boat costs, did I?'

She said nothing back but I felt the reproachful vibes. 'I'll get a boat,' I said in her ear. 'Just you see.'

Secretly, though, I was glad. No boat meant no terrifying gun platform out on lonely sea. All right, so it meant Devlin would get away with murdering Drummer. All *right*. But why has it always to be good old Lovejoy doing the risky necessary? What the hell's the bloody Old Bill for? They cost enough. Let Maslow do it. I beamed all this psychic logic into Germoline's head but only got accusations of cowardice psyched back.

It was in this happy situation that Maud joined us, arriving in a pink sports Lotus. A mile of engine soldered to a hutch.

'Lift, Lovejoy?'

'Not you again, Maudie.'

She smiled up from her reclining position, looking

ready for blast-off. Earrings, cleavage, I got the whole
treatment. I'd never seen so much thigh, and she'd made
no move to get out. Why are fast cars only knee-high?

'It's you and me, Lovejoy,' she said calmly. 'We both
know it. Don't bugger about.'

The engine went thrum, thrum. I knew how it felt.

'And your pal Devvo?'

'He's playing it too close.' She was delighted at the
obvious effect her presence was having on me. 'I *know*
Uncle Bill's cage was some sort of clue. To a fortune. I
think you know how it links with Devlin's deal. The point
is, we've not much time left.'

I didn't let on I'd learned about the deadline from
Mannie. 'I do?' All innocent.

'You're the only one, Lovejoy!' Her tongue raked her
mouth, wet her lips. Trying to look away didn't help.
'You're crazy for me, Lovejoy, and I want you. Admit it.
Between us we'd clean up.' Her face was lovely in that
instant, a revelation. 'Not a one-night stand, Lovejoy. I
want you for good. Ten minutes of me and you'll never
look at another woman.'

'First things first, Maudie.'

If she'd been anyone else I'd have thought her look full
of compassion. 'What *is* first with you, Lovejoy? That fat
geriatric mare Dolly?'

'Antiques, as always.'

'You're wrong, honey.' She revved her engine. 'It's
hate. You'll not rest till you've killed somebody.' Her car
slid into a slow reverse and her pretty head tilted. 'My
offer refused?'

'What else?' What did she expect? It had felt like a tax
demand.

She smiled brilliantly. 'We'll see.'

I climbed angrily into the cart, nodding to Harry
Bateman who was just pulling in for a feebly earned
whisky. It was Harry's chance remark that put me back in

Germoline's favour—and back on the warpath, through no fault of my own.

'You ploughed that profit quick enough, Lovejoy,' he called.

Ploughed? I asked Germoline to cool it a second. A pause. I gazed about and saw Liz Sandwell arrive, chatting Mel Young up about his watercolours. He's English watercolours, and currently had one by Edward Dayes, who taught the immortal Girtin. She was doing what we are all doing these days: going after the early lesser-known watercolourists. While they're still seriously underpriced you can still make a killing—I mean a fortune, of course.

Harry and Mel zoomed past into the tap room when I collared Liz. 'Your village show this Saturday. Going?'

'Hello, Lovejoy. Yes, all of us turn up.' She gauged me coolly. 'Thinking of setting up a stall?'

'The ploughing competition. A friend,' I lied brightly. 'He wants to enter. Is there a prize?'

She laughed. 'Tell him not to bother. A handsome blacksmith wins them all.'

'What's the prize?' I asked casually.

'A new car,' Liz said. 'Wish your friend luck.'

I nearly fell off the cart but clung on as Germoline trundled us out into the stream of traffic.

A whole motor-car, I marvelled. For driving a grotty tractor up and down a field a few times? A gift. A new car. I ask you. Well, I can drive a tractor. Drive it straight and you've won. Get your furrows parallel—bingo!

'Hear that?' I chirped at Germoline as we went. 'I'll win the valuable new motor Saturday morning—boat hire Saturday afternoon. Wealth and justice Saturday evening!'

We clopped merrily home. I stopped in our village post office and phoned Mrs Hepplestone to tell her that by Saturday she would be the ecstatic possessor of the ploughing championship trophy that had long evaded her. I'd drive her estate to victory.

She was doubtful. 'Are you quite sure, Lovejoy?' she asked uncertainly. 'They're very difficult. When Miss Smith gave me your offer to plough for me at the contest I naturally assumed it was some kind of joke.'

So had I, then. I chuckled lightly. 'Never fear — Lovejoy's here,' I cracked. 'As long as there's no rule against antique dealers . . . ?'

She assured me there was none.

'See you Saturday,' I promised.

We paused at the White Hart, Germoline's unerring intuition at work. I decided to say nothing about my forthcoming triumph to my mates in the saloon bar. I've driven tanks in deserts, halftracks in swamps, once a hovercraft on an ocean, and sundry tractors in the apple harvest. Claude might be a tough blacksmith but I was sure to be odds on.

That night I was the last of the big spenders and got sloshed. Germoline had a forgiving pint too. We reeled drunkenly home at one in the morning, me singing 'Farmer's Boy' and Germoline's hooves scuffing happily in time all the way down the lane.

CHAPTER 14

It was a fighting day. Thankfully I was fresh and wide awake. Germoline snickered as I fed her; she too was raring to go. We were on the Dragonsdale road by nine.

I don't know if you've been to these fairs in East Anglia. They're a real yawn. You do nothing except hang about and try the odd shilling on catchpenny stalls like rolling wooden balls at hoops and such enthralling pastimes. The money goes to some dubious charity, though all charity's dubious. There's sometimes racing, occasionally a few tipsy knights jousting each other off tubby nags and women selling hot grub. If the weather's fine everybody tends to dress up. What with the green grass and the flower show and the bands it's really average, especially if nothing else happens for the rest of the East Anglian year, which it doesn't.

By the time Germoline pulled us in I was unpleasantly aware of the disadvantages of donkey travel. Most of my mates had overtaken us, honking hooters noisily as they burned past. You know the kindly way friends do. I told Germoline what a drag she was but I could tell from her ears she wasn't taking a blind bit of notice. I tethered her to a handy tree in the car park, just a field with cars in it.

'Watch her, mate,' I told the attendant, a shapely bird in wellingtons. 'I'll reward you afterwards.'

'How sweet!' she cried, promising to feed Germoline at halftime. I left the bag of oats in the cart with a plastic raincoat in case it rained. She was about to say more when Liz Sandwell hove in to leave her motor near the gate.

' 'Morning, Lovejoy,' she interrupted sweetly. 'And Viv. Working hard, Viv?'

' 'Morning, Liz,' Viv said, moving off with a glance that meant I had rotten friends.

Liz slammed her door and we set off across to the marquees. 'She's engaged to the vicar, Lovejoy,' Liz said with relish. 'Incidentally, is it true you're going in for the furrow match?'

'*Win*, Liz,' I corrected. 'I need the money.'

'You don't stand a chance. You're a million to one.'

I shook my head disbelievingly. I can never understand these country bumpkins. Anybody can drive a blinking tractor, after all.

The crowds were gathering. It was something past ten and the judges were already writing those rude remarks on the flower exhibitors' cards. Two bands were practising the same melody, their fine uniforms laid across their knees. As they played their eyes flicked across to the opposition, sussing out the strengths of the enemy. Later in the day the adjudicators would come and be imprisoned blindfolded in the small caravan, so as not to be able to bias their scores in favour of their own village band. Like most good theories, this has never worked because people balls it up. I suppose that's why they stay theories.

'Your friend, Lovejoy,' Liz warned me. Across the open car park a great square-looking Rolls had drifted silently into a spare acre, dwarfing the rest of the motors. Devvo. I checked Viv's whereabouts. Fortunately a small throng of infants had materialized and were crowding round Germoline. She would be safe. Oddly, I saw her looking across at the Rolls. Funny if donkeys had good memories.

'Did you get in trouble saying those things about Devlin?' Liz couldn't avoid asking.

'Just because he murdered Drummer?' I shot back. 'Where's the harm in a little gossip?'

She gave me a peck on the cheek. 'I like you, Lovejoy,' she said. 'You're a big softie, but I'm afraid you're going to make a fool of yourself today.'

'Stick around, baby,' I growled, doing my Bogart.

We had stopped by an open roped circle in the centre of the show grounds. A notice announced 'Drivers this way' with arrows. The circle was crammed with monster horses, great things the size of a bungalow. The tractors were probably in the other field. I for one was walking round, not elbowing my way through that lot.

'I'll stroll round, love.' I backed away as one great beast ambled closer. Horses and things always come up to me. 'I know they're supposed only to eat grass, but—'

Liz looked at me, stricken. 'But, Lovejoy. *They're* the teams. For ploughing.'

'Eh?' I almost fainted. 'I'm driving a frigging tractor, you stupid cow,' I bleated.

'No, love. You plough with horses.'

'I'm here to drive a tractor,' I insisted.

'But *anybody* can drive a tractor, Lovejoy. Horses are the test.' I flopped on the ground, broken. Liz sat beside me. 'Does it matter so much to you?'

Claude the blacksmith and a few gnarled farmers were strolling among the giant beasts, patting and prodding and lifting hooves. No wonder people had thought my entering the competition was a joke, especially when I'd gone bragging I'd win hands down. I couldn't even drive Germoline, let alone these beasts. I put my head in my hands. I could have wept.

'I can hook Devlin for killing Drummer if I get the prize. I need the money.'

'How?' she asked, but one glance at my face told her it was no sale. 'Look, Lovejoy. Can't you borrow the prize from Claude? Or money from somebody?'

'Look at me, Liz.' I held my hands out to make the point. 'Who'd lend Lovejoy Antiques a bent penny? Would you?' A bit cruel, but it drove it home. After yelling blue murder in the middle of town everybody must think I was off my head anyway.

'Haven't you anything to . . . ?' Liz tried to help.

I had the antiques, at least, even if they were not paid for. But getting round the dealers on a Saturday would be hopeless. Still, I had to try. Tonight was some sort of deadline out on the old sea fort.

'And there's your little donkey,' Liz was saying.

'I couldn't sell her.'

'No,' Liz exclaimed impatiently. 'Donkey rides. The children love her. Drummer used to bring her to village shows.'

It was true. One thing Germoline knew about was giving donkey rides. I grabbed Liz and hurried her back through the growing crowds as they began to pour from the car field.

'How do I do it? How much do I charge?'

'You remember, as a kid, for heaven's sake,' Liz said, exasperated. 'You mark a place out with those little coloured flags and Germoline takes people round.'

I glimpsed Viv's blonde hair in the distance and whistled urgently. 'Will you help, Liz?' I asked feverishly. 'I'll nick some flags if you'll shout—'

'Honestly, Lovejoy. You're hopeless.'

In about half an hour I was doing brisk business among the marquees. I'd pinched several small pieces of bunting. With string I got from a woman in the grub tent and a few sticks off the hedges I manufactured quite passable marker flags. Germoline was brilliant. She knew the game all right and enjoyed it except when a crowd of yobbos came scurrying through the mob once. Apart from that I did a roaring trade for over an hour, and started doing great.

Helen came and had a cart ride, tipping Germoline a quid which was decent of her. I saw her deep in conversation with Liz and caught her glancing my way. Maybe she thought I'd gone bonkers too. But I forged on, working the crowd and trying to look all paternal the way Drummer did, a sort of cut-price Santa Claus. I got the children rolling in by letting my own supporters, those who'd backed me up when confronted by Hepzibah Smith in my garden that time, have free rides. Germoline occasionally gave extra distances, moving to the band music in and out among my stolen flags. She was great value, Germoline, that morning. I have to give her that. Probably knew it was in a good cause.

A few of the lads hove in to give the bric-à-brac stall the glad eye. This is practically routine among even the most expensive antique dealers. Don't laugh. The only genuine Elizabethan gold and garnet ring in our museum was bought on such a stall last year—for fifty pence. And I once picked up enough profit for a new thatch on my cottage from a set of four Mayer plates which I got for less than a pound. Antique dealers underrated them because *Hausmaler* work is thought to be beneath posh dealers (though nobody turns a nose up at the vast profit they bring these days). A *Hausmaler* is a home painter of white porcelain, usually bought from factories as 'seconds'—ie: faulty. The home painter flourished in the eighteenth century. Franz Mayer was the best of the Bohemians. He bought rejects from Meissen to decorate. He was mad on flowers. People say his enamels aren't up to much but I like them. One tip: if you see a painted insect (beetle, fly, butterfly) on a decorated plate, with nothing at all to do with the theme of the plate's painting, have a quick shufti to see if the insect is painted over a small defect. If it is, you probably have in your hands a *Hausmaler* work. For some reason they're particularly common in East Anglia. They're the first thing I look for at these village fairs. You never need pay more than a tenth of their value. Dead easy profit.

I'd quite forgotten the ploughing by twelve. I was made to remember it in a particularly unpleasant way. Germoline had just taken off with a cartload of four children and one infant, with Liz laughing exasperatedly in close attendance and myself keeping a queue of kids under a semblance of control. Then the sun went out of the sky.

' 'Morning, Lovejoy.' Maslow again. 'Step this way.'

'Don't jump the queue, please,' I said, quick as a flash.

'Make him, Constable.'

George Jilks, my own treacherous village nerk, took my arm. I stepped aside from the children. Maslow had a second constable rocking on his heels nearby, thoughtful lad.

'Licence?'

'Eh?'

'You need a licence for trading, Lovejoy.' He grinned without humour. 'Don't tell me you've forgotten another point of law. And can I see your declaration of income tax—?'

'Cut it, Maslow.' I shook George's arm off and shoved my face at Maslow's. 'I'm doing this for a good cause.' Then I paused. Ho hum.

'What good cause?' He peered at me. 'I'm waiting. Would it be anything to do with Mr Devlin?'

'Er . . .'

'And while we're at it, Lovejoy,' he added smoothly, 'I want to know by what authority you maintain a commercial animal for hire.'

'Don't tell me I need a licence for that too?' The creep. 'Liz,' I shouted. 'Over here.' Liz put an older girl in charge and came back, sobering as she saw my visitor and the uniforms. A small crowd was gathering and was listening curiously. 'Liz will vouch for me, won't you?'

'Er . . . for what, exactly?'

'For . . . well, giving a safe, er, desirable service to the, er, community . . .' I halted lamely. Maslow was grinning now.

'Book them both, Constable.'

'I'm nothing to do with this,' Liz cut in, backing off. 'I was just, er, helping . . .' She merged with the crowd, giving me a mute glance of apology.

'Thank you, miss.'

I saw Helen and waved urgently but she avoided my eyes. You couldn't blame them.

'All right, Maslow,' I said softly. 'Do what you want. But I'll kill Devlin if it's the last frigging thing I do.'

'I'm going to have you certified, Lovejoy,' he said, just as softly. 'And I'll see they stuff you away for a thousand years.'

'There you are!' a voice cooed, and Dolly, beautiful

loyal Dolly, all dressed up with a flowered hat, slipped between me and the Old Bill. She took my arm. 'Now it's really time we moved on, Lovejoy—' She broke off, noticing the bobby. 'Oh *dear*! There hasn't been an accident, has there?'

'Er, no,' I said, bewildered, wondering what the hell she was up to.

'Thank heavens!' Dolly said. 'Is this your friend?' She reached out a gloved hand which Maslow shook mechanically.

'I'm police, lady,' he managed. 'Lovejoy's under arrest.'

'What?' Dolly went all aghast. 'But . . . not for giving donkey rides, surely? In that case, you'll have to arrest me. I own the donkey and the cart, and it was at my instigation that Lovejoy kindly agreed—' I listened, stunned.

'You can only do this for a registered charity,' Maslow snapped.

'Here's our charity number,' she said sweetly, pulling a card from her handbag. 'Lady's Guild for Church Maintenance and Structure. Would you like to contribute?'

'Is there any trouble?' The vicar showed, bless him. And his fiancée Viv with him. My allies had pluralled.

'None, Reverend,' Dolly gushed. 'Lovejoy here has done a perfectly delightful thing, collecting for our church funds. Isn't that marvellous?'

'I'm deeply moved,' the padre said. I entered into the spirit of the thing and hauled out my ill-gotten gains. I even felt all choked up as I passed it over.

'That's that, then,' I told Maslow, smiling to nark him. 'Look, pals,' I said to the children. 'Look after Germoline. One ride every time the church clock strikes a quarter hour, in turn. And feed her in thirty minutes, all right?'

Having successfully swindled the shrieking mob of volunteers into serving Germoline's interests, I took Dolly's arm, leaving Maslow and his soldiery.

Dolly was really great, keeping up a meaningless chatter all the way. We flopped down exhausted as soon as we were in the shade of the tea tent.

'What was all that, Lovejoy?' she asked faintly. 'Did I do right?'

'Thanks, love. You were superb.' I kissed her feebly. At least I wasn't arrested. 'I was trying to get some money to get a boat.'

'How soon?'

'Tonight.' I saw from her face it would be hopeless. To make matters worse the tannoy croaked my name. 'Plough teams please check in,' it squawked. There was nothing for it. 'Come on,' I said. 'I've a field to plough.' I was shaking.

The improvised paddock was crowded with men and shire horses. They looked bigger than ever, and one or two seemed decidedly bad-tempered. A lot of good-natured ribbing was going on from the onlookers as I pushed my nervous way through to the ropes. Mrs Hepplestone was sitting with Squire Wainwright. Both gave me a wave. I waved back with an arm that suddenly felt rubber. Dolly was pushing my arm.

'You can't, darling,' she was saying, aghast. 'They're like in *Gulliver's Travels*.'

'Don't remind me,' I said, shaking her off. 'I've got to try.' Then I stopped, gazing quizzically back at Dolly.

'What is it, dear?'

'Gulliver.' That name. 'Wait, wait!' Wainwright's men had said there was this old bloke called Gulliver, the best ploughman in the business . . . who used to win all the competitions. I struggled to remember. That day in the burning fields. Claude was best *except for Gulliver*, who was now a drunken bum round town, a useless gambler, decrepit. It couldn't be. *Lemuel* Gulliver in Swift's famous tale. And who else knew to an ounce what a donkey ate? *Old Lemuel was the ploughing champion!*

I grabbed Dolly. 'Love, for Christ's sake,' I babbled. 'Get on the phone. Do anything—you understand, *anything*—to phone the White Hart and find Tinker. Tell him to get Lemuel here *now*. Got it?'

Her eyes were wide and alarmed. 'What if I can't?'

'Do it. Tell them to pinch a car, anything.'

She ran off towards the marquees while I swallowed hard and climbed the rope. There seemed to be a lot of chains and iron things about on the ground. People cheered raggedly as the horses were walked about in front of the stand. A group of some five men were there, Claude among them. We shook hands like wrestlers do.

'All right, Lovejoy?' he asked kindly.

'Fine, thanks.'

I was to go third. I got in the way, risking life and limb. I talked incessantly. I mislaid people's harness and lost my entry papers twice and finished up waiting while the judge irritably wrote my entry out longhand. I was frantic, struggling to spin the minutes out. You take turns, I was pleased to hear, one team going at a time.

The game consists in driving these monsters into a field and ploughing a stetch—that's a strip a few yards wide, all furrows parallel. Judges sit and watch your skills. The trouble is you have only the old-fashioned plough to do it with, one furrow every trip. For God's *sake*.

Claude had drawn first. I refused to go into the paddock to be with my team of horses, though the other drivers did. I sat with the crowd glumly watching Claude do his stuff on the sloping field. Even Jethro Tull, the great ploughing modernist of two centuries back, would have been proud of him. Half an hour and he came off his stetch sweating like a bull and sank near me like a small earthquake. I passed him my brown ale which he drained.

'You're next after this, Lovejoy,' he gasped. 'Watch the field. There's a dip midway over.'

'Thanks, Claude.' I rose miserably as the tannoy called. If I didn't go now I'd be disqualified. I had to have my team strapped together, God knows how, by the time the second team came off.

I went over to the paddock sick to my soul. The shire horses looked at me with disbelief as if asking if this was the goon they were landed with. 'I know how you feel,' I told them bitterly. I swear they almost laughed.

'Second team, now entering,' the tannoy squawked, 'is the Ashwood-Pentney team driven by Harris. Spectators please make way.'

I was stepping over the rope when a miraculous croaking cough froze me in mid-straddle. Tinker and Lemuel were pushing through the crowd beind me. Lemuel could hardly stand and Tinker looked knackered. Dolly was with them, sickly pale but pleased.

'Tinker!' I rushed at them, babbling. 'Lemuel! Is your last name Gulliver? Are you the Gulliver who—?'

'Give us a drink, Lovejoy,' he whispered, trying hard to open his eyes.

'With sugar?' Dolly asked. I love her, but Jesus.

'A drink!' I screamed. '*Beer*! Listen, Lemuel.' I grabbed him and pulled him to one side. 'Can you do this? We've got to enter and win it.'

'Fall down,' he wheezed blearily.

'Eh?' I thought I hadn't heard right.

'Fall down, you thick burke,' Tinker rasped.

I fell spectacularly, groaning. Tinker was quicker than me for all his hangover. He was already waving to the judges. They started impatiently across the paddock. I groaned, holding my belly.

'Here, sir,' Tinker was calling when Dolly trotted back

with two bottles of brown ale and a cup of tea, the innocent. 'Lovejoy's got his appendix again. He's entering a substitute.'

'This is a nuisance,' the head judge said coldly, a testy old colonel who'd hanged men for less. Charming, I thought indignantly, doing my stricken act. I really could have been dying. 'Lovejoy's done nothing but procrastinate. Who's the sub?'

'Him.' Tinker pointed to Lemuel who was busily soaking the ale back while Dolly, ever the optimist, held the cup and saucer.

'Gulliver?'

Even in mid-act I couldn't help hearing how the judge's tone changed. His impatience became respect. I let myself recover enough to see Tinker push the tottering Lemuel under the rope into the paddock. Please God, I prayed fervently. Let Lemuel get among the prizes. so I can hire a boat to kill Devlin tonight. I admit it wasn't much of a prayer.

There's a saying, isn't there, horses for courses. It applied to Lemuel like nobody else I'd ever seen before. Three parts sloshed as he was and probably never having handled a nag for some years, what he did was quite uncanny. He sort of shook himself and just walked— swaying unevenly a bit, but definitely casual—into this massive shifting mass of horses and said, 'Come here, you buggers. Let's have a gander at the lot of you.' And the horses looked round and simply did as they were told. I swear they nudged each other, pleased at having swapped a nerk like me for an acknowledged master. The crowd stilled reverently and silently paid attention to the shapeless heap called Lemuel.

He must have been some champion in his time because word shot round. Farmers poured from the beer marquee to the ploughing field. A murmur of approval rolled round the crowd as Lemuel did the oddest things, like

squeezing the shire horses' knees and smacking their
chests, really giving them a clout. Whereas I'd kept out of
their way when they showed the slightest hint of
friendliness, Lemuel just mauled them about. Like
gigantic infants, they tolerated him happily as he
prodded and thumped and strapped them. I noticed the
judges didn't shout at him like they had at me when I'd
taken my time. That's discrimination, I thought irritably.

'Ready, sir,' Lemuel called at last. He took up some
straps and flicked, and the whole ponderous team
thundered slowly from the ring towards the field, hooves
thudding in time and great heads nodding together. It
was a magnificent sight, almost beautiful. Before that I'd
always thought horses really mediocre but Lemuel,
shuffling along behind and swearing abuse, made them
almost dance. I had a lump in my throat as the spectators
rippled applause.

'See that, one-handed out of the paddock, first time?' a
farm man exclaimed near me.

'Better, Lovejoy?' Claude was by me, all eighteen stone
of him smiling in a hurt kind of way.

I was in no fit state for a scrap so I instantly showed I
was still unwell by doubling up again and groaning. Dolly
believed the act and helped me off to sit on an exposed
mound where we could see Lemuel in the distance.

'Go for some more ale, love,' I told her, making sure
Claude could see my face screwed up in pain.

'I don't think you should. They may want to operate,
dear.'

I looked at her. She was serious, actually believing my
act. 'It's for Lemuel,' I explained, making sure Claude
had gone to see our champ. 'I'm only pretending, love.'

'Thank heavens for that, Lovejoy!'

I watched her go, marvelling. Well, it had taken me
some years to link the drunken figure of Lemuel with the
mighty champion ploughman of the Eastern Hundreds,

so who was I to criticize. Smiling, I lay back peacefully, the roar of the distant crowd music in my ears.

At two o'clock the delighted Mrs Hepplestone was presented with the rose bowl for her team's success at the ploughing championships. Lemuel got the keys of his new car. I made Tinker tell him of a certain important matter of murder which I had in mind, and that his prize was required as deposit. We drove grandly down to the estuary and hired a motor launch from Terry's boatyard. Terry showed me the controls and I signed the papers with a flourish. Lemuel's new car went as security and deposit combined. Dolly drove us back to town, and then took me home to the cottage for a quiet rest before tonight's action. I promised I'd make a meal for us both when I got a minute.

CHAPTER 15

Dolly promised to stay at home all evening and all the following day in case I had to phone urgently for anything. She was white and worried, but I was beginning to think that was par for her course. We had a long snogging farewell at my gate before she drove off and I invited Germoline to crack on.

I boxed clever choosing my route. I had more sense than go along the main roads, and selected one of the old cart tracks between the farmlands. Only three miles out of our village there's a turning through the woods where the American War Cemetery stands, which saved me and Germoline miles. The wind was fairly whistling across as Germoline plodded between the rows and rows of sad heroic crucifixes. We made fair speed and reached the estuary a few furlongs below the Staithe about dusk. The big Yank's posh boat was there again, I saw in the lessening light. Mended.

The place looked as peaceful as any holiday cove, with a few noisy families packing up for the day into cars ready for home. Two yachts were riding in, just starting to show lights. An inverted cone was hoisted from Joe's station, meaning I supposed some sort of weather. The radio's always on about them, onshore winds near Dogger Bank and all that.

We went to Drummer's old hut. Germoline's ears pricked and she stared around at me as if asking what the hell. I explained as I undid her cart and stuffed her manger full of some granular material Lemuel had got her.

'It's this way, Germoline,' I told her. 'I'm going to the old fort. There's a load of nicked antiques out there, in the fort's lowest concealed room. I happen to know that because Mrs Hepplestone's old man made a model as a clue. Maybe he was in on it too; I don't know. You saw them doing the ferrying bit, didn't you, cock?' I went on. 'It's reprisal time, Germoline.' She snickered approvingly at this. She was bright for a donkey—just how bright I was yet to find out, and in the most horrible way possible, but at the time I was so full of myself I thought I was in command. 'See?' I said, patting her neck. 'Devvo will come to ship his stuff out to the continental buyers tonight, the deadline. I learned that from Mannie. And *I'll* have pinched it all!' She snickered again, over the moon at my plan. In my innocence I scratched her shoulder and added, 'Of course, he'll come for me, but I'll ram the bastard in the dark. It'll be an accident. I'm not sure if Devvo can swim, but let's hope, eh?'

This was all right, because I can swim like a fish. Anyway, I'd hoped by then to have unloaded all the recovered antiques.

'And when I come sailing back,' I chuckled, 'guess

which clever little donkey will be waiting here to cart the goodies into hiding, here in the hut?' I winked. 'I'll rescue Devvo if he confesses, by which time there'll be enough rescue boats on the scene to witness . . .'

It seemed foolproof to me then. No wonder I was grinning all over my face. I went inside and lit the lantern in Drummer's window to guide me home, and splodged my way back to the Staithe. Terry had said the boat would be all stocked up and full of petrol. I had the keys.

It was a grand thing, long and white. These modern fast craft always seem taller than necessary but I suppose our boat-builders know what they're doing. They charge enough. It had radar, and a mast with a great bulbous thing at the top and a lot of wires. 'Radar's hazy inshore, but invaluable,' Terry had said, showing me how it worked. The idiot had wanted to show me its insides. The point was that none of it seemed missing. I'd got more maps than the Navy. Anyway, I knew where I was going.

I got the engine going by simply pressing a knob by the key. The last family carful was leaving the Staithe as I moved the boat into the channel, carefully keeping my lights off though some white riding lights were showing in the lower creeks. As I turned my craft into the sea lane I could see the single flash of the lightship miles down the coast where the treacherous sands steadily ingest coastal freighters year after year.

I put her at low speed between the promontory of the clubhouse and the shipyard. Somebody flashed one handlamp at me. I ignored them. In the dusk a wind was rising steadily. That tinselly tinkling was beginning to sound again, the wires tapping on the metal masts of the yachts pulled up on the hard. Somehow comforted by the din, I smiled and glanced round at the little harbour. Plenty of lights, street neons reflecting well on the darkening sky. I was reassured. There would be plenty of help there should I need it. Surprisingly how easily lights are seen over a black sea.

'Devvo,' I bleated joyously, 'here I come.'

As I left the shelter of the harbour and the wind's force began tugging for the first time I admitted that I didn't really intend to kill Devvo or his two goons. I'd only be troublesome if they started anything. Otherwise I'd bring them tamely to justice, which was after all what it's about, isn't it? Germoline would be narked because I'd this funny feeling she wanted blood, but women are like that. Even if it did mean helping Maslow to get promotion . . .

The boat started rocking up and down on the choppy sea. Watching the waves rising against my hull made me giddy as I started out between the long dunes into the open sea. I began to discover one thing after another, all vaguely worrying. You'd point the boat at some distant light, and after a minute you'd find your bows sideways on even if you'd kept the illuminated compass perfectly still along one of the lines marked on its glass. Presumably all sorts of nasty currents moving about under the water. I had a chart telling you which way they went but hadn't time to study it seeing I'd spent the afternoon resting, so to speak, with Dolly at the cottage after my exertions of the morning's ploughing.

I must have gone zigzag for more than a mile, correcting every furlong or so on the lightship as the sky darkened. The speedo said I was going about six knots, whatever they are. I tried to make this reading sensible by spitting over the side and watching it float past but got into difficulties by not steering straight so gave it up. The cockpit had an interior lamp which I switched off. If Devvo's boat overtook mine in the darkness I didn't want him spotting me.

The motion of the boat was making me feel vaguely queasy. And I suppose the knowledge that I was drawing near to that enormous great concrete monster out there in the ocean wasn't doing me any good. Anyway, I had a knife with me, a modern piece of Scandinavian metal ten inches long which I'd nicked from one of the tacklers' harness racks that afternoon. I'm like that, a real planner. No doubt Devvo's goons would be knuckled up and maybe armed with a pistol or three. Devvo naturally would be clean as a whistle. My boat chugged on.

My face was wet from spray. The wind was cutting across me now, making my eyes water with the cold, but I could make out the red light on the old sea fort's mast. Was there some gnarled old salt left on the fort to tend the light? Nowadays they were automatic, I supposed, though you can never tell. My spirits rose. Some poor sod stationed on the wretched thing meant at least one guaranteed witness.

I decided to curve right round the fort and come at it from seaward. That would give me less of an edge by reducing the time I'd have. Devvo's merry crew would probably come direct from landward. I cracked another couple of knots on the speedo and turned south-east or thereabouts.

Coming up to a big solid mass sticking menacingly out of the sea in the dark's a frightening experience. It's also very sudden, which sounds odd unless you've done it. I'd kept my eyes on the red beacon that meant the sea fort, which had climbed slowly up the black sky the further out I got. Then it started disappearing and only coming back again when the boat rose on the swell. I tumbled that I must be getting very near and that the lip of the fort's main platform was cutting the beacon off from view. I wished now I'd had the sense to take some daylight measurements.

It was then I heard the rushing, sucking sound of those vast legs of the fort, sloshing in the water. For a moment I almost gave up and turned back. God knows what made me soldier on. It might have been lust for the antiques I

hoped were concealed there, or maybe love of Dolly, to
show what a hell of a bloke I was. The funny thing is that
it might actually have been hatred of Devlin, as Maud
alleged, a curious concept. Anyhow I kept going, cutting
my speed. I felt stalled but the instruments showed
otherwise. The wind had crossed me again and was now
whipping at the other side, stinging my eyes with spray
and making my face feel cut to ribbons. I was shivering.
No wonder these yachting types dress like astronauts.
Dolly had brought me a woollen hat and muffler and I
have this thick short coat for long drives from the days
when I had something to drive.

When the sounds got unpleasantly close I put the beam
lights on, and almost swooned. I'd thought I was being
careful, but now, with the yellow lamps illuminating the
huge fort, I knew it had been cowardice, my typical trick
of postponing anything unpleasant. I was about fifty
yards off, the boat already being tugged and shoved with
the crushing spread of waves round the nearest of the vast
legs. There were four, of enormous girth, draped with
green weeds and discoloured from corrosion. Metal
stanchions had trickled their oxides like blood down the
slimy legs, creating an impression of straddled limbs
impaled by some giant stapler causing dirty haemorrhages
towards the fast sea. I switched into reverse and for a
horrible instant thought she wasn't going to pull away.
Then I was standing off about a hundred yards, pushed
by the currents in a way I hadn't expected. I wasn't really
frightened, but what with the cold and the rising wind
and the frigging noise, not to mention that fearsome
monster looming above, I felt like staying away at any
price.

I was still to seaward. The noise from here was somehow magnified, caught up in the hollow under the belly
and funnelled out in a succession of squelches and sucks.

I managed it without much difficulty, except that my

hands were freezing and unbearably sluggish. Once one end was tethered I only had to rush back to the cockpit and throw the gears into neutral then pull her round on the rope the way I wanted. Doug had explained about the rocks between the seaward pair of legs. Modern oil rigs mostly float. These old sea forts are actually built on the ocean's bedrock, with a protecting line of concrete or dredged rock on the side away from the land. In wartime this served both as a breakwater and as a mooring line. Rough, but effective. If I'd worked it out right, the breakwater would hide my boat from direct view from anyone tying up to one of the landward pillars—and the right-hand pillar was the special pillar Hepplestone's model had indicated. I switched off and pocketed the keys, gave one last despairing upwards shine of my torch to fix the layout in my mind and put the boat's lights off.

There were projecting iron handholds from the pillar. Not the easiest climb, but I suppose that was the intention. The first step was about chest height. I'd brought a clothes line and some old gardening gloves, but how the hell you lowered a score of antiques down from a thing like this fort into a bobbing boat on your own without help . . . I climbed. They say don't look down when you're up high, but nobody tells you the other most important climbing lesson, which is: never look up, especially if you're climbing the underbelly of an old sea tower.

The handholds were rusted and slimed. I stopped and shone my torch every three or four just to make sure there was something to grab and that my hand wouldn't be left waving in the air when I needed support. I ought to have kept an eye out for approaching lights at this stage but I was frightened enough. There was this moaning, faint and fairly quiet, as if the wind was hurt at not being allowed in. Give me land any time.

At the top, flat surfaces stretched away into the

distance. I shone the torch only once, clinging on like a tick on a bull. Above me the handholds led up into a rectangular hole like a loft ladder does into an attic. I beamed upwards. The light hit nothing but space, which gave me hope there might be a respectable floor for me to stand on. I climbed in, shaky and trying not to look down. It stank of must and seaweed. Holding on with my left hand I shone the torch on a level with my face and almost shouted from relief. There was a rectangular room about forty feet by forty, almost as if I'd simply climbed into a barn loft. I hauled myself in, scrambling away from that horrible edge and the sea's noise beneath. For a minute I wheezed on my hands and knees, partly relief. Behind me, what had been a hole promising safety had now become the start of a bloody great drop and I didn't want any part of that. I got away from it fast and tried to control my shaking limbs. No wonder Lemuel had looked decidedly grey with fatigue after the ploughing. Until now I'd regarded myself as fit as a flea.

I started first on the flooring, treading carefully, then pushing the walls to make certain I was in something really solid. The feeling of emptiness was all about, as if I'd come to a deserted city. I tried to sense if anyone was here or not, and got no vibes. The fact should have reassured me and didn't.

I walked round and round coughing on the dust. A big empty room with a hole at one corner and a metal door at the other. No windows, no footmarks in the dust except mine. I reasoned that, if Drummer had been killed for seeing them load the stuff in, their route would have to be up one of the landward side legs. Logical. The walls were covered with graffiti, testifying to some intrepid holidaymakers getting their money's worth out of the hired powerboats from Clacton or somewhere. A few faded scrawls from soldiers fervently marking the days off to demob, and that was that. I crossed to the door and pulled it back on its crossbar.

It led up five steps to the start of two corridors. The left one. My torch flickered ahead. It looked about two hundred feet long and was littered with debris, though God knows where that came from. Pieces of planking, some glass and a bottle or two, even a brick. The ceiling seemed to be made of crossbeamed concrete and the walls were the same endless fawn coloured tiers. I trod cautiously along it, realizing that the sound of the sea was getting fainter with each step.

About halfway along, a double entrance led into what must have been some sort of briefing room. It was low but wide, with a central spiral of stairs upward round a thick circular pillar. I vaguely remember the silhouettes of these forts. They all have a flat tier, then a somewhat bulbous turret structure like the highest bit of a lighthouse. There were footmarks in the dust round the stairs, showing that Devvo's happy band had been here. I climbed slowly, holding on to the rail. A metal door blocked the way about the level of the operations room ceiling but it answered to a hefty shove, and I was through into the top of the fort. The lookout room was no more than thirty feet in diameter. Slit windows showed the distant shore lights directly opposite, the lightship's signals from the Sands, and I caught a glimpse of the sea lights shining where the oil ships steamed north-south from the fields and refineries along the coast. I could even have picked out Joe's station and the harbour lights of Barncaster Staithe, but I felt too vulnerable in this derelict place. It was beginning to give me the willies. Perhaps Devvo had heard of my renting a power yacht from Barncaster and was coming without lights, same as me. The slimy creep, I thought indignantly. Just the sort of rotten filthy trick he would get up to. The trouble was I had no real plan, which was what was making me mad. I'd assumed that if I'd got here first I'd somehow be in control, able to dictate terms to Devvo. Now I wasn't sure I'd done right.

I could threaten him with the police, of course, though Maslow was about as useless a threat as you could imagine, and Devvo had already got away with murdering Drummer. After a few times I decided to change my original non-plan to a new non-plan. The thing was to try to find the antiques first, maybe shift them to some place in the fort where I could keep them under lock and key, for use as a bargaining counter.

Time was passing. Nervously, I hurried down from the turret into the big operations room and began an urgent search of the rooms leading off it. It was a huge place, bigger even than I had imagined. Like a ship, always so much more space than you dream of. I raced from one place to the next, shoving metal doors open and spluttering on the dust that hit me every time. A third of the way around, I was soaked in sweat, and realized I'd never get round the place in just a few hours. I had to think. Of course I'd known it would be a big task but assumed that my luck would carry me through. Maybe, I began to think, I'd trusted luck instead of brain.

There was only one thing I hoped I had that Devvo and his goons hadn't, and that was a knowledge of the deep chamber waiting for me in that special pillar. Maybe it was where the antiques were waiting . . . ? There was only one way to find out, though I hated the idea. Logically, any search had to commence there.

I entered the rectangular room shining my torch every inch of the way. I didn't want to touch anything until I was sure I wouldn't go hurtling down into any abyss I couldn't get out of. Despite my fear I felt a twinge of excitement. Plenty of signs of activity here. It was an isomer of the room I'd climbed into at the other corner of the fort. The same rubbish, same design—but here the dust was trodden and most of the debris had been shoved aside into one corner. There was the same dark rectangle, with ugly sea sounds loudly echoing up through it. This must be Devvo's regular way in. I followed the treads easily, back into the corridor and along to a trio of steel doors. The adjacent enclosures were marked 'Latrines' and 'Ablutions'. Most of the piping had gone and the doors hung askew on rusted hinges. I shivered. The idea of soldiery long gone was too spooky for me. I turned my attention back to the three rooms. The doors were solid metal, curiously new. My heart sank, though I'd have done the same thing. If I'd been Devvo and my mob were robbing all the country houses in East Anglia and wanted to stash the loot away, I too would have found which rooms were situated near to one of the pillar climbs. Then I'd have built my own new steel doors in, just as he obviously had, and simply used the place as a castiron cran, a drop. Safe as houses—in fact safer.

I shone my torch obliquely under the door and peered through the keyhole. It didn't give much light but enough. By waggling my head I could spot the stuff. A load of small cases, wooden crates, even a few ordinary suitcases. Of course. Everything had to be small. You couldn't winch up a suit of armour. Half of it would drop off or it would swing and be damaged. The room was some fifteen feet from door to wall, perhaps a former store room. The second too was packed, every sort of packing case, crudely nailed tea chests, brief cases, shopping bags taped up into ball shapes. And the third. Dog tired, I sat on the floor. This was Devvo's cran all right. Now the enormity of the task came home to me. I'd found Aladdin's cave but no trick to get the solid steel doors open. And it would take a handful of men some time to drop that much down into my waiting boat. Ludicrous even to imagine one bloke trying it on his own, even if I could get inside. There was no way to snaffle his loot. And simply watching and reporting back to Maslow would be pointless. All evidence would be gone.

My tired mind told me, with the heat on over Drummer, all traces of Devvo's connection with the fort would need to be removed. And it had to go tonight, fast. It's well known that antiques robberies are a summer pastime, ready for the relatively high prices of autumn auctions. It's also the season when new deals brings money flowing in from the 'nick trade', as we call it.

I'd lost my edge. Now I was waiting here with no advantage. Devvo would clear off laughing and leave me to trail home with my tail between my legs. Not even having to lift a finger, the bastard. I'd assumed I would pose a serious threat. Now I was no threat, not even a faintest irritation. Yet . . .

I got up wearily and went back to examine Devvo's route in again. This was the way he'd come, where his goons would drop the crated antiques into his boat. Easy with a net. The place was cold as ever, but there was something, something different. I shone round and walked every inch. Then I cursed myself for not having spotted the obvious. A notice in faded paint, letters two feet high no less. I'd walked past it for a quarter of an hour without reading the thing. 'Ammunition winches not to be used for the carapace retraction.' I had to think about that. There was a winch support projecting from the wall, its chains rusted and old but looking pretty serviceable. I tested it, swinging on it cautiously and trying to dislodge the projecting girder before searching for the iron rings. If they'd gone to the trouble of telling soldiers not to use this winch for shifting the piece of flooring, then it was proof that it could be used just for that purpose. I wound them round the wheels and pulled them through the iron rings in the carapace. Easier if I'd brought some oil. There were three rings set in the floor. A fourth was rusted to blazes.

Good old Archimedes. I practically flayed my gloves

pulling the link down so the concrete paving rose to lean on the wall beneath the winch. A space was left about four feet square, exposing quite respectable steps, suggesting that nothing here was meant to be hidden so much as preserved. Perhaps in the event of enemy forces attacking, and the defenders having to retreat like Douglas Fairbanks doing his sword bit on the staircase? I descended slowly, my torch pointing ahead. They were ammunition vaults, a core of chambers placed vertically alongside stairs and a lifting well as if for a regular elevator. Warning signs were everywhere. As soon as I'd realized what the chambers were I dashed back to the winch and dismantled its chain. I was in a nasty sweat. If Devvo turned up while I was down there I didn't want him gently nudging the slab in place and leaving me entombed. That precaution gave me confidence as I decided to go further down. In any case, if Devvo's loot was in the sealed rooms up top, what was in old Hepplestone's concealed chamber down below at the bottom of this pillar's steps?

I went down scared in spite of all my precautions. The place looked untouched for years. No footprints in the dust, no graffiti, and no rubbish. Therefore Devvo had not been down here, either. And the winch up top had been practically unserviceable. At every level I checked in the ammunition rooms, one to every landing on the stairwell. Empty, just faded War Department instructions stencil-painted on the walls and doors.

It was then that I realized I must be about the level of the sea outside. It felt horrible. Above the water you feel there'd be something of a chance. I stopped and pressed my ear to the concrete wall but jerked it away the same instant. It sounded frigging awful, as if the sea were trying to get in, the swine. I shone down and realized I was near the bottom of the pillar. Another couple of floors and I'd be on bedrock. But if anything valuable was hidden down here, surely decades of scrounging idle soldiers would have found it?

The stairs came to a dead end at a door, metal and reinforced. A notice read: 'C.O. or authorized Acting C.O. only.' I felt something, steadily but gradually begin warming me. There was something down here, something worth coming for. I cleared my throat and shoved but the door wouldn't give. I returned to the ammunition room on the landing above and set to on the door hinges with my tacklers' knife. They are the usual military projecting pin type. I got the door off but clobbered my knife. Well, easy come. Gasping, I dragged the heavy door down the concrete stairwell, getting my arms practically dislocated at each bump and making a hell of a din.

The door would do as a battering ram, seeing I had nothing else. About six feet from the lowest stair to the block room, just too much. I'd probably rupture myself but what the hell. With the torch lodged on one of the stairs I took some deep breaths and dragged the door up three steps. Holding it against the wall I undid my belt and got it round one edge. Not much of a sling, but it might give me a bit of extra leverage. I inhaled, heaved on my belt in an ungainly lift and staggered down the three remaining stairs, the strap cutting my hand. The full slanting weight of the bloody door was on my shoulder as I swung it forward. It took me about ten minutes and seven more goes before the obstructing door yawed inwards and I could clamber through. I'd nearly creased my back.

Light reflected from the whitewashed interior. It was a small chamber, the first room of circular design I'd seen in the fort, with the single word 'Counterbalanced' painted on the wall. A red arrow indicated the flooring. Not concrete in regular rectangles, I observed, but evenly laid around a central void about three feet wide. Something was so important that only the commanding officer was allowed in — or somebody he'd appointed to do a special job. And *here*, not anywhere else. I felt suddenly uneasy. A sealed room, restricted access, deep down where any intruder would hardly bother to look . . . And situated underneath a tier of rooms which in wartime would have been packed with ammunition. It had all the hallmarks of a place you retreat from, where the departing officer could create an explosive exit. I swallowed, dry as a plank, thinking how carelessly I'd slammed the door in with my improvised battering ram. I could have been blown to blazes.

A ladder projected from a central hole. A mournful wail sounded outside, a ship of some kind. Whatever it was up to I fervently hoped it steered clear of the fort. I didn't want it careering into this particular pillar while I was in its base. Other horns were sounding now. Stiff with goose-pimples I shone into the hole and saw the ladder end about twelve feet down on the bedrock. I almost yelped from fright. It was horrible, gazing down on to solid rock. Actual rock's not bad in itself, but this bit signified the bottom of an ocean and I was down there, at the end of a great concrete tube.

The sickening realization froze me. *Sea bed.* I moaned and backed off. No antiques, no valuables. Time for me to be off, I was thinking, when something flashed in the darkness, from a stray torch beam. I found I'd shot off to the doorway in a panic, one foot on the first upward step on the way out of the wretched place. Like the fool I am I dithered, my torchlight wavering shakily on the wall. A quick listen. Nothing except the distant muffled hoots of boats, more and more of them now. That gleam. Now I'd come so far, what's another few feet? I flashed my torch up the concrete steps. Still alone. There was still time.

Practically creaking from the frigidity fear always brings, I lay on the floor with my head hanging over the edge and waggled the torch round. A concrete slab projected into the cellar from its wall, probably a support, but what for? I decided I was wasting time. Better to be frightened quick and get it over with. I got up and tried the ladder. It felt firm. I went down, prickling all over, and stood petrified on the living ocean bed. You could only call it a cellar with a knobbly floor, the remaining space where the hollow pillar had been constructed to stand on the sea bed. Quite empty.

Nothing. Just a circular room, concrete walls, that one projecting slab. But a gleam *had* shone back at me. And it had come from down here. Faint, yet rich and lustrous and . . . *and mauve!* Like when I'd opened the little hollow leg of Hepplestone's coal cage. I stepped about on the uneven floor, shining my light at the rock. It was so raw and irregular it appeared quite randomly cobbled, yet all of a piece. The engineers must have simply decided to build where they found a solid upthrust on the sea bed. No good doing it on sand. Even I could see that. They'd probably just blasted it to solid rock and built like mad. The North Sea in 1939 had been no place to dawdle. And one or two of the areas seemed faintly goldish, faintly green, shiny. I knelt to look. And suddenly knew. Goldish *and* green. Greek. Chrysos and beryl. *Chrysoberyl.* 'Ooooh,' I moaned, frightening myself by the chamber's resonance.

I'd been a fool. Chrysoberyl, the natural metamorphic rock which mothers alexandrite. One of the first things you learn in the antiques game is a list of old tricks and legends. I'd stupidly forgotten one of the commonest sayings, remember alexandrite is *emerald by day, amethyst by night*. I could almost hear Blind Benny's voice, drumming his teachings into me night after night in Petticoat Lane as a lad. Take an alexandrite ring into daylight and it glows a perfect emerald. But dance in the glittering artificial lights of a ballroom and it transforms into a luscious deep amethyst. Old Man Hepplestone, one of the workers building this fort in the wartime rush, had put a flake of it in the bottom of the copied cage's hollow limb to show not only *where*, but *what*. I'd seen it flash green in the cold sunlight when Maudie had chucked it on the fire. And by artificial torchlight in my cottage I'd seen its mauve gleam.

I sank back on my heels, kneeling on a fortune. Weakly, realization began to come. I had everything. At last I had money, power, wealth to set up in London. Dear God, I could practically buy out Christie's. I was rich as Crœsus. Made for life. My hands were shaking as I fondled the craggy protuberances of the floor. The whole floor was chrysoberyl, one of the most valuable minerals on earth, worth every antique I'd ever handled—

'Found anything, Lovejoy?' a voice boomed suddenly from above me.

I jumped a mile and found myself babbling at the shock. 'Who's that?' I knew perfectly well.

'Me. Devvo.' The ladder twisted suddenly and crashed down, clouting my shoulder and knocking the torch away.

Blackness enveloped the cellar. I scrabbled helplessly for the ladder. Just as I felt it a dreadful slithering sound shook the cellar. The faint rectangle above where a torchlight was suddenly wiped out. The darkness became total. For a second I could not understand what had happened. Then even when I realized Devvo or somebody had shoved the enormous iron door over the manhole it took me a full minute to realize I was sealed in. More slithering sounded. I could hear two voices.

'What are you doing, you bastard?' I bellowed, deafening myself.

Devvo chuckled. 'Fixing your tombstone, Lovejoy.' A feeble line of light showed and was gone.

'Let me out,' I yelled, disgusted at my fear. The vicious pig had sealed me in, maybe wedged the metal door some way.

'No, Lovejoy.' Devvo sounded breathless from his exertions. 'Serves you right, nosey sod. Going to hide down here and bubble me, were you? You can frigging well stay down there for good. Snide bastard.'

'I'll get you, Devvo,' I screamed. I flung the heavy ladder upwards, nearly braining myself as it clanged on the door and crashed back. It caught my leg a chance swipe. Cloth and skin tore.

'Keep trying, Lovejoy.' Breathless but calm.

'I'll help you nick antiques, Devvo,' I babbled, ashamed at myself. I'm pathetic.

'Not now, you won't.'

'Please, Devvo. I'll take back what I said about you killing Drummer.'

'That old fool had to go, Lovejoy,' Devvo called back. 'Like you, mate. I've too much to lose.'

'You're not going to leave me, Devvo?' Crawler.

'I am that.' His voice was receding.

'I know where there's stuff worth millions, Devvo.' My screech echoed within the cellar. 'Please, Devvo. It's here. There's a ton of chrysoberyl—'

Aghast, I heard them talking about fog outside as their footsteps sounded above. I even heard Jimmie the goon ask Devvo for a match and Devvo's reply, 'No smoking till we're outside. We don't want Old Bill finding clues all over the place.' He didn't believe me, the moron, the sadistic killer.

The steps sounded fainter. I thought, this can't be happening to me. Not to *me*. It can't happen. People will come. Devvo will turn back. Maudie will arrive. Dolly will bring the police. The Navy'll see the boat . . .

Then they had gone and I was where I'd always feared. Finished.

CHAPTER 16

Darkness is the worst. Well, second worst. Second to being entombed.

I'm not scared of dark places. No, honestly I'm not. No more than anyone else. And solitude's a precious commodity, if you like that sort of thing. But being at the bottom of the sea bed sent me demented. I sweated and shivered, shouting and pleading though Devvo and his goon were no longer in earshot. I yelled incoherent explanations of the chrysoberyl, promises, bribes, anything.

Sobbing in fear, I hurled myself repeatedly at the ceiling, foolishly hoping to reach the rectangular opening's margin. Once I even thought I touched it but nearly broke my bloody ankle falling on the rock. I battered upwards with the ladder. I begged and pleaded, wept and screeched abuse. In those few minutes I regressed from *Homo sapiens* through a few million years, finishing up a shambling whining hulk whimpering and scratching in a cave. I became again a feeble thing of reflex, *Homo neanderthalis*, an animal with less brain than Germoline. Utterly disgusting. Fright made me pee repeatedly, hardly a drop every time. I almost knocked myself senseless against the projecting slab. I cursed it soundly, regaining my old anger. Stupid bloody army engineers, leaving one great slab like that sticking out. You could brain yourself on it if you weren't careful. And what for? Typical, just typical. You'd think they'd have just built this lunatic place and got the hell out.

Then gradually I was brought back to my senses. Perhaps it was rage at the fort's builders. Or at Devvo. Or at the plight I was in. Or just me. Or at everybody in good old East Anglia beering up and snogging and going about their lawful business, selfish swine, with me left to die miles offshore out there—*here*—under the ocean.

'Oooh,' I moaned, terrified.

Whatever else, I had to keep that horrible thought from my mind. Ignore the reality of cold, of silence and darkness. Think. *Think.*

Think of Germoline, waiting out there by Drummer's shed, trusting in me to come back loaded with antiques. Think of the engineers under the impetus of war, slogging night and day in the cold and mud out here. I sat on the fallen ladder and slowly and ever so slightly began to cerebrate.

My head was still ringing from catching it on the projecting slab. What was it I'd just said to myself? . . . You'd have thought they'd just have built this lunatic place and got the hell out? But they hadn't. They *hadn't*. They'd most carefully made, deep down at the bottom of one supporting pillar, a single projecting slab. Apparently for nothing. Nothing could lean on it. A winch bar, then? No. Nothing could be winched up to it—you build winches at the top of places, not in cellars. Some architectural necessity, then . . . but what? I know nothing about architecture, especially of sea forts, but no amount of thinking could explain the projection. The fort itself was huge. Its four supporting pillars were huge as well. This projecting slab, big as it seemed, was relatively small compared to the fort.

A strange unease settled in my belly. Whereas I'd been scared out of my skull a few minutes before, a coldness came in me now, fear of a totally different kind. Something horrid underlay all this. Something old man Hepplestone possibly knew about and which was gradually starting to dawn on me. My white-hot panic vanished. My mind plodded on to a clear frosty logic.

A construction team, labouring hard out in a

dangerous ocean, struggling to erect this sea fort in the
hectic rush to war, doesn't pause to build something
useless a million fathoms down. Local legend says they
lost a man a day from drowning or injury on every single
fort. Add to that the bombing, the worry about enemy
ships . . . I was suddenly too scared to move. Counterbalanced. Exactly what was counterbalanced?

'Keep calm.' My voice echoed funereally, scaring me
worse. Hepplestone's cage. You pressed it down, and a bit
of the floor had pivoted aside. *Counterbalanced*?

The way down had been carefully locked so that I'd
had to improvise a battering ram to get in. And only the
C.O. or his aide were allowed down, even though it led
nowhere. Cellars *never* go anywhere. Everybody knows
that. The glamorous image of a retreating swordsman
came back to me again, retreating stair by stair. Suppose
the fort was stormed. A brave C.O. might want to
sacrifice everything to save a fortress falling into an
enemy's hands so close to shore. Or he might have *orders*
to . . . to . . . Jesus. I swallowed, my throat dry. No
wonder it was locked, the doors solid metal. Something
was mined, or self-destructive. And I was in it. And I
knew now what was counterbalanced. It was the slab.
Somehow it pivoted. And it could be done by one person,
'The C.O. or authorized Acting C.O.', the notice had
said. *Or*. Therefore not both. Therefore even a
knackered Lovejoy could unbalance it on his own, after
which . . .

I went 'Oooh', sitting still, frightened to move a
muscle. Supposing I did manage to turn it. What the hell
happened then? Maybe it would prove a way out — into
the frigging sea. Who needed that, for gawd's sake? I'd
seen enough films to know that the bloody sea's crammed
with sharks and tentacled monsters. A pivoting slab in a
wall would let the whole frigging North Sea into my black
prison — definitely bad news. Worse, supposing it *did* let

me out? *What else did it do?* That ghastly feeling of being
in a mine recurred. How long did mines take to blow up
once you set them ticking? Or do mines only tick in
comics?

I tried to talk myself out of it. 'It's all make believe,' I
said aloud. Sweating clammily, I brought up perfectly
sound reasons for the War Department being too careful
to leave sinister explosives in our trusty old sea forts.

Aren't they?

One thing I could do, meanwhile. If I was going
anywhere I'd at least take a piece of the chrysoberyl with
me. The ladder would help to bash a piece of the scaggy
rock floor free. Careful, though, to stay away from the
projecting slab in case I unbalanced something in the
darkness.

I got down on my knees and began feeling the rock. My
torch was broken. I'd have given anything for my pencil
torch. I laid the ladder pointing at where I remembered
the projecting slab to be and took bearings from that,
using feel. Then I quartered the cellar in my mind and set
to, my fingers fumbling across the rock inch by inch.

Chrysoberyl looks like nothing on earth, just rock with
faint greens and yellows and the odd brownish creamy
material. You feel for smooth areas the size of your
fingernail, especially where they end in crazed bits as if
somebody had criss-crossed the rock with a file. There
were several excrescences feeling like this. I finally chose
one about a yard from where I guessed the room's centre
was.

A small fissure extended to a depth of about my hand
to one side of the rock piece I'd chosen. It was as wide as a
fist at the top, just big enough to ram my broken torch in
and leave it sticking upright. The ladder was easy to lift
but difficult to keep on its side edge. I held one end as
high as I could, over the torch. I stepped aside and let go.
One would be the hammer, the other the nail. It took me

a dozen or so goes before the ladder's plunging metal side hit the torch with a dull clack and I heard the chrysoberyl splinter. A few chips spattered about my cell but I could ignore those. The biggest piece was about a couple of pounds, an unimaginable quantity. I got it into my lap, gloating like a delirious miser, though God knows what I had to be pleased about.

It was a winner. Irregular as hell, the lump had nine facets with smooth silky flat surfaces. Three of them led into gritty crazed patches. I could feel the delectable richness of the beryllium salt and its violet lustre. Supposed to be unlucky for sailors, it is none the less sought after, and the clearer transparent stones are very valuable. Most come from the Urals, Ceylon and parts of Africa, with a few from Colorado. A single 10 carat natural would buy a family house. Not antique, but I was in no position to argue against free wealth.

The question was whether to wait and rest or to waggle that slab and hope for the best. But wait for what? Death in this cellar? Devvo would return my boat, simply make sure it was found tied up at Terry's when dawn broke. Everybody would reach the same conclusion as Maslow—that Lovejoy had scarpered with a load of nicked antiques. Devvo would be thoughtful enough to leave a giveaway antique in the boat. I was done for in any case. Nobody would come after me. That was the truth.

I put the chrysoberyl piece in my pocket and, hands reaching out in front, stumbled carefully across the uneven floor towards the wall where the slab was.

I knew that you breathe *out* when rising in deep water. How many steps had I descended? Maybe about ten flights or so, say, a dozen steps to each flight. Say about eight inches a step. That's ten times twelve times eight over twelve, in feet. I worked it out as best my incoherent

mind would allow. Eighty feet. Christ, it seemed a hell of
a lot of water. I resolutely avoided working it out in
fathoms. I'd learned too many grim fathomy poems in
school to do that. Fathoms always sound to me distances
you sink, not distances you float — and I badly wanted to
float.

My heart was banging almost audibly and my palms
were hot and dry. The cellar was freezing. I'd been a fool
not to bring Tinker. He'd have been useless because he's
always even more scared than I am but at least he could
have kept watch. I'd been thick, as usual. I peed against
the wall. There was enough water out there without
carrying some with me. I undid my shoes, took them and
my socks off and stripped to my underpants, replacing
only my jacket. The lump of chrysoberyl stayed with me.
At least human beings float. I hesitated. One more worry.
Is there such a thing as a non-floating man? If so, I was
bound to be it. Oh God.

I felt the projecting slab. The floor beneath it seemed
solid rock, like the rest. Supposing it didn't move?
Supposing it wasn't the slab which was counterbalanced
but some other thing elsewhere? Fear made me reach out
and pull the slab the instant the thought came. And I was
engulfed in water, roaring, howling water.

I was buffeted and knocked, pulled and swirled. Water
forced into my nostrils. I hadn't got a decent breath in. I
tried to open my eyes but saw nothing. I didn't even know
if they were open. I was spinning. Something seemed to
have hold of my right arm. I screamed into rushing
bubbles, threshing and kicking in the vortex, perhaps
some instinct not to die from nitrogen bubbles in your
blood, diver's disease. I didn't know which way was up.
All I could hear was the terrible rushing noise, hissing like
a steam train. Things seemed to keep on pulling at me,
my arms and legs and shoulders. I kept trying to kick
clear, as though at clutching enemies but the water

tugged a million ways at once. A minute was too much. I
needed to breathe but to do so would mean drowning. I
kicked madly, flailing arms and legs and doubling my
body in agony. My head wanted to burst.

Something belted my neck and scraped my shoulder. I
clouted it back, not feeling the pain. I felt a hard smooth
surface and me sliding along it curving upwards. How did
I know it was upwards? Breath came into me, pressing me
out and setting me choking. I choked and retched and
choked.

And floated.

It was odd, that first breath. The air was curiously
warm. I wasn't able to believe it actually was air. For a
moment I wondered if this was drowning, that this stuff I
was sucking in and gushing out was actually water. The
fact that I was floundering dizzily beside one of the great
pillars and on the sea surface, being lifted and lurched
tantalizingly near to the metal stanchions, seemed
somehow irrelevant for an instant. I realized I was
delirious for a few seconds. Reflexes kept me surfaced.
Not drowning but floundering. Great bubbles heaved
and popped about me. The trouble was I couldn't see far.

'What the hell was that?' a voice shouted. Devvo. I
couldn't judge the direction.

My choking stopped but I was splashing like a
flounder.

'Some boat, maybe.' That was Devvo's goon, breathless
from lumbering the antiques.

'What d'you expect me to do, in this frigging fog?'

'Can it or I'll can you.' Devvo.

Fog? A wave slammed me against the pillar. I was lucky
not to be brained. Fog. That explained the horns from
passing ships. It also explained why the sea was not
running murderously high. Thick fog, low waves, they say
on the coast. Noises sounded close to, thumps and a
creaking, presumably Devvo's boat loading up. I peered

stupidly about, lifted and sloshed down by the swell. As if
anybody could check position from distant lightships in a
fog with a ten-yard visibility. My mind was too stupefied.
Simply to strike out might be suicidal because I could be
swimming away from the fort. Above and around a great
greyness. No lights. Merely me heaving near a vast pillar
in the endless bloody ocean. Distant foghorns wailed
again making me shiver more.

Driven by fear, I told myself angrily, cerebrate, you
idle sod. *Which way?* I turned my head. Foghorns. Where
else but further out to sea? You don't get ships on shore.
So left was land, right was east. I listened, tugged and
shoved by the heaving sucking sea. An intermittent
shushing sound came from the right. Rocks, the ridge
protruding from the sea between the seaward pillars. I
drew breath and let go, flailing towards the shushing. It
was less than a length and took me years.

I don't even remember reaching the rocks or finding
the rope. Maybe I blacked out or, knowing me, fainted
from relief. Blokes shouting brought me to, a shout of
directions and an insult.

'Last case, Devvo.'

'Thank Christ. I'm frigging frozen.'

'Slowly, you stupid get.'

My boat. I couldn't see it but there was a rope in my
hands, and I was sprawled on sea-washed rock. Only a
terror-stricken idiot like me ties eleven knots in a single
rope to moor a boat. I grasped it one-handed and tugged.
Something out in the grey darkness nudged my leg. I just
kept from screaming and leaping away. Surely to God
after all this it had to be my boat and not a shark.

I stuck my foot out at the sea and hit something solid
but which moved as a body, undulating with the sea.
Benign but definitely there. Like an ape, I swung one-
handed, pulling like mad.

It made me remember sharks again. I splashed like a

drowning rat, finally getting one leg over the brass rail and feeling my way back until I reached the glass windows. I was safe. Nearly frozen to death, but in my own boat. I should have danced with delighted relief. Instead I retched up the other half of the sea.

It can only have been a few minutes. I'd cut the ropes first with the ship's knife and pushed away from the fort's pillars before scrambling into some clothes. The sea drift seemed to be swirling past me away from the sound of Devvo's men. I judged it would take me away from the fort pretty quickly without the engine. I was useless, unable to stop sicking up water and shivering.

I counted to five hundred before finding a handlamp and looking round the cabin. That was probably far enough. The engine caught first go. I don't know why that's always more astonishing than it would be in cars but it is. I found myself grinning in a kind of astonished ecstasy. I could simply go home if I wanted. I was free. Out and free. There was a quarter-bottle of brandy in a cupboard but I didn't feel like celebrating that much. I let the engine idle while I did exercises to thaw out, and sussed out the radar. Fog means radar. The fort stands a good three miles from the coastal sea lanes, and about five from the Sands lightship, so there was time despite the speed of the sea.

You switch on and a greenish radius appears, belting round and round this little telly screen. The whole cabin becomes ghostly, something out of a horror film. It leaves a faint green outline, the shape of the coast. You can alter the scale with a few knobs but I didn't touch those after one hesitant go, scared to damage it and finish up blind in the fog. There were several extra dots about that weren't on the map. I felt terrific, really proud of being in charge of my own destiny. I could head for the estuary, there on the screen, any time I wanted. But I didn't.

I did a few turns, using minimal throttle for quietness and watching the small screen. It was quite simple. Turn one way and the screen stayed conscientiously drawing the coast always in one direction. By this time I'd identified one green mark as the fort. If I watched it carefully it would show Devvo's boat too as it pulled away. I hadn't a clue what I'd do then.

The centre of the radius on the greenish screen practically joined to the fort's dot before I heard it, that terrible swooshing and slurping noise of the sea against the fort's pillars. Cutting the engine down, so as to just about keep me stationary as far as I could tell, I settled down to wait. Warmer now, and thinking at last. Thinking and listening. Devvo couldn't have left yet. I heard a couple of shouts from up ahead.

I honestly swear I intended no harm. Cross my heart. Honestly, I mean it. I was so thankful to have got out of that great monster I'd have been daft to go risking myself again, just for vengeance. Vengeance is a motive to be avoided. Too costly. Probably I was waiting to see what would happen to the antiques.

I found a score of plastic-wrapped pork pies in the diminutive fridge, Terry's boatyard's idea of nautical cuisine. It was also mine. I wolfed six and polluted the North Sea with wrappers.

Sailors trust radar. I'd heard them talk about it often enough. So when I saw a small green dot leave the solitary larger dot I decided I'd have to follow across the oily sea. It could only be Devvo's boat, loaded with its crated cargo. It stopped for a full five minutes, then moved a few hundred yards and stopped again. I followed it but cleverly kept at the same distance. The screen helped me to judge, and finally the dot began to move steadily. I couldn't hear an engine, so they couldn't hear mine. I followed, honestly still intending no harm. I'd be the perfect bystander.

I straightened up at last and settled on the same course towards the estuary. Say ten minutes and I would be in the mouth of the Barncaster creeks.

And so would Devvo, which would be his tough luck.

CHAPTER 17

Time often has a will of its own. Some hours go like a bomb. Others trail past like clapped-out snails, like now. My boat was static. I'd been stuck in one position for hours, about a mile offshore as far as I could estimate.

Devvo's boat had slowed down, then stopped. Naturally I'd stopped too, reversing to kill the speed, then holding her in neutral. A few times she needed a touch of the propeller to keep station but not often. Once I heard Devvo's boat throttle up loudly and saw the radar dot move to stand offshore a furlong further or so. I instantly pulled out a similar distance. Maybe he was afraid of being swept in by that sinister rush of the dawn tide when it came.

To still the engine would leave me dawdling if Devvo shot off fast. Even then I wouldn't lose him altogether but I wasn't sure how our boats compared for speed. I'd risked too much to let him get away now. I remember thinking this quite clearly despite not knowing why I simply wasn't trotting home to a hot meal.

Through the hours we had drifted steadily southwards along the coast in the thick fog. Now I was completely safe and a winner I couldn't help gloating, believing Devvo was now in my hands, virtually my prisoner. Perhaps lulled by the reassuring sense of security I began to nod off. Every now and then I caught myself snoring and frightened myself to death by jerking suddenly awake. When that happened I scanned the radar screen feverishly to make sure Devvo's boat hadn't given me the slip. I invented games to keep awake, and very exciting they were. Counting foghorns, a real gripper. And seeing how many different tones I could detect—high, low, gravelly. Every now and then I gave the throttle a nudge just to keep the engine on its toes. Everything had to be ready for it, though what 'it' was I couldn't imagine. Once I was pulled from a personal twilight by a deep muffled *crump* from seawards. I listened hard and peered blindly about but the sound didn't recur. A single swollen wave lifted the boat a minute later, then was gone. Sleepily I put it down to an extra-super supertanker passing and went back to waiting.

I'd hoped for the fog to clear as the night wore on, but if anything it grew thicker. Maybe the after-affects of my immersion and the fright I'd had were greater than I thought. Anyway I grew so cold towards dawn I went to sit inside the cabin for a few minutes. There was a kettle and one of those gas-burners, with clean water from plastic pipes. It took some time but I made hot water. Teeth chattering, I took it and a couple more pies back to the cockpit. Maybe I'd caught malaria from the sea, or was that polio? By then I'd ripped a blanket into an improvised poncho. I felt like nothing on earth. A sartorial mess, but drowsily confident. I nodded off a little, fell awake, checked the screen. Devvo was still there.

'And, Devvo,' I said quietly, 'so am I.'

A seagull perching on the cabin roof gave me a momentary thrombus about an hour later.

'Watch it,' I told it laconically. 'Stuffed case-mounted seabirds have gone up thirty-seven per cent.' It eyed me hungrily and I chucked it some pie. Watching it go made me realize I could see it. The elementary fact forced itself into my sleepy brain. *See?* Seagulls don't fly much in fog. Therefore as I'd dozed the fog had started lifting. And dawn was coming.

I wearily rubbed my face to alert myself. My engine's deep mutter sounded strong and quiet as ever. A few exercises standing up in the cockpit did nothing to help my stiffness so I stopped that and got some more hot water, hurrying back to watch the screen.

Gradually the darkness lessened. I knew that the boats tend to move about the estuary even in the early hours. Our few fishing vessels would be easy to spot on radar. They usually headed straight out, Indian file, and I knew from Joe there were only four in harbour.

As dawn came, today merely a sulphurous yellow version of darkness I realized the boat was now rocking more than it had, perhaps some sign that the tide was on the turn. I was too tired to start looking tide tables up at this stage. I just wanted to get the whole thing over and done with, but exactly how I did not know.

At exactly six-thirty by the cockpit chronometer Devvo's boat started up with a roar. It was too near for my comfort. Maybe my vigilance was going. I heard it quite clearly and moved sloppily into pursuit. Of course they didn't know they were being followed so it wouldn't seem to matter much. The screen showed them heading southwards, not steering into the estuary but going parallel to the coast. Maybe they were looking for their rendezvous. A freighter from Holland, perhaps? Or that big grey coaster which people rumoured made pick-ups for the Hamburg antiques trade? Port Felixstowe is rumoured to be cast-iron so it would have to be in one of the creeks. Probably Devvo had waited because he was early. Why, I wondered idly as I steered a following course south, was the stuff not transferred out at sea? Easy enough when it was calm like this, and much less likely to be sussed out by the coastguards, fog or no fog. Two knots, I observed. They must have time to spare.

At this funeral speed keeping Devvo's dot tracked was

easy. By guesswork I was some three furlongs from him, hardly more than a stone's throw. We seemed to be a half-mile off the estuary now. As the choppy water began to rock me unpleasantly side to side the sound of a bell came clearly across the harbour mouth. That would be one of the buoys which lined Barncaster's lower reaches. Once I heard an engine start and the sound of a car's horn. I even glimpsed a tall mast's riding light. The screen wasn't much use now. It had blurred into a haze of green. I didn't much care, because any company meant safety.

The sky was lightening with every second. Dense fog everywhere still, but things were definitely looking up. Land and daylight. Those plus my—well, somebody's— precious load of antiques equalled success. And my precious chunk of chrysoberyl, with private knowledge of a King Solomon's mineful in my own private spot on the seabed. With the loot I could easily hire a couple of professional divers . . .

I was gloating like this when I noticed a green blip moving quickly out from the green haze which indicated the crowded estuary. A shrill engine was audible, and getting nearer. Well, I thought resignedly, it's about time Joe Poges showed up. I'd done nothing wrong so far, or so I thought. If anybody was in the clear it was me. Devvo would get ten years, richly deserved. The engine sounded closer. And the police would prevent anybody doing anybody else any GBH, right? Maybe it was all for the best.

Suddenly uneasy, I noticed Devvo's boat had slowed. I cut speed, if you can call a slow drift speed. From the rate at which he was now going it looked as if he'd slipped the engine altogether. After a hesitation I too went into neutral. The green blip from behind was coming on faster. My boat was between the two. And now Devvo's boat was moving again—*northwards*? Towards me.

Slowly, but definitely with deliberate intent. I could hear both, and see sod all. Worried, I looked up and swung my head to listen. Maybe I should try the radio now, raise Joe Poges and say what was going on but I didn't know how, and wavelengths are Greek to me. I'd actually bent to fiddle with it when a boat hurtled at me out of the fog roaring with bows raised like it was taking off. I had a single second to shove the gear lever forward. The boat crumped against my boat's side, flinging me off my feet with a numbing shock. I wobbled upright into a world abruptly gone mad and grabbed the throttle, bellowing in alarm.

The bloody boat was the same one I'd used to rescue Germoline, the big Yank's estuary yacht, flying its commodore's flag. I'd seen it all in a millisec as it loomed out of the fog. I yelled frantic insults and slammed some way into my boat. The quicker I was out of this the better. I glared around into the thinning fog but saw nothing. The boat had vanished. In my sudden fright it seemed to me that engines sounded from every direction. I was just taking off landwards when I saw on the screen that Devvo's blip had gone. But between the estuary and me a steady blip was slowly circling, probably Devvo, waiting over there in case I ran for land. And another was closing swiftly at me. I shoved the throttle and headed for Devvo's blip, cursing myself at the chances I'd now have to take.

How thick I'd been. It was so obvious. If my hired boat possessed one of these radar gadgets, it stood to reason Devvo's would. Of course he'd have seen me on his radar and simply led me on. Then he'd waited until one of his goons could row ashore—maybe on an inflatable dinghy of the sort my boat carried—and nick a boat, by merest chance the Yank's again. Unless the Yank too was in on it?

The following blip was closing fast, now in earshot. I

glared around into the fog like a cornered animal. Nothing. The sea was increasingly choppy now and I was finding standing difficult. The tide must have started. And Devvo's blip was starting at me. There seemed no way home. Whichever way I steered I'd get trapped between the two of them, a bobbing walnut in the jaws of a seaborne nutcrackers. My only advantage was that my boat was as big as the commodore's. I risked a glance at the radar screen. My own engine's sound dulled theirs, and I'd lost all sense of direction. Nobody would see us from the shore. Worse, the nearer we were to land the more blurred the screen. There'd be a real risk of running aground on one of those frigging sandbanks. I'd be a sitting duck. After all this.

In a sudden rage I burst the throttle into life and felt the deck lift as the boat accelerated into the estuary mouth. In for a penny in for a pound. No use looking at the hazed radar screen now. The rocking and shuddering practically flung me out. I realized in fright that I hadn't even donned a life-jacket, and the boat carried six. Going so fast, the bows lifting and juddering nastily, I could do nothing else except gasp at the speed and hang on to the wheel to keep her straight. I gaped at the fog ahead, hoping I'd guessed the distance right. The fog rushed past me, parting and flinging past my face. Fear of what I wanted to do was draining me of willpower. Any strength I'd possessed had been left in the fort back there. Another glance at the screen. The swine following was as fast as me — and so close. Devvo's blip was rapidly closing from ahead. I cut the speed back with a jerk.

They came at me simultaneously. Jesus, but Devvo's boat looked big, a destroyer compared to mine. It came suddenly cutting the water into great level spouts through the fog, its engine deep with intent and power. In that second I glanced from front to back, judged the relative speed. The commodore's boat was in line, coming at me, about twenty feet to go. I cracked the throttle ahead, curving to the right in the start of as narrow a circle as I could go, screaming abuse at the engine to move us.

'You idle bastard,' I bawled at it, terrified. The commodore's boat tried following, hurtling round into a great banking curve and spraying a wall of sea up on to Devvo's advancing bows and lifting its pale side. The crash wasn't so much a crash as a clang with a muffled clatter. I was too busy wrestling with my steering-wheel to see much of what happened behind. I could again see nothing when I'd recovered and got my own boat slowed and straightened up in the choppy water, now surging unpleasantly high. The fog was light yellow now, pale, quiet. And empty. Engines muttered nearby. Somebody shouted.

While I was checking the screen a sudden whoosh sounded. I swear I even felt the heat. A reddish glow penetrated the fog for just an instant and was gone. A swift turbulence rippled across the sea, the blast tapped against my face, and that was that. Somebody's boat had exploded, maybe the commodore's again. Dear God. That's all I needed. I headed out to sea again, with the blip I guessed to be Devvo somewhere among the green haze that was the estuary's banks. Which one was he? This close inshore the radar seemed sod-all use. I cut the engine and peered at the screen. Twenty, there must be twenty discrete blips there, if not more, and a haze that could mean anything. A bell was clanging. Somebody must have heard the explosion and be calling the men out to help, though exactly where was difficult to tell. They'd see as little as me in this fog, I thought, though the more boats put out from shore the merrier, as far as I was concerned. All I needed was one friend. The trouble was I'd got none. My belly was cramped and my chest still thumping from the realization that the explosion might have been me.

At this point I seriously considered standing some miles offshore till the fog cleared. It didn't take much to make me realize what an error that would be. Devvo's boat was bigger and faster. Nothing would please him more than having me out there with no witnesses and no chance of assistance. This fog was a blessing for him. For me it was yet another danger. So it had to be inshore, and soon.

I swung round, slow but steady. The radar swept the coast in a great blur. I decided to ignore it. The tide would be running, filling the inlets and creeks and bringing up the boats as distinct radar points. But which of the fleet of static boats would turn out to be Devvo's?

Then I had a brainwave. Drummer's creek, where the commodore's boat was normally moored, where I'd struggled across to that sandbank. It filled at the tide. Only a short distance over the mudflats to Drummer's hut and Germoline. I could make it safely to land, moor there, dart across the mudflats past Drummer's shed to tell Joe Poges and simply have him arrest Devvo! Once I reached land there'd be no problem. I could of course cruise boldly up the estuary, but I knew Devvo well enough by now not to do the obvious thing. He would get me for sure, probably ram me, claiming that stupid Lovejoy — that clumsy, dangerously unskilled sailor — had made some mistake and caused some calamity. His boat would cut mine in two like it had the commodore's, and I'd go for a burton. And the fog, thinning all too slowly, would hide all.

I guessed I was almost about the spot where I'd escaped from between the two boats, and flicked out of gear to search for debris. Maybe the explosion had been both of them after all, not just the commodore's boat alone. My spirits rose. I might be free this very moment. A loss of a lot of antiques, but I would survive.

Something floated close by, wood maybe. A clue to who had suffered the destruction. I leant down to peer at the water and an oily hand rose from the sea and grabbed at my arm. '*Ooooh!*' I flailed back, screaming and gasping and beating at the horrible thing. It was coated in black slime, blistered almost beyond recognition. I screeched in terror, lashed out at it with my feet as it kept coming, lifting out of the heaving sea in a mad benediction and finally clinging to the brass rail. I kept kicking and screaming from fright until it slipped away leaving a ghastly bloodstained oily mark on the gunwale. I flung the gear in and roared away fast as I could go. My teeth were chattering and my hands uncontrollable.

The boat had bucked a good half-mile with me whining and shivering at the wheel before I got my mind back again and cut speed. Thank God no innocent boat was in the way or I'd have bisected it without a chance. While she slowed to idling I struggled to regain control of myself. My hands were jellies and I was cursing and blinding about being out on the bloody ocean in the first place. It took me ten minutes to steady up and stop shaking all over. I couldn't even look at the smears on the gunwale. The terrible fact was I'd just killed a man. Killed. Whoever it was had been a shipwrecked mariner, and I'd just killed him. He'd reached for help and I'd . . . and I'd . . . I heard myself moaning and tried to stop. All right, I'd panicked, been terrified. But my instincts to help had been submerged—I swallowed at the word— well, overcome by horror. And what was worse I'd felt the propeller chop, pause, jerk before pushing the boat on, as if it had . . . almost as if something in the water had fouled the propeller and been cut . . . been cut . . .

Naturally I made excuses. I told myself it had probably been Devvo's goon, and he'd been armed. I told myself it was a boarding attempt and not a plea for rescue, but I knew I was lying. How much of my savagery had been Lovejoy the buffoonish antique dealer, and how much sheer hate? It might even have been envy of Devvo's

wealth, his birds, his power. I had a splitting headache.
I'd have given anything just to reach land and go to sleep.
But a living man, badly burned from the explosion, had
been reaching from the sea for help, and I'd killed him.
Being scared's no excuse. Vengeance isn't, either.

An unutterable weariness settled on me. Maybe it was
the cumulative exhaustion, maybe the permeating cold.
But maybe it was the wretched suspicion of myself. As I
said, I've always believed that there's nothing wrong with
greed. Nowadays it's one of the few remaining honest
motives. But I'd always thought myself a pretty kindish
bloke, even if some characters get on my nerves. Well,
whatever I thought, being depressed was only stupid. I
had to go through with it. No escape out to sea. Staying
here meant that sooner or later I'd run out of petrol,
wreck myself or do something just as hopeless in the fog.
Nothing for it. I'd turn south, aim for Drummer's creek
fast as I could go, and get the hell off this ocean to turn
Devvo in.

As I spun the wheel I somehow felt I was cutting my
losses.

I took bearings from the radar screen. Its haze had
diminished and I was able to spot the seaward bulge,
south of which Drummer's creek started. Despite this,
heading inshore in fog's hair-raising. East Anglian sea
fogs are famed for density and patchiness. Several times I
let the way fall off until my confidence returned.
Tiredness and cold were taking it out of me and
concentrating on the screen was proving difficult, though
I hadn't been scrapping Devvo on the ocean as long as all
that. Collingwood in his wooden sailing ship had waited
for the French fleet three years without a break.

My instincts were dulled, practically non-existent, but
something made me uneasy. By rights, the nearer I got to
Drummer's creek the more relieved I should have been.

Instead I grew increasingly edgy and fidgety. Once I even started whistling, nervous as a cat, stopping myself as a precaution. The screen was now only guessing where the long sandbanks lay, though I wasn't unduly worried. From the time I'd pulled Drummer off I remembered that the sea flooded swiftly in from the south until the sandbank was cut off. I could easily find my way by letting the ocean do it for me. On impulse I cut the engine. A gentle waft of air cooled my cheek. Maybe that would lift the fog, another worry. Another ten minutes and I'd be opposite the southern arm of Drummer's creek. I felt the erratic seas swirling me on, pulling jerkily as the dangerous undercurrents competed for the boat. The only benefit was I knew which way the tide was going.

It was then I heard that familiar tinkling of the wires on masts. The faint breeze was helping. I could use the sound as a crude direction-finder. I began to hear the sea's sounds, until now suppressed by the engine. I stood upright at the wheel, stupidly wrinkling my face as if that would let me see through the fog better. Telling if you are actually drifting in a fog's one of the hardest things on earth. The sea doesn't help because it moves like you do. Instinctively I found myself keeping quiet and just listening to that magic tinselly sound, my only guide.

Despite my caution the sense of unease persisted. Something was wrong, horribly evil. I took off my plimsolls and padded carefully around the boat, peering nervously over the side to make sure no oily hands were planning to crawl up like blistered crabs and come scrabbling at me . . . I became so apprehensive I switched everything else off, too: radar, lights, cockpit light, cabin bulbs and chronometer light. The boat drifted on. Once I panicked, feeling sand or something scrape the keel. Another silent creep around the boat to peer over the side at the water to make sure . . . but of what? I returned to the cockpit and sat nervously by the controls. Ignoring the cold, I stripped completely except for my jacket with its weighty chrysoberyl lump in the pocket. I could easily chuck it off if anything happened.

The boat began swirling. Even though I could see damn all I was sure she was swinging round as well as being pulled forward into Drummer's creek on the tide's flood. If I lodged on a sandbank now it would be no real hardship. I'd have to splash over the side as soon as I grounded, and wade inland for Joe, just walk across the mudflats, home and dry. A bell clonked once, mournful over a considerable distance. No use. I considered going forward to sit on the front but decided against it, seeing I didn't know which was front any more. I might be drifting into the creek backwards.

Feeling sick's natural when you're scared, and nausea was welling up in me. I felt I'd kept quiet so long I must have forgotten how to speak or whistle. The fog was no lighter, and the sea gave nothing away, just floating about looking enigmatic. I was almost in despair. There seemed no end to my frigging messes, one after the other. Fright's a ridiculous thing. I told myself this so often I became fed up and stupidly reached for the starter, rather do something than nothing.

Then almost within reach somebody went, '*Shhh . . .*'

CHAPTER 18

I froze, hand outstretched. The sound had come from behind me, obliquely left . . . about sixty feet off, maybe? But sounds in fog . . . The cold blank air was moving against my face but was opaque as ever. I swung around, heart bumping, desperately trying to see and sickened at my ineptitude. All I could remember of my entire life seemed fright, far back as I could go. A grown man terrified of shadows, of fog, of sea, of oily hands and now speechless with terror at a whisper. Anybody's whisper.

'Let's go out and find the bastard,' a voice growled. From the *right*.

'Wait.' Devvo, definitely Devvo. Quiet, assured. 'Lovejoy'll come. I know him.'

'We could do him easy out there.' A complaint, the burke's voice louder, closer, and this time from over my bows. I must be going round and round on the water like a top.

'We wait here. And he knows it. That's why he'll come this way. He's trying for us as much as we are for him.'

Another grumble. 'Let's get it over with.'

'Shtum it. Sounds carry in this.'

It was here, and now. No escape, no chance of quietly escaping in Drummer's creek. I felt clammy. How odd that Devvo believed I was the hunter and not hunted. Maud had said something similar. Yet I'd been like a rabbit in a barrel of ferrets since last night.

I was done for. To wait would be useless. To run for the open sea was equally hopeless. I'd known that all along. To drift meant sooner or later our boats would come together by chance in this creek. It wasn't as wide as all that after all, and when all the sandbanks and flats are submerged a quick sweep of the radar would reveal me, a precise dot on a spread of an otherwise empty screen. To shout for help would simply tell Devvo where I was. I contemplated swimming for it, but in what direction? I might head blindly out to sea in this fog. How stupid to think of missing East Anglia by miles. I'd drown, and I'd done enough drowning for today. I closed my eyes wearily. Finished after all. And in the most pathetic, hopeless way possible. To go out whimpering and useless. Maybe that was me through and through.

'Give uz a light,' I heard somebody say in a low voice,

closer, the burke just wanting a fag, casual and sure. The sheer frigging effrontery of his calm certainty was suddenly galling. I felt heat rise in my throat. My cold vanished in a sudden burst of hatred. If I was going to get done I'd take one of these bastards with me, maybe both. I thought in a blistering blaze of white-hot fury, all *right* — let's frigging go. I slipped the clothes from round my shoulders and slithered down into the cabin, tiptoeing feverishly about, opening drawers and cupboards and stupidly almost clunking myself unconscious with a great flat board thing which fell outwards from the cabin wall. I caught it in time and hoped I'd concealed the sound. A few pieces of cutlery, a series of plates and a stove with that gas thing. Gas? I ducked back to it, getting down to look at it under the sink. Gas is liquid, in a flatish metal bottle with brass screw top. Compressed. You release it by turning the valve. I screwed the brass nut closed and waggled it free of its tube and restraining clamps. It was unbelievably heavy. So I had a metal bottle of compressed gas. I felt the boat swing suddenly and scrape, a creak from somewhere. The boat was slowly being pulled over the flooding mudflats.

I swallowed hard to get my mind moving. Flame-throwers. They were only big cylinders of gas, weren't they, with some kind of lighter at the front end, and a valve with a trigger. I'd seen them in the army. Nobody liked using them because of what they did and the risks you took. People were always getting burned in training. But I didn't even want to be on the cold end. I wanted to be nowhere near it. Everybody knows that these characters that make homemade bombs are always the first to get themselves crisped. What a rotten thought. I was shaking still, but rage had taken over. I wasn't thinking so much as doing.

I reached up and shut the water off at the cock. That left a long plastic tube, transparently full of water itching

to run into the sink. I opened the tap and it glugged
noisily out, air bubbles blubbering upwards.

'Hear that?' somebody said nearby.

'Shhh.'

They'd heard the waste water fall into the sea. I'd not
had the sense to plug the sink as I'd run the water tap.
The boat swung suddenly again, sending me off balance.
My knee caught on the bloody bunk. It wasn't much of a
noise, but in the state I was in it seemed like the clap of
doom.

They'd know by now. I tore the plastic tube away from
its fixture and bit savagely through. The end went on the
gas bottle's nozzle. No time to fix it there for good with
wire, even if I had any wire. A light. I needed a light. I
searched frantically, throwing caution aside and
scrabbling in the supplies for matches, a cigarette-lighter.
The bent plastic tube was about six feet long. I needed a
pole, a boathook, anything. Surely there'd be a boathook
on a stupid boat? I found an unused mop and tied the
tube along its length with a feverish series of twists, using
the orange-coloured strings from a life-jacket to keep it
there. I emptied the quarter bottle of brandy over the
mophead. Brandy burns. But I still needed some means
of igniting the thing, preferably when I was some distance
away. I found matches, the sort you have to strike and
keep hold of when you're setting fire to something.
Sodding hell. I really was a goner.

Lugging the mop and the gas bottle I crept out into the
cockpit. I couldn't let it slip at this stage, not now. Then I
had a brainwave. Collingwood, Nelson, the fireship
tricks. If I was going to go I could go as a fireship. The
least I could do for Drummer. And up here there were
plenty of ropes, wires and a railing I could tie my weapon
to.

Fog all around still, but thinning. I peered about and
wobbled precariously forwards, never thinking that they

might come at me from the side or behind. I'd have to get the engine started up again if I was going to do any good — or any bad, whichever way you saw it. Silently as I could, I lashed the mop pole to form a kind of bowsprit, sticking out at the front. Once tied, it projected somewhat sideways, but that would have to be. That made it easier to strap the gas bottle through its brass screw top and round its neck to the low railing that ran round the boat's entire edge. Great. I was almost pleased.

'Over there!' The shout came from behind. 'I saw something!'

'Where? Where?'

They hadn't started their engine, which meant they weren't certain yet. I crouched by the gas bottle with my matches, wishing I could be at the controls as well as up front. Then I might have stood some chance.

The fog swirled, waved across my tired eyes in great clouds. A definite wind was coming up. People often say the tides change our weather. I peered about, but only saw that terrible daunting opacity. The sea was gurgling now, and the waves had decreased into millions of rapid ripples. The tide race was starting, washing into the creeks and obliterating the coastlines again with its sinister swift onslaught.

Another shout from one side but I was too exhausted and bewildered to make sense of it. My mind had one scheme and this was it. Any further planning was beyond me. I clung miserably to the railing while the boat scraped and rocked its way helplessly into the reach, whisked in on the speeding tide.

'Got him!' They'd seen me. I looked frantically about. An engine roared so close it sounded on board with me.

For a second of panic I almost left my matches and leapt over the side. If I hadn't been so weary I probably would have, but my mind was programmed to its single plan. As it was, I saw Devvo's boat loom out of the fog some forty feet off, going past at slow speed. It looked enormous. The wave at its front showed they were moving against the tide. I saw a dim dark blob of grey in the cockpit cabin. Another was holding on at the front. I struck a match, let it fall and swore. I turned the brass screw on the gas bottle and heard the hissing sound of the escaping gas at the front of the projecting mop. And I couldn't reach the frigging thing. It was sticking so far out from the bows that I couldn't reach where the gas was escaping. Flame-thrower, match and fireship, all together, and I couldn't use any of them. I moaned at my stupidity.

'I see the bastard!'

'*Take him!*'

Devvo's boat suddenly sounded different. The engine roared, settled into a deep thrum as its screws churned the sea. I swore and clawed at the mop, pulling it back through its lashings. I'd light the bloody thing if I had to hold it in my teeth. I cursed and swore. I'd done it in a hurry but the bloody thing wouldn't come back in. I struck another match and held it out, clinging with one hand to the brass railing and trying to reach from the front. And I did it. But I'd never checked to make sure the gas being released was a reasonable jet. The whoosh of the igniting gas flung at me. I let go at the shock, away from the roaring heat, and fell with a splash. I was in the sea, done for differently but just as surely finished. They'd get me now.

I came up spluttering near the boat. It wasn't moving and I could see it clearly by the furiously roaring spray of fire in the bows. Something was dripping from the mop head, maybe the plastic tube melting under the flame. I felt the heat and flailed clumsily away. Devvo's engine shook the water. The vibes trembled through me as his boat neared mine. Somebody shouted again. I struck out for the opposite side away from the sound of the engine, using breast stroke because it's what I'm best at and it shows least when you are in the water. The flame's sheen on the sea gave me some guidance but only relative to the boat. Something bumped.

'Pull her in. He'll be in there—'

Metal clanged on metal. Boats rubbed. A bump of fibreglass on solid wood or something. Another few clangs and scrapes and the engine muted to a mutter. It was exactly then that the explosion came. I was lifted by some enormous force, the sea squeezing me before I heard anything at all and the blast thumping on the back of my head. The sea sank almost the same instant, plunging me under and setting me fighting for the surface and air. Suddenly things were spattering about me. And behind a sustained roar and heat and noise, a screaming and somebody splashing in that roaring. I thought I heard somebody scream a name but wasn't sure. The ochre-coloured blaze made the sea visible underneath the fog for some distance. I was too bewildered to reason what might have happened. I knew that somebody else was in trouble out here in the fog-filled creek besides me. For once I wasn't dying on my own. From the horrible sounds behind me somebody else was at it too.

I struck feebly away from the fire, never mind where. Another, less intense whoosh sounded. The sea sucked, dipped, swelled but less severely this time. I couldn't keep swimming for long. The cold and my tiredness were making it difficult enough to float, let alone move. For a second I trod water, peering underneath the fog with the gilded sea surface reflecting the fires. I had to look. The boats seemed gigantic, piled almost in one heap. Both were blazing. Even as I looked some glass shattered with a crack, perhaps the heat. I don't know what had caused the explosion, whether it was my gas thing or the boats colliding and the petrol . . . *Petrol*. Terror-stricken, I saw it on the surface, a pure yellow heat spreading towards me. I gave a squeal of alarm, tried to turn feebly . . . and then I heard it. A donkey's coarse braying, up and down, over and over, to my right. It sounded near, very near. Germoline's voice.

I tried to shout again, excitedly drawing in a breathful of sea in my anxiety to get Germoline braying again, and almost sank. I splashed up again coughing and vomiting water, weakened further. I tried using my hands merely to keep me level, drew a long breath and yelled at the top of my voice: 'Germoline!' Almost instantly a succession of donkey brays came, but I was on my back and couldn't place the direction. Stupid. I struggled wearily vertical, treading water again, but she'd shut up again, probably listening as hard as I was.

I tried shouting from this position but was too breathless to get up steam. I flopped exhausted on to my back again, to draw breath, let out her name in one despairing bellow and pushed myself vertical again, treading water.

'Keep shouting,' I yelled, turning towards the bray. 'Germoline!'

She gave three steady brays almost as though she knew what to do. I homed on them, finding after each one I was successfully pinpointing the next.

'Germoline!' I gasped. 'Germoline.'

I couldn't shout any more. I floundered blindly on, flopping my arms over and splashing like hell. I kept trying to shout but managed finally nothing more than a sort of weak talking, gasping out her name as I went. Several times I thought I saw something up ahead but no longer had the strength to hold my head out to see. I felt I'd been going for days before I realized I could not hear her braying any more. Gone. I must have lost her. I gave up, stopped swimming, lying on the water and trying to concentrate all my energies in keeping my face up to breathe. The current was pulling me now, probably running round at the full of the tide inside the creek and starting me out to sea. I swear I'd practically nodded off, when I was swept against these four hairy legs. I was so frightened I let out an almighty yell, but it was Germoline, standing in the tidal shallows. I clung gasping to Germoline's lovely legs and flung an arm over her neck, standing rocklike on the mud-covered flats.

'Darlin',' I gasped. She stood there, bracing breast deep against the flood. 'Up, love,' I wheezed. She was just turning, her tethering rope trailing where she'd pulled it away from her stall, when I heard a cry from seawards.

'Lovejoy!' Devvo's voice.

'Devvo?' My shout back was a mere wheeze. I tried taking a few waded paces but fell and had to sprawl against Germoline for support. My legs were rubber. I couldn't move without Germoline.

'Lovejoy.' The voice was feeble but real and solid. He always did sound in charge, Devvo. Always so bloody sure of himself. 'Lovejoy! Help, for Christ's sake . . .'

'Keep shouting!' I yelled, finding some strength from somewhere. 'Keep shouting! I'll get a rope.'

'My leg's gone, Lovejoy,' Devvo shouted in a hoarse gurgle. 'I'm burned . . .'

'Hang on, hang on!'

I turned Germoline and urged her out of the sea and up on to the flats, geeing her more decisively than I'd ever done. She splashed across the muddy shallows with me clinging to her neck. We came to the hut before I had time to focus. I staggered inside, grabbed a couple of rope hanks, and drove Germoline down the way we had come, following our trailing marks back towards the water. I could still hear the crackling of the blazing boats but could see nothing. I rasped a bit but got out a respectable shout.

'Devvo! Where are you?'

Nothing.

'Devvo!' I screeched. '*Devvo!*'

A feeble shout came, sounding some thirty yards off. 'I'm here, Lovejoy. The water . . . I'm burned . . .'

'Which way are you going, Devvo?' I shouted. 'Looking towards me, which way are you going?'

'It's pulling me . . . left, left.'

'I'll wade out, Devvo!' I got hold of Germoline's mane and urged her to our right, tying the rope round her neck as I splashed along the sea's edge. I got her maybe a hundred yards, shouting all the while, before taking hold of the free end. I reeled out into the water, all but knackered. It was surprisingly shallow, coming slowly up to my chest as I flopped and waded out. And I found Devvo, or rather Devvo found the rope.

I felt a weight behind me on the rope, simply turned and there Devvo was. He'd drifted against the lifeline which linked me to Germoline. At least, I thought it was Devvo. He was a ghoulish mess of blisters and burned skin, blackened around his face and all his shoulder, floating on the surface about ten feet off and just keeping his mouth up. His hair had gone.

'My legs, Lovejoy,' he groaned. 'I can't move.'

'Here. It'll hurt.'

I slid along the rope and tied it round his waist, lifting it to settle under his arms the way seemed best. He cried out in agony a few times as the rope bit. The sea was just too deep for me to stand. With each attempt I became weaker. I hooked my arm under the rope and let it come on to my shoulder. My arms wouldn't work any more. Germoline brayed again, worried for me.

'One more second, Devvo,' I gasped, craning my neck up for air. 'I'll go and we'll pull you in, mate.' I called him mate. Him, that had murdered Drummer.

'I can't hold on . . .'

'We'll get you in.'

'I can't see, Lovejoy. You won't leave me, eh?'

' 'Course not.'

I dragged myself weakly along the rope until I touched the bottom and crept forward, utterly done, pulling myself weakly back to the fogged shore. Germoline was waiting patiently as I crawled on to the mud beside her. I honestly thought I was dying from exhaustion. I lay there, unable to move a muscle. I couldn't even support my own weight, but I'd done it. I'd saved Devvo, atoned for killing the owner of those oily hands out there on the black sea. All it needed now was for Germoline to pull him in. And thank God Germoline was there, bracing solidly against the rope as the tide tried to drown Devvo. She was just waiting for my command, bless her loyal little donkey heart.

'Right, love,' I gasped up at Germoline's dependable form above me. 'Pull.'

Nothing happened. Not a muscle.

'Germoline,' I wheezed. 'Please, cockie. I can't do it.' I was looking up at her.

'Lovejoy!' came weakly from the sea. '*Lovejoy*. For Christ's sake.'

Something spluttered out there in the creek.

'Germoline,' I bleated. 'Pull, lovey. Pull. Please.' Didn't she understand? I tried to get up but my muscles weren't moving. I felt indiarubber, like those elastic toy things you put into different shapes for children. Maybe she didn't know what to do.

I struggled up her forelegs and sagged over her neck, too done even to straddle her. She felt so warm and Strong. All that power.

'Fucking gee up, Germoline,' I gasped in her earhole. 'Please, lovey.'

Not a twitch. Her head was turned seaward, almost as if she were listening to that awful burbling.

'*Lovejoy*!' came again offshore. 'Please . . .' A gagging sound. I knew it well. I'd been making the same sound for what seemed hours.

I found tears running down my face. I wobbled off Germoline's neck and tried pulling on the rope, the seaward side. It barely lifted out of the water.

'Please, Germoline,' I said. 'Sweetheart . . .'

I was helpless. The rope sagged, tugged a few times, drifted, sagged. Once I looked into Germoline's eyes. She gazed back with that calm with which an infant watches another who's crying, almost dispassionate and without the slightest sympathy. I suppose cold's the word I'm looking for, something like that. Once or twice I shouted for help, that Mayday thing, without any real hope. In any case Drummer's creek was nothing but a waste of mudflats at the best of times. Flooded at high tide, it was even more desolate.

Numbed, I found myself sprawled on the mud, leaning against tough little Germoline with tears streaming down my face and those horrible sounds growing fainter out on the waters of the streaming creak.

There came a time when the rope stopped tugging, but it must have been an hour before I could move. Every muscle I had was screaming. Even breathing was painful. As soon as I could I left Germoline there, tethered to something unspeakable floating out in the creek, and followed the marks back to Drummer's hut by crawling, stopping every few yards to recover.

It must have been a good two hours later that I returned, clumping across the receding tidal lip to where Germoline waited. She said nothing. I was still falling a bit and my muscles weren't coordinating too well, but at least I was clothed and in some of Drummer's old garb and had got warm. I'd even brewed up and tried a slice of bread with some cold samphire on it but fetched that up.

I unlooped the rope from Germoline's neck, and pulled her round to face the land again. I simply let her end of the rope fall and left it as it had been, trailing into the ebbing tide.

I didn't get her straps right on the cart, which is something that normally makes her irritable. This time, though, she was as good as gold and tolerated my clumsy fastening while I got her roughly hitched. I had to sit in the cart then and just let her get on with it. I couldn't have gone to report to Joe Poges at the Staithe for a gold clock. The straps made it hard for Germoline but she seemed to know the problem and struggled gamely across the mudflats on to the hard with me in the cart. We came upon a man from the lobster fishery chipping and bending away over some of his pots. He looked up as Germoline clopped on to the stone staithing.

'Good heavens,' he called pleasantly. 'Bit odd weather for donkey rides, eh?'

'It is that,' I said. He straightened up and watched us go past.

That was all that was said until we reached home. I took the same way I'd come, through the American War Cemetery and back into our village through the woods. The cemetery looked more heroic than ever in the changed light, but I'd rather have the people any day.

When we reached the cottage I was too far gone to unhitch the straps. My joints seemed to have stiffened all everywhere. I fell out of the cart whimpering with aches and hurts.

I looked at Germoline. She gazed steadily back with that cold look. I noticed her eyes were a brownish grey.

'You're as bad as me,' I croaked, and went inside.

CHAPTER 19

I woke into sunset, disorientated as hell and aching all over. Little Ginny was shaking me with the self-righteous face of a child aware that somebody was neglecting their duty.

'You have to get up, Lovejoy,' she was saying.

I growled, 'Sod off.'

'Ooooh,' from little Dobber, eyes wide.

I creaked upright and tottered out after them into the garish sunlight. I was surprised. The world was still there, Germoline was plodding round the garden and three children taking turns to walk her. The trees were still hanging around. Everything really average as ever, almost as though it was only to be expected. I sagged on to my unfinished wall, feeling about eight hundred. An evening breeze whistled round my limbs.

'What did you get me up for, you pest?' I demanded, avoiding Germoline's eye — as Germoline was avoiding mine.

'Tinker sent Harry to say get out of town, Lovejoy.'

'Eh?'

I was shivering. Surely to God things weren't going bad even further? I felt I'd done enough. Harry's our famous flower-pincher, a six-year old liberator of floral tributes from their churchyard pots. He escapes them back into the forests and woods, a one-child anti-liturgical plague which has struck as far as three whole villages away. It was his turn with Germoline. I shouted — well, croaked — him over.

'Tinker says they're coming to arrest you, Lovejoy.' He was quite calm about it.

'You've to hit the road and get out of town,' Ginny

confirmed. Telly Westerns.

'It sounds like it,' I said.

The children were looking doubtfully from me to Germoline and back again.

'Don't worry,' I said reassuringly. 'I'll get a bigger one. For speed.'

I heard Ginny's mother calling them back for their grub.

'We hope you make it to Utah, Lovejoy,' Ginny told me gravely. 'And that the Red Indians don't get you.'

'Can we have Germoline if they do?' little Dobber asked.

'I'll talk to her about it,' I told them, and saw them off up the lane.

I wished getting away from Maslow was so easy. I went in to make some grub, wondering where the hell's Utah.

Maslow came about five o'clock. He didn't come in, just stood grandly at my door. He informed me that certain investigations were proceeding concerning certain events related to certain deaths concerning certain antique dealers. While insufficient evidence was available on which to base an arrest, he wanted me down at the police station to help him and others with their enquiries. I said to get stuffed. He smiled at that, and said I was not to leave the cottage under any circumstances without notifying him or his duly authorized deputy. I watched him go, knowing that Constable Jilks, our flying peeler, would be hovering in the lane.

I stayed at home, resting some more, and then strolled up the lane at a geriatric limp for a pint at the White Hart. Word had got round about my escapades. I was treated like a mild explosive. Tinker was there. Ignoring his air of despondency, I got him into an alcove.

'This rock piece, Tinker.' I passed the chrysoberyl over. He turned it in his mittens. 'To Silver Joe.'

'What the bleeding hell is it?'

'Never mind. Ask Silver Joe to price it. Then pass word to me. I'll be in prison. If the price is right I'll let you know, and you can have the commission on the sale. Joe can chop it for me.' I meant to divide the proceeds, not the rock. I'd give half to Terry for his rotten old boat and half to Lemuel for his car. The value of the rock should cover it, with luck. I didn't tell Tinker the value because prices tend to show in his face more than mine at times like this.

Silver Joe's a reliable old rogue given to homemade jewellery. His brother works in London, though, and I knew he'd dance with delight at the sight of the precious mineral. If Maslow had left me alone I'd have loved a crack at the piece myself, but it was better this way. At least I'd go to gaol not owing everybody on the outside. Tinker went a bit white about the gills when I said that about the car and the boat, fearing the worst. He didn't ask after Devvo.

The pub was quiet that evening. The dealers left me alone, only Tinker and Lemuel bravely coming to cadge a drink or several. Helen and Brad looked in for a minute but left after a bit of whispering together in the somnolence. It was a real mortuary. I explained to Lemuel that his car was a goner owing to an accident with Terry's boat. Seeing that his car was the deposit . . . Lemuel took it better than Tinker, funnily enough.

Finally I told Tinker to get me two hundred ounces of pure silver from Silver Joe and to leave it in my converted garage. It's the sort of thing you can still do in our village without any risk of theft. Keeping alive and trying not to commit murder are a lot more difficult. I've found that.

I did the work three days later. Dolly was with me and I felt fresh and in reasonable health. Dolly respected my long silences, seeming to understand what was about to happen. The police had called several times asking me to make statements. I'd refused, even when they brought Maslow. I wasn't having any, and they were still in the lane, nodding to Dolly and eyeing her legs every time she went out. Once she came back from town looking fraught, but that was maybe her husband creating hell. Constable Jilks tried to come in once when it was raining, and several times I'd caught Dolly brewing up, feeling sorry for him stuck down in the lane while everybody else was in their warm house, but I put a stop to that. He wouldn't bring me one when I was in the nick, that was sure. Let him do without.

The silver was oval, done on an improvised sandtray, heated by my foot bellows of leather and hollowed ash. I'd have liked to use elder, like some of the northern men, but you can't get that too easily in the south, not of the quality. I'd got Ian, Andy's lad, to bring me all the dense logs he could find from the tithe cuttings, when all the extra wood in the village is given to the church. God could spare it. I had a pile as high as the garage when the time came.

The die was the easiest part, as with most dies that aren't too recessed. I used hard steel on account of the wear it was going to have to take. A piece as thick as a finger, made convex at one end, the sides filed flat to allow a good grip in the vice, and then cutting and filing the dome into a firefly pattern. I wanted it very stylized. After much thought I chose one of the patterns from traditional Chinese fireflies, more symbols than actual drawings. The mood was on me, and I knew it. I was in a trance, hardly eating, dreaming hours at a time between filing the metal tip into a firefly.

That took the first day and half the next. I tried to rouse myself then, for the coming ordeal. I paced myself because of the state I was in, took decent rests and had good meals in between.

Dolly was great, bringing grub and never asking what I was doing. Several times she fended people off and had one nasty fight with a pretty young reporter called Liz. I wasn't too sure I wanted her to win that one, but thought maybe later, if . . . The rest of the second day I saw to the silver, making certain the edges were stencilled, the base clean and the casting of the dish impeccable. Casting's fairly easy. I had to sand one small nick in the oval's centre, but didn't have time to repeat the whole thing. Maslow would be along for me any day once he'd gathered enough lawyers against me. I was for it, just as he'd said. I'd be lucky to come out at the other end.

I slept late that third day. Dolly didn't put the radio on, just let me go out after breakfast into the watery sunshine and start. I walked about nervously to keep from distractions, idly kicking sticks and grass, going round and round the garden as the mood came into me. Now and then I returned to the garage and bellowed the fire up. I always use the old charcoal-burner's trick of banking the furnace up with clods, forcing the heat to stay alive yet closed during the nights. I'd uncovered it and got the fire drawing easily within an hour of getting up.

The silver was in my hands before I'd made any conscious decision to start the Reverse Gadroon. It was heavy and ponderous, hellish difficult to control. On any normal day that would have put me off, but today I was above everything and simply went on, fixing the firefly die into my vice and getting the angle right. I began practice with a quick tap, using the sheet metal to get my arm going and make sure the die would hold nice and tight. The fact the marks showed neat and precise through the metal was no surprise to me, not on that magic day. Oddly, it was like watching Drummer.

I hitched the huge silver dish to the hanging pegs and

got the homemade pulleys running free. It took the heavy silver oval beautifully. One rapid dash to the furnace for maximum heat, and I laid the hammers out on the improvised benching. I have this great iron stool and perched myself on its edge. My throat was dry as hell and my eyes gritty from the sand table, which smoked and flickered behind. I spun the great silver oval, flat as a pancake, on its suspending clothes pegs. All ready. One more hitch at the stool to centre me against the die's position, and I was off. I was in a dream, floating. I even wondered if it was me there.

I simply watched the firefly gadroon come through the silver. One hammer blow, almost as if done by somebody else with me looking, fetched the indentation through the silver, impressing the firefly design. A smooth movement to one side a fraction of an inch and the hammer fell again, a loving stroke, not a blow. And again the impression came, meticulously in position against its neighbour. And another blow and another. Another. Another.

The hammer's sound drugged me. It was true love, the silver assimilating into itself the heavy loving strokes. And somehow, with every stroke of the hammer, the great silver oval spun itself that fraction of a turn into position to receive the next loving penetration of the rigid die. Round it spun, flashing reflections of the golden-red furnace colours. The hammer lifted and fell. The great dish spun. I heard somebody singing and only dimly realized after some minutes that it was me. My arms that had been arthritic and hopeless for the past three days were doing the silversmith's work of their own accord. It was as if I were simply watching Drummer's gnarled hands as, time after time in this same spot, he'd shown me the wondrous gift of the gadroon. I slammed on in the smoke, oblivious of aches and weariness, sometimes shaking sweat from my eyes and hefting the hammer

down again and again as my hands flicked the ponderous
dish in the air before me. It was beautiful, this spinning
for the act of love, the silver seeming to quiver and move
of its own volition as the hammer bore down and down
again upon its gleaming surface. The last stroke brought
the patterns into one circumferential oval, precise and
ideal. Without a second's pause I saw my right hand flick
the heavy hammer aside with a crash and bring the
lighter hammer into position, starting off round
the silver's edge again with the same loving actions,
spinning and beating.

It must have been less than half an hour but when
finally the sounds ceased I couldn't believe that my
private blissful eternity had come to an end. The silver
had spun the last time, and now hung there. I dropped
the last hammer and sat there looking. The furnace
flickered and darted colour off the silver surface. Its
margin was indented now, the firefly design meeting
exactly in its brilliant dance round the edge. The
distances were right. The small markings where the
design had to be fetched into precise line were there. It
was magical, as beautiful as any gadroon design I had
ever seen. And it was a reverse design, the most difficult
of all. Done blind, guessing exactly for every one of the
several hundred glittering impressions.

I had done it. I found I was drooping over the bench,
wheezing like my old leather bellows. The exaltation left
me gradually. I got all my creaks back. I straightened and
turned to place the dish on the sand tray, ready for its
three silver ball-and-claw feet.

Tinker was at the pub when I phoned and told him to
bring the big Yank urgently, tell him I'd done the Reverse
Gadroon. Dolly and me sat waiting on the divan.

She knew there was something wrong. I suppose I'd led

her on a bit, for the sake of peace. I decided now was the time.

'They'll come for me soon, love,' I told her. 'There's an order out for me. I'll have to go with them.'

'But for how long, darling?' Dolly was instantly worried about socks and things for me to take. She's great. I had to grin.

'Some time,' I said. I told her about the silver dish in the garage. 'Tell Tinker to take it to Silver Joe and see its claw feet are put on, properly finished.'

'Silver Joe,' she repeated for memory's sake.

Somebody was at the door then. It was the big Yank, the commodore whose boat I kept wrecking. He came in smiling, refusing Dolly's coffee as he sat. I didn't blame him because Americans are used to the proper stuff.

I said, 'It's too much of a coincidence that your boat was around so much, Mr Naismith. Am I right?'

'That's right, sir.'

I sighed. That's all I needed, I thought wearily. This New World politeness when my world was crumbling. Despite all, he was watchful as a cat.

'Tell me one thing. Drummer's death.'

'None of my doing. I'm nothing to do with that side.'

'You're the broker for the nicked stuff, right?'

'That's so, sir. Only the business side.'

I kept gamely on. 'And your position at the yacht club's a front for popping the nicked antiques to the Continent. Right?'

'Correct.'

'I'll tell nothing of it. But on your way out step into the garage. You'll see a Reverse Gadroon, silver, two hundred ounces, on the hot sand table. I've not time to fix its feet, but it's handmade. By me.'

I saw his eyes widen in astonishment and he made to speak. I cut him short. He'd have to suss the rest. This wasn't the sort of conversation that could be finished with

Maslow in the room. 'I can do it,' I said. 'Again and again. Drummer taught me. And they allow arts and crafts in clink, where I'm going. *You* could provide the blank cast silver bowls, dishes, anything. If there's any difficulty tell them it's only plated, or maybe pewter. They won't know.'

'I see.' His brain was on the go. I knew he was thinking of the laws in the USA, where possession of a genuine antique silversmith's personal marking die is quite legal. Here it's a criminal offence. 'I see,' he said again.

I drew breath. 'Er, about your boat. It wasn't intentional. I didn't mean to sink it. They came at me.'

'I accept that. I'll prefer no charges.' He leant forward. 'The idea is that . . . er . . .' he glanced at Dolly, pausing. Dolly was already packing some clothes up for me but she was in earshot. 'Er, you might consider making some items for shipping abroad, by any means I chose?'

'Maybe,' I said.

'A handmade Reverse Gadroon's unbelievable.'

'Check on it,' I told him. Drummer would have been proud.

'Can I take it with me?' he asked.

I thought on this. Maybe he'd better, seeing I expected Maslow to put me in a cage. I nodded. 'But I want Tinker here, until we agree a price. Silver Joe as referee?'

'Done.' His grin came back and we shook hands. 'Maybe I'd better wait outside,' he added, getting the feeling between Dolly and me.

I let him go, a nice bloke full of politeness still. I accepted his version. Nothing was further from his behaviour than aggro. He was the antiques broker for the nick trade all right. And I was sure he'd had nothing to do with the killing of Drummer, especially seeing how well he had behaved when I'd rescued Germoline that time.

Tinker came shuffling in while Dolly and I talked on

the divan. She was crying and saying I could get a lawyer.
I didn't know any so I'd have to leave that side to trust.
Tinker was jubilant.

'I seed it, Lovejoy!' He meant the gadroon. 'Drummer'll
be smiling all over his face, Gawd rest him. And that
Yank's dancing wiv delight, mate.'

Mate. I let him prattle on for a while but I had called
Devvo mate while he'd begged me for help. And I'd let
Devvo drown, me and Germoline. Maybe I deserved gaol,
or maybe I was just tired.

Something was on Tinker's mind. 'Here, Lovejoy. Did
you really do for Devvo and his burkes? I'll say you was
with Lemuel and me.'

I gazed back at him. The loss of his principal source of
income for booze — namely, me — was practically the end
of his normal everyday life, but he was still in there
sticking up for me, the stupid old get. I went to look out
of the window at the garden for a minute.

'Leave it, Tinker,' I said when I could speak the words.
'Look after yourself while I'm in the nick. The Yank will
see you get your lolly.'

'I could tell the Old Bill we wuz at Sotheby's.' He was
all eager, but I shook my head. Just as well I did for
Tinker's sake because just then Maslow walked in. No
knock, notice.

'Get your coat, lad,' he said to me. 'You're under
arrest. Among other things, for destroying a sea fortress,
property of our Sovereign Monarch — '

'Eh?' It had damned near destroyed me, never mind
the other way round. Then I remembered that ominous
crump out to sea, and the single great swelling wave that
lifted my boat . . . Oh hell. The 'counterbalanced' exit
from the chamber must have been a destruction device. If
I'd half the sense I was born with I could have worked
that out.

Maslow was deliriously happy watching my face. 'And,

he said, grinning some more, 'complicity in the murder
of —'

'Don't bother,' I said evenly. 'I'll come quietly.' I've
always wanted to say that.

I had quite a send off. Germoline looked at me as I went
towards the police car. Our worthy Constable Jilks was
there, important but embarrassed at all this. I told him it
was all right, George, and not to worry. Maslow ordered
me to get in, but I went across to say so-long to
Germoline. She was grave, thinking whatever were things
coming to, but aware there wasn't much of a way out for
either of us.

I told her, 'Germoline, I've made arrangements with
Lemuel to take you to Mrs Hepplestone's.' I scratched her
neck and left her there, kissed Dolly and got in between
these two constables. There seemed nothing else. Dolly
was weeping. Well, I wasn't too happy either. I wound
the window down.

'Oh, love,' I called to Dolly. 'Count the teaspoons after
these coppers have gone. Okay?'

She nodded, sniffing into a hankie. I sighed. It had
been a joke. The trouble was Dolly *would* count them all,
and keep a list at that. Germoline watched us go.

We rolled down the lane. I noticed the big Yank had
vanished and that his car was nowhere in sight, a shrewd
nut if ever I saw one. You can't teach the Yanks anything
about running a business.

'What the hell?' Maslow muttered.

As our car turned towards the chapel there were two
grotty figures waiting by the side of the hedge. There was
hardly room for our big police motor to squeeze past. I
saw the pair of them, tatty as ever, come to attention as
the car cruised slowly past. Lemuel had his medals on
still, and Tinker was looking his worst. The silly old fool
presented arms with a stick.

Maslow had reached out furiously and wound his window down, when I leaned forward and tapped his shoulder. Hard.

'You dare, Maslow,' I said softly, my hand resting casually near his neck. 'You fucking dare.'

He paused. The two old fools were standing there at the salute, the wind flapping their tattered coats. A few of the villagers were watching in astonishment by the bus stop. Maslow looked angrily across at his apprehensive driver. 'What are you waiting for?' he snarled. 'The Guards' band? Get on, get on.'

I didn't look at the ridiculous pair. It was hard to swallow. The car edged past and we drove off, but Maslow had the last word. They always do. By the main town road he'd recovered and was smiling at some secret success. He unleashed it as we settled down towards town.

'One thing, Lovejoy,' he said. 'It'll be hundred to one, you getting off.'

'Them's bad odds.'

'Either way we'll have you,' he said pleasantly. 'Oh, incidentally. One of the court's advisers has asked personally to take your case. Social worker with a special interest.'

'They're all the same to me,' I told him.

'Really?' he said cheerfully. 'Tell you one thing. The last thing I'd want is five years' court probation in Maud's tender loving care.'

Maud? That cannibal? I croaked, 'Maslow, you wouldn't . . .'

'Wouldn't I, Lovejoy?'

'Look, Maslow. Please . . . *please* . . .'

The swine said nothing. He just laughed and laughed and laughed, and we drove on to town.